Minyan

Ten Jewish Men in a World / That Is Heartbroken

Eliezer Sobel

Winner of
The Peter Taylor Prize for the Novel
Co-sponsored by the Knoxville Writer's Guild and the University of
Tennessee Press, the Peter Taylor Prize for the Novel is named for one
of the South's most celebrated writers—the author of acclaimed short
stories, plays, and the novels *A Summons to Memphis* and *In the Tennessee
Country.* The prize is designed to bring to light works of high literary
quality, thereby honoring Peter Taylor's own practice of assisting other
writers who cared about the craft of fine fiction.

Selected passages from *Minyan* also won the 2003 New Millennium
Writings Fiction Award and appear in the 2004 edition of *New
Millennium Writings,* a literary anthology published in Knoxville,
Tennessee by Don Williams.

Chapter One of this book is reprinted from *TIKKUN Magazine* 12, no.
4 (July-August 1997); 58-62. www.tikkun.org

**A Yiddish/Hebrew Glossary is included
in the back of this book.**

By the same author:

Manual of Good Luck

Wild Heart Dancing

The 99th Monkey:
A Spiritual Journalist's Misadventures
With Gurus, Messiahs, Sex, Psychedelics and
Other Consciousness-Raising Experiments

Why I Am Not Enlightened (e-book)

Blue Sky, White Clouds:
A Book For Memory-Challenged Adults

*For all of my Jewish male
comrades-in-suffering,
and in loving memory
of the two who left us behind:
David Gilbert
&
Shivaya Alan Cain*

The author wishes to thank
Richard Powers and Jana Wolff
for their insightful suggestions and generosity;
Max, Manya and Harry Sobel
for their unwavering love and support;
Sharon Lowinger and Eddie Greenberg
for their undying friendship, inspiration and humor;
and Shari Cordon for being
the light of my life
and keeping our home funny.

You can take a boy out of Judaism,
but you can never take Judaism out of a boy.
—Grandma Fanny Lerner

...Once one knows...that this upside-down world
can never be set on its feet — then one stands
on one's own head.
—Chaim Grade,
My Mother's Sabbath Days

CHAPTER ONE

Lipschitz

One by one we file into Finkelstein's living room (Finkelstein, the big shot): Goldberg comes with me, Greenblatt and Weissbaum show up together, everyone glum. Reb Miltie and Breshman arrive smelling of bagel, then Bernstein in his Hindu get-up with the orange shawl. Finally Moscowitz, looking pathetic. And that's it: counting the deceased, we have ten men, a *minyan*. You're not supposed to count the deceased, but what do we care? Nobody's standing on ceremony. What, God's going to turn a deaf ear on a technicality? The herring and the sponge cake can wait; we have to say *Kaddish* for Lipschitz.

Freddy Lipschitz, dead at thirty-five, found in a bathroom with a needle dangling from his arm. Who knew he was still shooting? Not me or Goldberg, certainly. Not Greenblatt. No one knew. Okay, Bernstein knew, because Bernstein with his Turkish connections and his hashish friends with their Tibetan Book of the Dead routine, Bernstein supplied him with the stuff. But none of the rest of us knew.

Poor Freddy, miserable his whole life anyway—everyone secretly felt he was better off. A guy with his talents, his gifts, still living with his parents. Broke, out of work, no direction, hadn't

1

touched a woman since the Beatles broke up. Plus ugly—pock-marked, big nose, a guy you'd be uncomfortable seeing in a public restroom. Death couldn't be all bad for Freddy Lipschitz.

Now, to the point: Assembled in Finkelstein's—the big shot's—living room are ten Jewish men. And *kibitzers*, every one of them. Listen to me, already mouthing off:

"Jesus said 'Wherever two or more are gathered in my name, there will I be also.' The Jews never had it so easy. They had to gather ten or more before God would show up. Nine other *shlep-pers* in the room and what you say counts. Otherwise your deepest soul cry is considered idle chatter upstairs. You want to talk to Jesus, that's a different story. You could be in the back room of the Ramrod Club *shtupping* a stranger in the behind and it still counts as two or more. But you want the king of Abraham and Strauss to listen, you need a *minyan*...is this right?"

Nobody is listening. They are all preoccupied with Freddy, and with the spread Finkelstein's wife has laid out on the dining room table, a little snack for the boys after *Kaddish*. Delicious-looking platters from Petaks. Kosher dills like they are going out of style. A feast for Freddy, heartburn for the dead.

And these guys were no strangers to deli. Real *fressers,* every one of them. Committed eaters, the cold cut for them was a religious matter. The Gentile kids may have rubbed their bloody, pricked fingers in secret rituals, but the Jewish kids were born brisket brothers. They may not have set foot in a synagogue since their Bar Mitzvahs, but show them a Jewish mother's pot roast thirty years later—any Jewish mother's—and watch them pray.

'Course there was a trade-off—along with the food they also had to listen to the litany of be-carefuls and watch-outs, all the play-it-safes: the ear muffs so you don't catch cold; the lock all your car doors in this neighborhood and leave a radio on in the house; the never order meat loaf 'cause you don't know what they put in it; the watch your step it's like a sheet of glass; the fear of Gentiles and Germans. And through some inexplicable alchemical interaction, this combination of Jewish food and Jewish fear led

2

to a wild sex drive most of them had for Christian women, all the girls who never drank Manishewitz, who couldn't pronounce the 'ch' in challah or Chanukah, blonde girls that made their mouths water.

But how can you possibly explain this to a mother when you imagine that she wants you to marry someone like the *zaftig* Friedberg girl and wind up being a *shlump* in a chair the rest of your life, stuffing your face on potato *latkes*? (Like the late *Mister Friedberg*.) You can't, and you don't. So as close to their mothers as Jewish boys usually are, is also how distant they can be when they become men—even if only on a purely *informational* level. There's just too much information about their lives that, from experience, is better left unspoken.

Which leaves, in many cases, only the very *brisket itself* as the bridge, the primordial place of connection—it is love on a pure and holy meat level. But the more stuff sons keep hidden from their mothers over time, the greater this *informational distance*, and that can cause lots of problems. Emotional problems, I don't have to tell you. *Tsores* in relationships—don't even ask.

Ten Jewish men with emotional problems like nobody's business. Okay nine, may Freddy rest in peace. And I grew up with most of these idiots. The playground at East Lake Elementary was our stomping grounds. We did recess. We did lunch. We stood on line together with our pants at our knees waiting for the school nurse to squeeze our testicles. (How many seven-year-old boys actually have hernias?) No wonder we were a bit off when it came to women.

Take Goldberg, a real nutcase in point—a composer, a doctorate from NYU no less—thirty-eight, still no wife, no kids, running after a *shikseh* who tells him she'll only marry him if he can promise to come up with $150,000 per annum. Why? Because "she likes clothes," he says. This is Goldberg the composer we're talking about, not some *putz* from Long Island who sells shoes. Goldberg, the man who read all seven volumes of Proust and will liberally quote from them to complete strangers—(*"Ah, there is no such thing as a bad choice in love, because if there is any choice at all, it can only be bad.* ") (Goldberg made a bad choice.) Goldberg, the man of culture, vitality, generosity and principles, who waited on tables for a living until he was thirty-six, who is reduced to tears by Olivier's King Lear. What does he know from money? Or clothes? He wears an NYU sweatshirt night and day. Even on first dates, he never thinks about how he looks, greeting a new woman with a dirty wrinkled handkerchief dangling from one hand, not afraid to perspire in mixed company. Not like me with my deodorants and scents, my musk oils and breath mints. Goldberg could stink to high heaven and still charm young music students with his sheer enthusiasm.

But this is the woman he wants to marry, come hell or high water. Why? We don't know. All we know is that at the beginning they were spending entire weekends in bed and Goldberg confessed in a moment of sexual candor, that he was "learning to receive." What does this mean? Phil Goldberg finally learns to enjoy oral stimulation? Anal? Is this a reason to marry a wardrobe nut? I don't think so. A little poke in the tush is not a life commitment.

Goldberg had a paper route, for crying out loud. To this day, you drive with him through the old neighborhood in Jersey and he'll still show you each house on his route:

"There, the Hollers," he'll say, "the house on the corner, the Taylors; across the street, the Grisattis—lousy tippers," and so forth. Anywhere in East Lake, New Jersey that he ever tossed a *Daily Record* from the basket on his Schwinn, he remembers today like there was going to be a test. Why am I telling you all this? Because Goldberg was a boy who counted his pennies—Jewish boys didn't have paper routes, ordinarily. That was for the Velano boy, the Dominguez kid; Phil was the exception. So this is not a person you demand a $150,000 income from, somebody who ran his *kishkehs* off, sweating profusely, serving fifteen tables at a time to pay his way through a doctoral program. Plus all the student loans, the work exchanges, the graduate assistantships, the stipends—what he didn't do to make ends meet. Not your typical, well-to-do East Lake Wilner-type Jew (me) who, to this day, has no resume and never had to work. (Only to say now that even when the bucks finally stopped coming from Dad and it looked like I would have to get a job, what happens? Uncle Izzy eats a little too much sour cream and has a heart attack and leaves me twenty grand to keep puttering away at finding a life. But I am taking steps. I received an invoice in the mail recently that stated, "This copy is for your personal files," and I panicked. I had no personal files. I ran out that very day and came home with a huge filing cabinet, which remains empty except for that one invoice. At least I know where it is now.)

No, Goldberg doesn't know from money. He's in student loan payments over his head, and you think a Ph.D. in composing music is a gold mine? Forget about it—there are no "composers needed" in the want ads; this is not a marketable skill by a long shot.

In short, Goldberg has to scrape together $150,000 a year or kiss his *shikseh* good-bye. We all say kiss her good-bye and relax:

"The way you live," we tell him, "you can get by on thirty grand a year, forty tops if you leave the house once in awhile."

But what do we know? Do we know what goes on in the bedroom? We don't. Do we know what shapes and drives a Jewish man's appetite for women? That we all know something about. Even Bernstein, with his long beard and the statues of Vishnu all over, knows something about it. Even Moscowitz with his committee of chiropractors and—God help us all—Weissbaum, the idiot with his baseball cards, knows about this. But we can't help Phil Goldberg. It would be the blind leading the blind.

Maybe his mother could have helped. All of our mothers could have helped, if they let us once go to school with a runny nose, let us once keep our shoes on in the house, let us once go out with wet hair. (Where is it written that you *must*, you *have* to, catch a cold if you go out with wet hair? The perversions these ideas lead to in adult Jewish men: walk by my house in the dead of winter, sub-zero temperatures, see me dangling my head full of wet hair out the bathroom window, laughing maniacally.) Maybe if our mothers, God love them all, didn't spray the whole house with Lysol everyday; if they hadn't started in with the lectures about intermarriage in the seventh grade:

"But I'm only taking Mary-Anne to the Thanksgiving dance, we're not getting married."

"Never mind Thanksgiving, this is where the trouble starts, don't tell me."

Who knew, at age twelve, that there could be a direct link between little Mary-Anne Hamilton and Adolph Hitler? But there was. The innocent Sunday school cross around her neck may as well have been a swastika, to anyone who survived the war, as my mother did. I saw a cute little girl in pigtails; my mother saw "Hitler Youth," saw ovens and smoke and her dead grandmother.

What's done is done, and our friend Phil Goldberg has himself an expensive, *shikseh* girlfriend and there's no talking him out of it. But I've known Goldberg for thirty years and it's very disheartening to see him so anxious all the time. Goldberg never knew from anxiety. That's my domain, and Greenblatt's, the anxiety experts. Like Eskimos with their seventeen words for snow, Greenblatt and I know the subtle gradations and textures of anxiety, from mild paranoia upon meeting someone new, to the unbearable sense of dread in the pit of your stomach upon awakening each morning (for no particular reason, it could be a Saturday, doesn't matter). Greenblatt and me, we know anxiety. That's our department; we're skilled in that area, we have a sense of mastery in our field—we can even diagnose and prescribe:

"What's the problem? Sweating buckets at job interviews? No problem, you wear sweats and make like you've been jogging, they think you're a fitness buff, you can sweat all you want...you don't like that, take half a Xanax twenty minutes before the interview with just a drop of Peppermint Schnapps."

Jerry Greenblatt, with his nervous habit of picking at his ear with his pinkie all day, and then smelling his finger—he has anxiety. Me, thirty-seven, who nearly blacks out when anyone asks, "So what do you do?"—I have anxiety. Not Phil Goldberg. Life, for Phil Goldberg, was no problem. Nothing he can't handle with a good-natured remark and a friendly gesture. Getting out of bed in the morning? Nothing to it, for Phil: "That's what you're *supposed* to do in the morning." He doesn't understand me, or Greenblatt. Job interviews? They have him managing the place before he finishes filling out an application. Charming, affable, generous. So maybe now you understand why I'm just a little disturbed to see him not only anxious, but bordering on tormented!

Yes, tormented, except torment is Moscowitz's department. Okay, sure, Greenblatt and I are no strangers to torment, but we generally stay on the periphery, hovering anxiously, fearing the descent into all-out torment. But Moscowitz is Mr. Torment, his soul tangled and anguished and desperate, all the lost opportunities, the too-lates and I'll-nevers, his dead child and estranged wife, the genital herpes and the back that twenty chiropractors couldn't help, spends half his life lying down, feeling lousy and thinking horrible thoughts. And worst of all—it'd be better if he was an atheist—he believes in God but thinks God hates him. Not a happy man, Moscowitz. And eating nothing but cakes and rich foods and sour creams like my Uncle Izzy, God rest his soul. He's trying to kill himself with Jewish food.

So enough already. Phil Goldberg is in rough shape because his girlfriend likes clothes. That says it all. In a few weeks, God willing, after this Lipschitz tragedy blows over, I'm going to see him, take him out for a nice lasagna—the way he likes to munch down the *goyishe* food—and I'm going to knock some sense into him. What have I got to lose? I've known him for thirty years; what, he's going to be mad at me? So let him be mad...after thirty years, let him be a little mad.

So "*Yisgadal v'yisgadash sh'mei rabbaw: May His great name grow exalted and sanctified...*" And so forth—we intone the traditional mourner's *Kaddish* for Lipschitz and move over to the dining room where Finkelstein's wife Lilah has laid out a spread. But delicious

7

stuff: cold cuts, pickles, fresh rye bread, cream sodas, you thought you were in a deli—at Petaks, maybe. Typical of Finkelstein, the big shot. Any of the rest of us would have picked up a dozen bagels, a container cream cheese and thrown it on the table. Not Finkelstein with his wife from Great Neck and her lazy susan filled with Nova Scotia lox, schmaltz herring and sardines, like one kind of fish isn't enough for ten Jewish guys? Okay, nine. I guess Freddy won't be eating. Who even needs fish when you have the corned beef and tongue, the cole slaw and baked beans? Not me. Moscowitz, that's who—lying on the floor in the corner with two plates of food like he's expecting company.

Does anybody notice, besides me, that the cream in the herring is dairy, on a *fleishig* table? Nobody. Or maybe nobody *wants* to see it, or they don't think it's important. If anyone should be aware, it's Finkelstein himself—his mother kept kosher just like mine—but the big-shot makes his own rules, looks the other way, the *gantseh k'naker* with his split-level house and the swimming pool, the rest of us in apartments, rentals, shares, walk-ups, adjacents. Only Finkelstein, out of everyone, went suburban. And how could he not with a girl like Lilah and her Great Neck-orthodontal background? He had no choice. The only joy I get out of it is noticing—you can't help notic- ing —Lilah is getting fat. Absolutely no question, Finkelstein's Long Island princess, slowly but surely, is blowing up like a balloon in the Macy's Thanksgiving Day Parade—serves the big *macher* right.

But I see the creamed herring standing out on the meat table like a Negro at Packanack Lake Country Club. Why am I so acutely aware of these things? Because I never had a cheeseburger until a gorgeous Gentile woman dared me in college, the mixing of milk and meat like a wicked sex game I couldn't resist. I never had bacon, pork chops, baked ham, lobster, shrimp, no veal parmigiana, not a glass of milk at the dinner table unless it was fish or Saturday night dairy—the hard-boiled eggs, halved or quartered, cottage cheese, plates of radishes—but no milk with meat in my house, ever. So there's no way you're going to sneak a creamed herring platter onto a table of cold cuts and have me look the other way.

But you gotta leave well enough alone...what kind of crime could a cheeseburger be, God, when you put it next to child molesting, or gas chambers? Can you really compare? I don't think so...a slab of red meat with a nice slice American cheese—not so terrible, in the big picture. But those little pink squiggly-looking shrimps people eat, those I'm not crazy about. I don't think I'm missing anything so fantastic or wonderful there...those I won't even taste (too pink, too squiggly.)

I approach Mindy Lipschitz, Freddy's overweight sister, to express my condolences.

"How're you doing?"

"How should I be doing? Not so good. I was just thinking about how Freddy so loved a good deli sandwich, and now we have all these beautiful platters from Petaks and he's not even here to enjoy it. It's just so sad."

I'm staggered by the mourner's psychology. The man's whole life, in the end, comes down to a hot pastrami on rye with a little mustard. On his tombstone they will write: "Beloved son and loving brother; enjoyed smoked whitefish." Just hearing Mindy Lipschitz mention the word "deli" in connection to Freddy's death throws me, and I start "going off" as Greenblatt calls it, but at least I have the good sense to wait until Mindy's out of earshot. But I go off nonetheless:

"My friends," I say to Bernstein and Weissbaum, "we are all but individual *noshers* in the collective Jewish unconscious...the Platter is bigger than any one of us; it was served before we were born, and Petaks will deliver after we're gone...do you follow? This is not merely about food; this is sponge cake as Holy Sacrament, Manishewitz the Jewish communion. I am the body of Abraham, I drink the blood of Isaac, I go into business with Jacob—catering the Jew's divine calling, hundreds of Rock Cornish hens on the sacrificial altar, the ritual slaughter of prime ribs, the 12 caterers of Israel...before I studied Zen, a knish was just a knish, and so on. Freddy is dead, Mindy Lipschitz is fat and insane, and the cold cuts lie there, broken-hearted, but *constant*. Am I making sense?"

"Mindy's insane?" Bernstein says.

"Try the salami and eggs," Weissbaum says.

"I nosh, therefore I am," I conclude.

And now eavesdrop on Greenblatt's conversation:

"So the old guy turns to me—I don't know him from Adam—we're at Petaks, waiting by the counter with our numbers, and he says, 'My wife and my doctor tell me not to eat this food, but the bagels with the *shmeer*, the brisket, the kasha, it's *so* delicious, I *have* to eat it.'"

Always the comedian, telling his stories, even at a friend's *Kaddish*. Better to laugh than tear your hair out when you can't do anything about it. Will being somber bring Freddy back? Do any of us really want him back? I mean truly? If it meant putting him up in any of our apartments, would any of us agree to take him in? I don't even want to think about it. Maybe Finkelstein and Lilah would take him in their fancy schmancy guest room. It's not even right to discuss such a thing—Freddy was a good boy, just a little *meshugeh*, confused. What are you going to do? For a lot of us a lot of the time, the world is a horrible place. I'm no exception, believe me. I think about Freddy and say to myself, "There but for the Grace of God go I." It's not easy, this living business, this human being stuff. It's no picnic, believe me.

Finkelstein holds up a shot glass:

"*L'chaim*, everyone, in memory of Freddy."

He sees me not drinking.

"Go ahead Wilner, it's on me."

What kind of thing is that to say in your own house? Of course it's on you, Finkelstein—what, you usually charge your friends for a glass of *shnapps*? You just want to remind us who's paying for Freddy's *shivah* spread? With your salary—between your office products emporium and the legal work on the side—you can afford some cold cuts for old friends, without rubbing it in our faces. But *nu*? I say nothing. Better.

"*Namaste*," Bernstein says. It's a Hindu greeting, like *Shalom*, but where does this guy come off, with a name like Bernstein,

10

pulling this wandering sadhu routine? Claims he walked around India for three years in a loincloth, no money or shoes, hanging out with beggars in Benares, the guys with no arms and legs, the lepers. He told me they were some of the happiest people he'd ever met.

"Why happy?" I asked him.

"Because they were God-ecstatics and when you're intoxicated with the Divine it transcends all conditions."

We all know how Bernstein transcends his conditions—he must spend upwards of a hundred bucks a week on pot, mushrooms, you name it. He comes back from India three years later with a beard down to his *pupik* and it's no more Alan Bernstein, it's "Arjuna," he tells us. How they got Arjuna from Bernstein I can't figure out. So Arjuna, the Jewish Shiva-*bochur* greets everyone with *Namaste* and stands there with a roast beef sandwich dripping with mustard in one hand, his *mala* beads in the other—little prayer beads like a rosary. He moves the beads with his thumb and repeats a word to himself for each one, a mantra, a name of God: "*Ram*," the Hindu Big Cheese. Alan Bernstein, Arjuna, the sadhu drug dealer; he didn't enlighten our Freddy any by selling him smack, that much I know.

But he's not the only one to renounce his heritage. Finkelstein himself, as Jewish as homemade gefilte fish in a thick jelly sauce, with a few pieces raw carrot, his parents Auschwitz survivors no less—but does Finkelstein think of himself as Jewish? Not on your life:

"Jesus is the Way, the Truth and the Life. The Lord has opened up my eyes. I have been reborn in the Light."

"He's kidding, right?" Bernstein had said when we first got wind of Finkelstein's conversion. Like Bernstein should talk.

Prior to Finkelstein happening upon Christ, he had been on another kick: "I'm a Transcendentalist, in the tradition of Thoreau and Emerson," he would spout any chance he got. "I believe in a Supreme Cause but self-reliance and personal integrity are the only authorities I answer to."

"Finkelstein, you spent three days alone in the woods on an Outward Bound trip when you were sixteen," I used to tell him, "and you've been *hocking* us about it ever since, trying to pass yourself off as a 'rugged individualist.' Thoreau lived at Walden Pond for two years, and they didn't give him an emergency whistle and Tiger Milk bars. He didn't read philosophy books; he chopped wood and fished...ah, why am I wasting my time? Congratulations, you're a Transcendentalist. Your parents should have only known from Transcendentalism at Auschwitz." (I later learned that Thoreau took his laundry home to his mother every week. As far as I can tell, he was marching to the same friggin' drummer as the rest of us *shlubs*.) But now it's Finkelstein, the born-again Christian.

And it's not only Finkelstein and Bernstein; there's also Greenblatt, the Sufi, and Moscowitz, with his New Age claptrap. That leaves Weissbaum, Goldberg and Breshman, and of course, Reb Miltie, the real thing, Jewish through and through. Weissbaum is a sports nut and a TV nut—so he's nuts, plural. The closest thing to God for Weissbaum was Willie Mays. When Mays retired, Weissbaum had a religious crisis. Goldberg's an atheist. Breshman? That's another story.

For years I tried to talk God to Breshman. I thought he might be the one friend I could bring back to Judaism. In fact, every one of us with our religious causes tried to win Breshman's vote, and to every one of us he gave the same answer:

"Oh, I did that already."

"You did what, Breshman?"

"Judaism...I did it. The whole bit, the *tefillin* in the morning, *davening* three times a day, two sets of dishes, timers on all the lights for Sabbath, *b'ruchas like* they were going out of style, plus, all the guilt for the 613 things you're supposed to be doing that you're not doing or *not* supposed to be doing that you *are* doing... yeah, I did all that already. It wasn't fun."

"Breshman, Judaism isn't something you *do*, and you're done with it, like two years in the service. It's who you *are*, Breshman, your *kishkehs* are Jewish. That's like saying you already did 'being a man.'"

"Yeah, I did that."

"What?"

"I did being a man already—you know, having a wife and two kids and a house in the suburbs where things break and you're worried all the time about everything and you hate your job and you go to conventions and flirt with other men's wives or maybe see a hooker once in awhile because you're totally bored in bed with your wife and the kids play in the sprinkler and you take out health insurance and fire insurance and theft insurance and life insurance...I did all that already. It was no fun—too much insurance. So I quit."

He gave the same story to all the rest. To Greenblatt, who tried to make him a Sufi:

"I did that—the whirling dervish bit, the '*la illaha il allah* ' for hours, tossing your head around in *zhikrs*, drinking tea with sheiks, telling Nasrudin stories...I did all that already. Too many head movements...made me dizzy."

To Finkelstein, when he tried to wax Evangelical on him:

"I did Christianity—the whole nine yards: I let Jesus into my heart, I loved my neighbor as myself, I took on the cross, I was saved, I was born again, I said '*Kyrie Eleison*' and 'Hallelujah,' I lost my life so I could have it, I confessed, I repented, you name it, I did it. I turned the other cheek...I couldn't handle being a sinner. Punishments too severe. Not for me."

And so forth. You couldn't find the thing Breshman hadn't done. Of course the truth was he hadn't done any of these things. He just knew enough about each one to imagine it all and then dismiss it, and in his mind, it was as good as if he had actually experienced it all. Probably was, too.

I remember the end of one of my conversations with Breshman, when I finally got who he really is:

"So, Breshman, you did it all already...tell me, what's your story? What do you do now?"

"I like to ski and play tennis."

And that's it. You got five religious nuts, counting me; Weissbaum, the sports and TV nut—or the *shportler*, as my

Grandmother would say, meaning "athlete," which Weissbaum wasn't; Goldberg the atheist; Breshman the ski and tennis bum; and of course, Reb Miltie, the real McCoy. Counting poor Freddy Lipschitz, it's a *minyan*.

Freddy, a member of the Bahai faith.

CHAPTER TWO

Wilner

When she was ninety-four and bedridden, she began to mutter "the Hitler, the Hitler," as she dozed off to sleep. This was fifty years after running from Germany with my mother and the rest of the family; fifty years since that "night of the shattering glass" when the Nazis broke down their front door with an axe that landed at my grandmother's feet, my mother clutching her from behind, terrified. My grandmother calmly picked up the axe and, as she put it, "returned it to the gentleman," and later that night snuck into the burning synagogue across the street to salvage the sacred Torah scroll which she would eventually donate to a synagogue in Watertown, New Jersey.

As a child, when my father was away on business, my mother kept an axe under her bed. This was a very scary world. I could not distinguish America in the fifties from my mother's Germany where the Gestapo could break through your front door at any time. "The Hitler, the Hitler."

My mother's family came to America on the Bremen, the very last boat that Hitler permitted to leave. They were unable to obtain a visa for my mother's grandmother, with whom they lived, and she insisted they leave her behind and get out while they could. She would be dead within months. No one ever truly got over it, including me. I'm still trying to get over it. Because it has taken me years to understand that although my mother's family sold most of their possessions before leaving Germany, they brought with them the one thing they should have left behind but couldn't: utter terror.

I had no idea what I was getting myself into, the day I was born. How could I have known I was coming into a world still in shock, poisoned by death and the machinery of genocide? Whenever our family gathered around the TV at night, and one of those '40s newsreels started to appear, showing the crowds screaming 'Heil' to their Fuhrer or the goose-stepping men in uniform, or the skeletal ghosts behind barbed wire, my mother would avert her eyes in horror and my father would quickly change the station. I had no idea what it was, but I knew somehow that the sitcoms we watched were a mask for something unspeakably dark living inside our television.

It's as if on the day of my birth, as I took my very first breath, I intuited—even then—the presence of something sinister and evil in the air. I was somehow aware that this was not a planet with a good safety record for Jews. I was born frozen with fear of the specter that had permeated the world, which had generated terror in the minds and hearts of all Jews everywhere, including the ones I met when I first got here.

I was the world's first paranoid baby.
And I've been scared of everything, ever since.

***

My name is Norbert Wilner. I once wrote a book that over 20 reputable publishers turned down with nearly the identical feedback: "Funny, good writing and interesting characters, but lacks narrative thrust, doesn't hold up as a novel." Which is the problem with my life. There is no narrative thrust. My whole life, in the end, is anecdotal, a series of vignettes. My life doesn't hold up. If it were a play, half the audience would leave at intermission.

Although parts of my story are identical to the author's, I am a fictitious character, and he can make me do and say things he would never do or say. For example, while the author actually takes very good care of his teeth, I myself never floss, even though every year Marvin Hellerman, my fat dentist, shows me the little chart with the giant tooth and the plaque creeping all over it like there's no tomorrow, and in the next picture, there's no tooth. I don't listen—I'd rather walk around worrying that I'm going to lose my teeth all the time.

This is despite the fact that when we asked my grandmother for some elderly wisdom at her eightieth birthday party, all she could come up with was, "Take care from your teeth." We asked her again ten years later at her ninetieth birthday, and she said, "I have no more teeth." Her last words to my mother as they were rushing her to the I.C.U.? "*Ich habe zahnweh.*" I have a toothache.

In the last months, my grandmother took to repeating a single phrase from a psalm, in German, over and over again, every day: "*Jung gewesen und alt geworden*" meaning simply, "I was young, and I got old." A barebones summation of a human life. Maybe that really does sum the whole thing up, in the end: "I was young, and I got old." All the rest is filler, like padding a story.

So *that* I listened to, carefully, because I too was young, and I hope, knock wood nothing terrible happens, I too will get old. And so my question is, what do I do in the meantime, when I'm neither young nor old? As a friend once advised me, "You need to find something to do between breakfast and dinner." What am I to do with myself? That's my main problem and it haunts me day and night.

There's a Chassidic story about Rebbe Zusya. When questioned about whether he feared being asked by God on Judgment Day as to why he hadn't been more like Abraham or Moses, Zusya replied, "No, I am afraid I will be asked why I wasn't more like Zusya."

I'm afraid that I too, will be asked why I wasn't more like Zusya.

What do other people do? They work, they marry, they raise children, they watch TV and they go on trips. I learned this from Arnie Weissbaum, when I once asked him,

"Weissbaum, tell me something...I've known you for fifteen years, yes? In all honesty, what do you do?"

He claps me on the back—always like you're in a locker room with this guy, a real *shportler.* Smiling broadly, he replies,

"I work, I marry, I raise kids, I watch TV and I go on trips. And I capture every minute of it on tape." The guy was never without his video camera, had not only filmed his own life, but most of ours as well—every gathering, every special event.

Grinning, he goes off to count his baseball cards. Thirty-nine years old, and you can still hear him muttering late at night, his wife asleep next to him,

"Got it, got it, got it, need it, got it, need it," going through his new pack of cards with a flashlight under the covers. This is a man I should ask serious questions about life? He only knows from baseball.

When his wife left him once, a temporary separation, was he worried?

"Where's Sally, Weissbaum?" I asked.

"Ah, we had to ship her down to Triple A for awhile, we'll bring her back up once the season gets going." Sally was actually Weissbaum's third or fourth wife—none of us knew for sure. This is not a normal person, this Arnie Weissbaum, who everyone thought looked exactly like Henry Mitchell, Dennis the Menace's skinny, bespectacled father on the original television series.

Now Jerry Greenblatt, that's a person I can understand, a man after my own heart. With his big nose and growing potbelly, he was always telling us that he thought he looked like "a young Abe Vigoda," and it was his fantasy that he'd someday be cast as the lead in "the Abe Vigoda Story." None of us knew who Abe Vigoda was but we all agreed that Jerry looked just like him. He actually was starting to get work as an actor, bit parts which usually involved big black guys beating the shit out of him. But ask him what he does and listen to his answer:

"Jerry, tell me, in all honesty, what is it exactly that you do? I mean truly?"

The beads of sweat pop out on his brow, the look of terror in his eyes—I can spot the symptoms a mile away.

"Me? What do I do? I, uh, I suffer, I struggle, and I torment myself mercilessly with regret, remorse, resentment and self-hatred."

Ah, music to my ears, I can take a deep breath, I can relax for a minute, I'm not the only one. Jerry Greenblatt, an angst-brother, a kindred paranoid, a fear-mate. The true test:

"Jerry, how do you feel about getting up in the morning?"

"It's a terrible, horrible thing. Unbearable. And then once you're up, you have to go outside and see all those little people scurrying around like cockroaches."

See? Let me tell you a little story about Jerry and me, to capsulize our relationship. This really happened: It's Christmas morning some year or other, and we've both volunteered to visit various nursing homes and mental hospitals, distributing gifts, singing songs and spreading good cheer. Us, the anxiety twins, spreading good cheer. We were doing it for ourselves, because it takes the back ward of a loony bin to make us feel like ordinary, miserable people.

So we're in one such ward at Creedmore, a genuine lunatic asylum, and a short, paunchy Russian patient—a girl, nineteen maybe—spots us across the room. She picks us out of the whole festive crowd—like a scene from *King of Hearts*, you don't know who's who, with the red stocking caps and tinsel all over everybody—and she calls us over:

"You two! Come here!" she orders, directing us with her forefinger to approach.

"I know the truth!" she says.

Greenblatt and I look at each other with...you have to understand, we're both die-hard truth-seekers, and we'll take it anywhere we can get it. The whole Guru-is-in-everyone *shtick* has made us vulnerable prey to all kinds of messages, God coming at us from all directions, relentless—we're continually bombarded with this stuff. So we give this girl our full attention:

"What's the truth?" we ask. We wait. We listen. We're *available*, is the thing. We're not humoring her, we really want to know. And she tells us:

"You're a nice guy," she says, pointing to Greenblatt, "and you're a *shtunk*," to me.

And that's it. That's the truth. And I *am* a *shtunk*, underneath it all, I'm the first to admit it.

But I also believe something else: To this day, I guarantee if you peel away some of Greenblatt's outer layers, you'll find that in his heart of hearts he believes the girl was wrong, that she got it backward, that *I'm* the nice guy and *he's* the *shtunk*. I know she got it straight. Jerry Greenblatt *is* a very nice guy. Very. A little hostile, maybe, that's all.

(I'm being polite—he's a mad, raving angry guy with a malicious mouth on him, he could kill you with a look, you want to walk on eggshells around him, but a *shtunk* he's not.)

(Ah, the hell he's not. Jerry Greenblatt, you are a Royal First Class *Shtunk* to the Nth Degree, and I, Norbert Wilner, am a nice guy! Now we're talking.)

But the question at hand was concerning what people do. We already know Moscowitz goes to chiropractors, healers and tarot card readers, and stuffs himself on kugels. He's also been working on his Ph.D. dissertation for six years, on "How Humor in the Helping Professions Prevents Burnout." He interviewed a bunch of people and concluded that the ones who laughed a lot at work seemed to enjoy their jobs more than those who were grumpy and unhappy all the time. Moscowitz, the Genius Sociologist.

Finkelstein sells office supplies, worldwide. He passed the bar but no longer practices law except when Bernstein needs him to beat a drug rap. Breshman you know. Weissbaum is primarily committed in this lifetime to memorizing sports statistics. He can tell you Juan Marichal's ERA from 1962, McCovey's RBI's, you name it. But the dramatic irony of his life is that he is surrounded by people who don't give a shit.

Bernstein you already know, sells drugs and lights incense at his little altar with all the pictures of Krishna and the Gopis. So that leaves Goldberg, the love-struck atheist composer—nobody really knows what he does. We know nobody ever pays him to compose. We know that his girlfriend with all the blouses and slacks drove him to a therapist for the first time in his life—a female therapist.

"How's your therapy going?" I asked him.

"Terrific," he said, "My therapist says she's been feeling a lot better since I started coming."

I told you, Goldberg will cheer anybody up. Even me. The guy's a laugh-a-minute. His favorite story? Listen:

"We're in fifth grade, and there's this short dumpy guy named Eli Pelta. He already had a little goatee, and his voice was about two octaves below middle C. Not a bright guy. Mrs. Baker calls on him during a grammar lesson: 'Eli, make up a sentence with the word pencil as the object.' Eli thinks about it, strokes his beard, takes his time, finally grunts, 'The pencil is a dope.'"

What'd I tell you? Goldberg, the funny-man musician. I too was a musician, once. (My teacher told me I had "negranotaphobia"—a fear of black notes.) But now, the big question, from Mrs. Lender, after Yom Kippur services at B'nai Shalom—I go once a year to sit with my parents. In front of my mother, no less, she asks me:

"And what do you do, Norbert?"

I perspire, I get anxious, I look at my mother, she's tearing her heart out.

"I'm in business for myself," stalling for time. "I'm a...funeral director! In fact, I heard that your Lewis isn't doing so well, maybe we should get together and talk. I'm running a special two-for-one sale now—how have *you* been feeling, Mrs. Lender? Sign up now and I throw in *shivah* benches free, plus I print up yarmulkes for everybody with the deceased's name inside, or you can go with the little engraved matchbooks. And I do my own eulogies, you don't have to pay for a rabbi—in fact, I'm training for ordination myself, I go to seminary nights, and I volunteer once a week to drive the Chabad Mitzvah Mobile around Manhattan...there's a lot of young Jewish boys walking around out there, Mrs. Lender, who never put on *tefillin*—I know, I know, it's a crime, but we nab the suckers and get 'em on board, wrap 'em up before they even know what hit 'em, before they can say '*Baruch Atah*,' they got the sign between the eyes and opposite the heart, and on the way out we give 'em a free *mezuzah*—nothing fancy, one of those little plastic jobs you can get in Chinatown, but a doorpost is a doorpost, and when you're coming in and when you're going out, you gotta remember God took us out of Egypt, etcetera and so forth and so on, Mrs. Lender, that's what I think..."

What did I really tell Lender?

"Well gee, I don't know right now, I'm sort of between things, if you know what I mean, trying to figure out what to do next."

Truth is best. But where did I get this bug in my head about going into the death business? At Freddy's funeral. Everybody was so morose and glum, you'd think nobody ever died before, that birds don't die, pet goldfish, flowers, that for every up there's not a down. "You take the bitter with the better," Goldberg's mother was always saying. At Passover Seders, when it came time to eat the bitter herbs, my grandmother would point her finger at us and solemnly instruct: "Never forget the bitter."

And we haven't.

Seven days and nights the Jews gather in mourning, *sitting shivah*. ("It's like a World Series of grief," Weissbaum once observed.) Everybody shows up the first night ("The opener," says Weissbaum) to pay their respects—-neighbors, distant relatives—then the crowd ("The gate") slowly dwindles as the week progresses. By Day Four it's just us, the core *minyan*, basically getting sloshed, and once again, I start making speeches:.

"You open a window, sooner or later you shut the window, it's a fact of life my friends," I begin. "A baby is born gurgling and drooling, eventually the baby grows old and dies. That's the best-case scenario. We're all living our lives inside one of those old black and white photos of high school championship sports teams on display in school hallways, that moment when you realize with a poignant shock that many of those young and bright-spirited high school teenagers have already gotten old and passed on...*jung gewesen und alt geworden* my friends, *jung ge-fucking-wesen und alt ge-fucking-worden*."

Bernstein, nodding in agreement, is high on Jamaican Gold, has already done a chakra-bypass and landed in the noosphere, he's with me, he knows what I'm talking about, he put in his three months on the banks of the Ganges, smoking hashish and meditating on the funeral ghats, the sounds of crackling bodies, the corpses floating by. He may have killed Freddy, but at least he had the good sense to wear his bright, orange-checkered *lunghi* and crimson headband to the funeral; everyone else in black, so depressing.

"Why do we rejoice at the *bris* and weep at the grave?" I continue, "It is only our limited human mind making the distinction. God makes no such distinctions—that a newborn baby is good, a corpse is bad, birth is happy, death is sad. The sensitive ones among us might just as well weep when a baby comes into this life—this miserable world, this vale of tears, this tale told by a *meeskite*, full of noise and hubbub, signifying *bupkis*, to paraphrase the Bard of Avon, and we could just as easily rejoice when a loved one leaves this world to join the happy souls on the other side, free at last of the mortal agonies, free to fly, to soar, to walk around in public in their underwear if they want to, no more fear of death. Though who knows, our dearly departed might well have fear of life to contend with, the terror of coming back here and doing all this again, in the unlikely event that reincarnation is as literal as all that. But my real message to you, friends, is that each and every day of our lives, while we are here, we need to, each of us, address ourselves with the very same deep question in the pit of our souls that the great artist Vincent Van Gogh asked himself..."

Dramatic pause. Silence. I had them.

"Well go ahead, Norbert, what was it?" asks Moscowitz. (Even Moscowitz stops stuffing his face for a minute, may his heart not explode like a gurgling vat of cholesterol.)

"It was simply this: Something is alive in me, what can it be?"

Silence. Then Finkelstein, the big-shot:

"That's it, Wilner? After the big build-up?"

"Maybe you didn't hear me, Mr. Finkelstein—you who once worshipped Thoreau, the man who went to the woods to 'live deliberately'—unplug your ears, Finkelstein, and the rest of you, listen up: Something is alive in me, what can it be? I leave you now to consider what I've said," and then raising my glass, "to Freddy Lipschitz, may his soul be blessed by *Hashem*."

"In the name of Allah," Greenblatt says.

"*Jai Ram*," chants Bernstein.

"Divine Light," Moscowitz the Aquarian kugelmeister pipes up.

"Thank you Jesus," prays Finkelstein.

"*L'chaim*," naturally, from Reb Miltie.

Breshman says nothing and finally Goldberg and Weissbaum offer the traditional,

"Cheers, gents," clinking glasses.

My Jewish buddies, my *minyan*. And like I said, I *grew up* with most of these clowns—I lent them milk money; we stood around together waiting for the bell to ring at East Lake Elementary; we played *Steal the Bacon* together. That should have tipped me off, way back then, the unkosher meat a smoking gun in this story, the pork product precursor of *trayf* travails to come. And now, thirty years later, forty, we have become a walking ecumenical conference for chrissake, a religious convention, a theology department, holy wars. A Jewish *jihad*.

And me? That was the day—a big moment, a turning point—when I decided two important things about my life: one, to become a rabbi and save other Jewish souls from bowing to stone Gods of other nations and offending our Lord, (who's not at all pleasant when He's upset—death by stoning, according to the Torah, for the tiniest itsy bitsy teeny weenie infraction) and two, to start the Happy Hearse Funeral Parlor.

And so I did. Both. Why, you thought I was all talk?

CHAPTER THREE

Gelberman

Does he have a congregation? No. Did he go to seminary or yeshiva and get ordained? No. Does he understand a word of Hebrew? No. Is he versed in Torah and Talmud, keep a kosher home, wear a yarmulke? No. What then, makes him a rabbi? Only one thing: He says so. And what Milton Gelberman says, goes.

I was on the #1 train, heading north towards Washington Heights. It was one of those cold, gloomy November Sunday mornings in New York, before the Christmas displays go up in the Lord & Taylor windows, before you need to put your name on a waiting list to shop in F.A.O. Schwartz. The #1 stops at 190th Street, famous for its pedestrian tunnel up to Broadway—the longest, darkest and most frightening walkway in any city anywhere; it's a nightmare getting out to the street. If you can manage, you always try to wait for other people to come along, because nobody wants to walk through it alone.

So I'm lingering near the tunnel entrance, waiting for someone else to come. This peculiar-looking guy shows up, wearing the traditional black garb of the Orthodox Chassidim, except instead of the big furry black *streimel,* on his head he has a New York Mets cap, and on his feet, rainbow-colored Converse sneakers. He's short—maybe 5'5", looks about sixty-seven with a thin, wispy grey beard and big bushy eyebrows, thick glasses with heavy black frames. Long, curly *payis*—the Orthodox sideburns. He's carrying a baseball bat and a shopping bag from Zabar's Deli on the Upper Westside. He sees me staring—who wouldn't? —and watches my eyes settle on the bat.

"It was bat-day at Shea," he says with a smile, a squeaky high-pitched voice, "Everyone under twelve got a free bat."

The fact that it was November and baseball season was long gone didn't occur to me until months later. By then, he would claim no recollection of the conversation, and say he had never been to Shea Stadium in his life, and what would an aging rabbi want with a baseball bat?

"Ready for the Tunnel of Death?" he asks. I nod, still trying to take the guy in.

"Let me ask you something, young man," he begins.

"Yes?"

Ordinarily, nobody in the tunnel made eye contact, or even acknowlåedged that they were walking together, or using one another for comfort and safety. Let alone get personal.

"Are you Jewish?"

"Am I *Jewish?*"

"You're *not* Jewish?"

"I *am* Jewish."

"Ah hah! I thought so...I could tell by the *yiddisha noz*—it's not such a bad one, you're lucky, but it's a Jewish nose, I knew it! I can spot one a mile away...my mother, she should rest in peace, had a nose on her like there was no room on her face for anything else."

"So?" I ask.

"So? So what?" he says.

"So what I'm Jewish?"

"So what you're Jewish? So what you're Jewish, he says. Are you blind? You don't see what I have here?" he says, holding up the bag.

"A bag from Zabar's."

"No! Completely wrong. It's what's *in* the bag from Zabar's—maybe you could make an educated guess. But enough with the quiz show."

He throws open the bag, holding it right under my face.

"Bagels and cream cheese," he says. "*Bagels and cream cheese*," this time raising his voice, excited. "This is it! The winning number! This is not the Tunnel of Death anymore, this is a Tunnel of *Chaim*, of Life, and let me tell you where this tunnel leads..."

"Broadway?"

"Again wrong! Completely! But it's okay, you're excited by the whole thing that goes on here. It's understandable, you're not thinking straight, so I'll tell you: it leads right to my apartment on 190th Street and Bennett Avenue, #6H, to my little kitchen table where I put out the bagels and the cream cheese and I make some nice coffee—or you like tea? I have tea also. And the two of us, we have breakfast, and you tell me everything there is to know about yourself and then I tell you where your thinking is all wrong and that's it! It's a beautiful Sunday morning in New York City, and we are joined by *Hashem* in a bagel-to-remember...come!"

With that he takes my arm and, humming a *niggun*—a Chassidic melody —he sweeps me along to his apartment on Bennett and 190th.

And that's how I first met Reb Miltie, as I came to call him.

Apartment #6H is tiny—one small room cluttered with old furniture and pictures and lamps, a pull-out couch that I gather is his bed, a tiny bathroom where you can lean your forehead on the sink while you sit on the toilet, and a kitchen just big enough for a small table with two folding chairs. Pictures everywhere—on the fridge, the table, the oven door—lots of children.

"You have a big family?" I venture.

"No. Never married."

"These are brothers and sisters then?" I ask.

"I was an only child."

"Cousins?"

"None that I knew—all my uncles and aunts died in the camps."

"So who are all these people in the pictures?"

He stops fussing with the coffee for a minute, stares long and hard at the photos as if trying to identify them, then shakes his head.

"Damned if I know. But they looked like such lovely people, I decided to leave them up, since I have no family of my own to speak of."

"What do you mean? Whose were they?"

"This apartment became available when the last tenant died—that's how you get apartments in Washington Heights. The landlord was going to throw everything away, I said leave it, and that's that."

"It's a little sad, I think, for you to have pictures of strangers in your home."

"Sad? *Now* we're talking. *Now* our breakfast discussion has begun—that's the first lesson Reb Nachman taught: The path to God is a path of joy. There's no room for sadness. The fact that he himself could have used a little Prozac is another story. Not a cheerful man. But you think you're going to attract the Almighty with self-pity? She doesn't hear it. Her ears perk up when She hears laughter, and dancing. She likes a good time. So, what you see as sad, my new friend, is *your* sadness. Go, eat, you like poppy? Onion maybe? Try the nice cinnamon-raisin. So tell me, Mr....what's your name?"

"Norbert."

"You have a last name, or is it just Norbert, like Dion, or Cher?"

"Wilner."

"Norbert Wilner....so tell me, Norbert Wilner, what do you do for a living?"

I choke on my bagel and begin coughing severely. He hands me a glass of water and claps me on the back.

"Okay, we talk about more important things—what's a living? You're not starving. You look healthy, you have a trust fund, am

I right? Doesn't matter. Let's get to the *kishkehs*, the important stuff...do you like God?"

I am stopped short by the question. Do I like God? What kind of question is that? Thou shalt love the Lord Thy God with all Thy Heart and All Thy Soul; who said anything about *like?*

"Sir?" I ask, stalling for time.

"'Sir' he calls me. Miltie. My name is Miltie. What? It's a simple question."

"I never thought about it quite like that—so ordinary and matter of-fact."

"Ah hah!" like he had struck gold, scored a point on a debating team. "Big mistake, Norbert Wilner. You've been thinking all wrong, then. I knew it! I knew it in the tunnel already. So, don't answer me then, if you never thought about it. Think about it, and next Sunday *you* bring the bagels—I'm an old man, why should I ride the subway to Zabar's and walk through the Tunnel of Death when you're a young man with two healthy legs and no arthritis eating the cartilage in your knees like it's a buffet? Okay? Okay...but before you go, let me read you something."

He takes down a book called *Chassidic Sayings,* flips it open and reads:

"Let everyone cry out for God, and lift his heart up to God as if he was hanging by a hair and a tempest was raging to the very heart of heaven, and he was at a loss for what to do and there was hardly time to cry out. It is a time when no counsel can help him, and he has no refuge save to remain in his loneliness and lift his eyes and his heart up to God and cry out to Him. And this should be done at all times for in the world a man is in great danger."

"Yikes."

"What?"

"What happened to the joy and laughter business? Now you're coming on with the heavy stuff."

"Heavy? What's heavy? Remind me to tell you the story of my life sometime. This is light stuff. Fluff."

"A tempest raging to the heart of heaven?"

"Piece of cake."

"A man is in great danger?"

"Small potatoes."

"Nevertheless," I said, "yikes." (Yikes, a philosophical position, an existential response: the human being stands alone at the edge of an Infinite drop, staggered, awestruck and terrified, and can finally utter only one word: Yikes.) I explain my theory to Miltie, and he says,

"Well there's the 'yikes' religion and there's the 'ahhh' religion," saying "ahhh" as if something miraculous and wonderful had just materialized right before his eyes. "It's called 'seeing the magic,' which you can't possibly do until you resolve the first question: Do you like God? I have another assignment for you: I want you to prepare a one-man show, music and stories, based on the life and legends of the Baal Shem Tov."

"How do I go about that?"

"You read about him and think about what you've read until you have a sense of your main character, and then you try to portray him, theatrically, but it must be convincing, it must be a great and brilliant acting job."

"And?"

"And? If you do this right, you will become *my* teacher...and listen: no one must know about this project...no one."

"Why not?"

"Because you must learn what it means to be a 'Hidden One,' like one of the thirty-six *lamed vovnik* who hold up the world. Contrary to everything they taught you in California, you must reveal your true Self to no one...not even you!"

At this Miltie laughs hysterically, at some joke I don't quite get. Then he pulls a second book off the shelf and says, "Now *you* read. It's a Jewish *I-Ching*, whatever page you open to is today's lesson."

32

Here's what I open to:

When the heart hurts,
chances are you're not breathing enough.
Have you never known what it is
to be done with grieving?
There is salvation for you,
but only when you are breathing deep.

Mordecai will tell you:
Breathe in the Presence of the Tender One now,
And your tears will feed the world.

Then we have a moment together where he is just kind of looking at me and neither of us speaks. I take a deep breath. Then I say, "Who wrote that?"

I look at the cover: *Mordecai's Book.*

"Who's Mordecai?"

"Moredecai, may his memory be a blessing, was a little-known Jewish mystical poet from the 13th century, a contemporary of Rumi's. There is reason to believe the two of them knew one another...you can read more in the introduction I wrote."

Sure enough, I had looked right at it: Introduction by Milton Gelberman.

"Take it, he says, then ushers me out as the buzzer rings and another guy comes in. Reb Miltie introduces us.

"Norbert Wilner, meet Miltie, Miltie meet Norbert Wilner."

He sees my eyes narrow in doubt and questioning, and he says, "What? Miltie's such an uncommon name? It's against the law for there to be two Miltie's in the world? It's such a miracle? Like the Red Sea parting? I say good-bye to you now, Reb Wilner. Have a good week, with only joy. *Zei gezunt!*"

I walk out onto Bennett Avenue and up the few blocks to my apartment, pondering a very unusual question: Do I like God?

***

I leave Miltie's place and go down to the New York Public Library, pile up six books about Chassidism and its famous founder, the Baal Shem Tov, on a table. But first I pick up the Mordecai book and read Miltie's introduction. Apparently the original manuscript was written in Aramaic, and was uncovered during one of Jerusalem's archaeological excavations in the Old City, in 1978. Like the famed scraps of parchments found in earthen jugs in Qumran which came to be known as the Dead Sea Scrolls, this too originally took the form of a rolled up piece of parchment stored in a vase, in what might have been a bathhouse of some sort at one time. Scholars had somehow established the author was a Persian Jew who lived in what today is Konya, Turkey, which was Rumi's home as well. Writings had been found by one of Rumi's early disciples describing "the Master's friend, the Jew known as Mordecai," and later references describe him as "the healer-poet." I read the first poem:

> *If you're running around in circles,*
> *like a white chicken in the neighbor's yard,*
> *maybe you, too, have lost your head.*
> *Sit quietly for a minute,*
> *and reflect on your situation.*
> *Nobody who goes in circles ever finds his way home.*

> *Mordecai will tell you:*
> *If you want to relax by the fire tonight,*
> *just stop everything you're doing.*

But I didn't, and spent the next six and a half hours reading about the Baal Shem Tov. I learned about the Jewish version of ecstasy, in which "the habitual is eternally new, and the future and past collapse into the glorious wonder of the Present Eternity."

It seems a tall order: to be ecstatic in the face of All That Is? For a Jew? What about our suffering? How can we give that up? It's who we are. What about "the Hitler"? But if it's true that it is possible to somehow choose and embrace an ecstatic mystical outlook, then I'm suddenly ashamed that I have wasted all those years being a selfish, suffering little shit, and I'm afraid God's gonna kill me when He finds out. "The jig is up, little *shlepper*," I imagine Him saying, or, "Your ass is grass, Yid."

Sitting in the reading room, I began writing a fictional account of the Baal Shem's childhood:

"Legend has it that when the great Jewish Rebbe, the Baal Shem Tov, was a child, his eyes burned with a radiance that set him apart from the other children, and, in fact, from all other people.

"Early one morning, as the great orange ball of the morning sun began to rise over the distant mountains, the young boy, Israel, son of Eliezer and Sarah, arose with a start. He sat up in bed, fully alert, the way you or I might if we heard a strange noise in the hallway and suspected an intruder, our hearts trembling.

"For in fact, there was an intruder—a Divine Intruder. An angel had been sent from on high, from the very Dwelling Place of the Unnamable, to rouse the lad, and beckon him out into the glorious morning at that wonderful moment of the pure dawn, the dawn in all its majesty.

"And now we must make every effort to look at this scene, this dawn, through the boy's eyes, and not through the habitual and dulled vision of our own eyes. For he walked out of his parent's house as if in a trance, and traveled another mile on foot along a winding country road, to a spot where a big boulder sat off to one side of a sprawling green meadow, a meadow dotted with thousands of burgundy, golden yellow, magenta and white wildflowers.

"And he walked through this extraordinary ocean of color, seeing also the crimson ball of light slowly rising before him and illuminating the distant horizon with an other-worldly glow, announcing one more day of life on earth. Young Israel, as if pulled by invisible

hands, climbed up onto the boulder and looked out over the sparkling meadow, each flower a bright, glittering diamond, and he looked at the red-orange circle of the sun as it finally appeared in all its fullness, and the boy experienced no distinction between that sun and the inner wonders of his own heart. His spirit literally rose with the sunrise, and he truly could not tell the two apart: the sun, and his soul. In some ways, it was, as the saying goes, 'the first moment of the rest of his life.'

"*When he returned to the breakfast table of his parents, he was not the same child they had raised for 12 years. Now his already-radiant eyes burned like a bright sun. Now Israel, son of Eliezer and Sarah, was gazing out at the world through* everyone's *eyes. No longer confined to the narrow vision of the individual self, his sight had become whole, and now included the myriad points of view of the entire creation in its totality.*

"*And from that day on, when the boy spoke, and especially when he sang, his song issued from the heart of creation, and his melodies had the power to heal the world.*"

That was my first attempt to fulfill Miltie's assignment, and I was pleased with it. But on my way home from the library, I remembered his other piece of homework, and it presented a much greater challenge to me:

Do I like God?

No; no I don't.

36

CHAPTER FOUR

The Greenblatts

"Gentlemen, I have a sexual problem," I announce to the group, hanging out at my place.

"Let's bond. Let's share. Let's be intimate," says Bernstein-with-the-beard, (as we sometimes called him, to distinguish him from Bernstein-without-the-beard, which is what we used to call him, before he grew a beard. Whenever he shaved it off, Phil would tell him, "You look exactly the same as you did *with* a beard, only without a beard.")

"The women with whom I feel a kindred spirit," I continue, "a compatibility—*simpatico* if you will—the ones I can talk to, enjoy being with..."

"The girls he likes," Weissbaum explains.

"Exactly. They are all roughly forty years old and up. On the other hand, the women who inspire sexual feelings to arise within me—who stimulate the dimension of Eros, stir the libidinal juices..."

"The ones he wants to fuck," says Weissbaum.

"...are all between the ages of about fourteen and twenty-six. There's a gap in there, if you've been following."

"Major gap," Greenblatt agrees.

"Sounds like you've got a serious gap problem," Goldberg concurs.

"So what do I do?"

"It's simple," Weissbaum says, "Find someone your own age who you love and respect and enjoy being with, marry her, and then *cheat*. Go at it like animals with a teenager."

"Definitely," Bernstein says, "Betray the wife with younger women. I'm in complete agreement with Mr. Weissbaum."

"Just keep the home satisfied," Greenblatt says (quoting his late father, Ed Greenblatt, about whom he had once written a poem which began, "Ed, still dead.")

"Listen," I continue, "Basically, I don't really feel sexually aroused unless I sort of hate the woman a little. If I like her, forget about it—who can have sex with someone like that?"

"Who did this to you?" Greenblatt asks. "Did my sister do this to you? You're twisted..."

"Nothing wrong with twisted," Bernstein says.

"...and disturbed."

"Disturbed's okay."

And actually, I think it *was* Greenblatt's *farbisener* sister who did this to me. Because I knew the first time we went to bed together, two weeks into the relationship, that she didn't interest me in that way—that I wanted out—but it took me three years to communicate about it. And in the meantime, our sex life deteriorated to the point where instead of asking each other to "make love" or "do the coochinadra" or "play moofkie poofkie," we were reduced to the rather functional, mechanical inquiry, "You want to have orgasms?" as if it was an in-dividual, but shared, act, like having ice cream sodas. Not even two straws in one glass. No whipped cream. Forget about the cherry.

Greenblatt's sister may have ruined me for all aspects of rela-tionship—not just the sexual domain. *Nothing* about our being together worked, except napping. We were big time nappers. I actually first met her when I was the editor of a monthly alterna-tive magazine. She joined the staff in the position of Managing Editor. As she would later tell people,

"I was the Managing Editor...I managed to put the magazine out of business."

Which she did, because our office was in fact my apartment, and while Greenblatt's sister was supposed to be on the phone with advertisers, she would instead, generally, be lying in my bed with me. And not because we were playing moofkie poofkie, or even having orgasms. On the contrary: it was because we were both strong nappers. We both preferred lying around doing nothing to working. This was our connection.

We soon began to run the entire magazine from my bed, and eventually we started going to movies every day, during office hours. She would make the trip uptown to "work" at my place, and immediately get under the sheets. In this way, Greenblatt's *farkrimpt* sister managed to put the magazine out of business. Naturally I didn't suspect at the time that what she could do to a magazine she could just as easily do to a man, but back then, at least for the moment, *I* was still in business, although she continued to torture me in our relationship by insisting that I be *in* it.

But after three and a half years, when it had become absolutely unbearable for us to be together, we went to a counselor to get an outsider's perspective. We did not go to see Myron Spotnick, although perhaps we should have. Myron Spotnick was the marriage counselor Jerry Greenblatt had gone to with his wife, after they had been married five years, and it had become absolutely unbearable for *them* to be together. (Although Greenblatt has privately confessed that he also finds it unbearable to be with himself.)

Spotnick was wearing two watches, which should have alerted Jerry and his wife as soon as they entered his office. Yet for a man with that name, who wore two watches, he was surprisingly effective as a marriage counselor. The session lasted exactly four minutes, and cost $100.

"Do you want to have children?" he asked Bonnie Greenblatt. "Do you want to own a home?"

"Yes," she replied to both.

"And do you, Jerry, want to have children and own a home?"

"No," he replied.

Spotnick advised them to be "just friends," and Bonnie left the marriage that night. Greenblatt has continued seeing Spotnick weekly ever since. One time, the *minyan* accompanied Greenblatt to his session:

"He really needs help," Weissbaum told Spotnick.

"This man is very troubled," I told Spotnick.

"Help him," Bernstein said.

"Help me," Greenblatt said.

"You're a shtunk," said Spotnick, and satisfied that Greenblatt was in good hands, we all left.

"Right on time, right on time," Myron Spotnick would greet Jerry, jovially waving his double-watched wrist in the air, amusing himself. "How're you feeling, Greenblatt?"

"I feel like there's a big hole in my being and I can't fill it up. I'm terrified of my very existence. I'm lonely and empty inside."

"You've come a long way since you first started seeing me..."

"I'm not happy."

"Why do I have to listen to you complain every week? Who told you that you should be happy? *I* never told you that. If you were happy, you wouldn't be seeing Myron Spotnick, Ph.D., am I right? "

"Yeah, I guess so."

"So, there you are: be happy you're unhappy, because you are. Now enough about you. I've got my own problems."

In his own way, Spotnick was not unwise.

"Time's up, time's up," the bi-temporal therapist said, and Greenblatt left the office. His sessions usually lasted three or four minutes. The brevity of Spotnick's counseling work had to do with his direct, no-nonsense approach, and the two watches were his way of reminding patients that time is divided. In ordinary, linear psychiatric time, a cure for mental suffering can take years and years of therapy and hard work. In Spotnick-time, most problems could usually be resolved successfully in under five minutes. He wore both watches because most of his patients, like Jerry, had a foot in both worlds: They saw Myron for under five minutes and resolved their problems, and, they did this for years and years.

"See you next week, next week," Spotnick said, said.

This style of therapy was remarkably effective for Greenblatt. He generally came out of his sessions glowing with a certain new-found clarity and strength.

"How'd it go?" I might ask him.

"Fantastic, I feel like a new man."

"What'd you talk about?"

"Myron."

Greenblatt's sessions with Spotnick certainly beat his first experience with a therapist. Jerry and I had spent enormous sums of money taking workshops that we hoped would make us feel better about ourselves. Each of these courses cost between $250 and $700. At one of them, part of the process was to have the shit kicked out of us by three very large men, one of whom would later be incarcerated in a mental institution. We put ourselves through the most humiliating situations, the most extravagant expenditures of time and money, trying to cure ourselves of feeling crummy all the time.

Then Jerry decided to try an ordinary therapist, a woman, and I saw him shortly after his initial consultation. He looked severely downtrodden. He told me that he had spent the fifty minutes telling her about all the workshops he had taken, all the personal work he had done on himself to open up and grow, about his meditation and his vegetarian diet, his guru and his mantra. He said that after he had gotten through telling this woman everything about his entire life, she had said to him, quite simply and matter of factly,

"You have no self. You need long-term treatment."

Poor Jerry. The rest of the night, whenever I would look over at him from across the room, he would shrug his shoulders helplessly and silently mouth the words, "I have no self." And after all that *self*-help, for crying out loud.

"Jerry," I said, trying to console him, "Just think of it this way...your whole life up until now has been nothing but a sham, a complete waste."

"Yeah, I suppose you're right."

Poor Greenblatt, he takes everything so seriously, everything to heart. It's what makes him a great comedian, I suppose. A sorrowful, nervous guy, making the world laugh. A sad sack in clown face, a tragic soul in a vaudeville get-up; you had to love him, if for no other reason than that he would go out to a sporting goods store in the middle of the day and come home with over a hundred dollars worth of fishing equipment. The man never fished. He rarely left the Lower East Side. He had no intention of fishing, ever. He just enjoyed buying things, "to fill up," as he put it.

Once I was at Jerry's house, observing him prepare for a picnic. He had all his things together, and then, as an afterthought, he showed me a beautiful, straw picnic basket that he had purchased recently.

"Should I bring it?" he asked me.

"Absolutely," I replied.

"Nah, it's too bulky, it won't fit in the trunk."

I pleaded with him: "Listen to me, Jerry, please, just once, for God's sake, listen to reason." (It was this sort of thing that could still move me.) "Okay, now follow carefully: you bought a new picnic basket, right? You're going on a picnic today, yes? You go on picnics once in a blue moon, maybe never again. If you don't use that basket today, Jerry, you may never use it. Please, for my sake, take the basket. Today's the day. It's picnic day. Take it, Jerry, I'm begging you."

Greenblatt acquiesced. Reluctantly. And he actually made matters worse for me by taking the basket, because although he took it with him, he didn't use it. He just brought it along for the ride, like a straw passenger. He stuffed all his sandwiches and fruit and cookies into plastic shopping bags, and then propped his new basket up in the back seat like it was on display at Woolworth's. As he drove off, he left me, deeply disturbed, standing on the sidewalk.

"I don't ask for much, God. All I wanted was for him to stuff a corned beef sandwich wrapped in cellophane into the basket. To carry the basket to the grass and place it on the blanket. To open it up, take out the sandwich, unwrap it and eat it. Period. That's it. A simple one plus one equals two. Finished. Not a big deal. Not like creating the heavens and the earth. Not making bushes burn without burning. I'm talking a few slices of corned beef on a decent rye bread, a little mustard, a soda to *shvank* it down. What's so difficult? I'm a little guy wanting a friend to act like a normal person. Strike me dead if I'm asking too much. I should drop dead if I'm on the wrong track here."

("And God said," I answered myself, "Let there be deli, and there was deli. And on the seventh day He created heartburn. He created families everywhere eating dairy for dinner, some herring, hard-boiled eggs cut in halves, some farmer's cheese and fresh radishes. And God saw that it was good...Good? It was delicious.")

***

But funnyman or no, one night I have an ominous dream that Jerry and I are walking the damp, dark, grey-blue streets of London on a chilly, drizzly night. I am clutching my chest, sobbing, and saying, "Oh Jerry, my heart is breaking," and I feel a wrenching pain; I am grief-stricken. When I tell him about the dream he dismisses it, says, "Everybody in your dream is you. Leave me out of it."

***

The man Greenblatt's sister and I went to for couples counseling was not nearly as direct as Myron Spotnick. He suggested that the two of us try an experiment: spend thirty days without having any contact whatsoever. This would be no easy feat for Greenblatt's sister who was accustomed to calling me three or four times a day, usually to discuss how miserable she was, and how miserable *I* was for making *her* so miserable. Our unhappiness together was very time-consuming; if we didn't work at it full-time, we ran the risk of feeling okay for a minute.

The thirty days of no contact worked. By the end of the thirty days, Greenblatt's sister was engaged to be married to the superintendant of her building, a Puerto Rican guy named, inexplicably, Marv Cohen. We needed closure, so I met her in a coffee shop where apparently the waiter knew her and had heard of her engagement:

"And is this the lucky man?" the waiter inquired, indicating me.

"Yes," I replied.

"Very funny," Greenblatt's sister said.

Don't get me wrong. I never said I didn't love her. I loved her with all my heart. I just couldn't stand to *be* with her.

Greenblatt's father used to call her "miserable" as a nickname. He died when she was nineteen, of a heart attack, in the middle of the night. If only Ed Greenblatt—("Ed, still dead")— could have known how miserable *that* would make his daughter. Whenever I talked about how attached she was to me, and how she probably wouldn't be able to bear the pain if we split up, she would say to me,

"If I survived my father leaving me, I can certainly survive *you* leaving me: What do you think, you're some great prize or something?"

I felt a very close kinship with dead Ed Greenblatt, whom I had never met: we both thought his daughter was "miserable."

So the screwball got married, somehow landed a husband who, fortunately, was not me. They got married in a tile-floored community center in Brooklyn with deli and paper plates. There was no musician present to play the wedding song, and I'm told that instead, the rabbi sang, to the tune of Here Comes The Bride, "Da, dum de dum; da, dum de dum." I wasn't invited to the wedding, but she called me four times the day she got back from her honeymoon in Asbury Park, New Jersey. I guess the honeymoon was over.

My elderly landlady was in my apartment to discuss something with me, and so I told Greenblatt's sister that I couldn't talk because "someone's here right now." To which she responded, "Oh who is it? You're *girlfriend*," saying "girlfriend" in a such a tone of contempt as if to imply that although she herself was now married, I was still not allowed to have any contact whatsoever with any other woman, ever, for the rest of my days.

When I gently shared my feeling that perhaps this was an unfair attitude, she said, simply, "So I'm a terrible person, I'm the worst girlfriend you ever had." I had no argument for that, and only reflected inwardly that it was a splendid turn of events—Divine Grace, surely—that I was free of Greenblatt's sister after three miserably torturous years. (I told her I was writing a book, and I was considering calling it, *Greenblatt's Sister: The Miserable Woman Who Wrecked My Life*. She suggested, instead, that I call it, *The Bubbi-Malachi Papers*, and suggested an opening line: "Celia is fat but she's no dummy." No explanation.)

I'm sleeping over Weissbaum's one night and we're lying in the dark discussing the phenomenon of Greenblatt's sister, trying to get a handle on her the way colleagues at a psychiatric convention might exchange views about a particular case history. I bring up the fact that she always told people completely different things about how the two of us met, where our first date had been, and so forth. She and I actually had absolutely contradictory notions about the entire history of our relationship: how it began, when it ended, and most of what happened in between. She will say that we broke up in July, I believe it was the preceding December. That leaves an eight-month gap under dispute. We once played an informal, at-home version of *The Newlywed Game* with several other couples, and we came in last, failing to agree on a single fact about anything, losing even to a couple who were on their *first* date.

Weissbaum brings up her preference for fighting only in public places—the many times she gathered crowds around us on the streets of New York, people leaning out their apartment windows, usually cheering her on. Once, frustrated that there was nothing I could do in such a situation, I abruptly turned around in mid-squabble and simply took off, ran away. She ran after me in a mad rage, screaming in the Village, "POLICE! POLICE! STOP THAT MAN!"

At the climax of one of our worst indoor fights, she ordered me out of her apartment. As I headed toward the door, she threw herself in front of it and screamed, "DON'T YOU DARE LEAVE THIS HOUSE." As I moved back toward the bedroom, she again blocked my way, screaming, "GET OUT!" As I headed toward the door, she again threw herself before me and said, "YOU CAN'T LEAVE HERE WITH THOSE JEANS ON, THEY'RE MINE!" which they were, so I took them off, and then, as I was standing there in my *gatkes*, she screamed, "NOW GET OUT!"

After tossing all these incidents back and forth with Weiss-baum for what seems like hours—neither of us even mentions the box of chocolate chip cookies she once smashed into my face while I was driving 70 miles per hour on the New York Thruway—we reject the hormonal explanation, we toy with genetics, and then the answer finally dawns on me. In the very moment I think of it, I just know it is right. It explains everything. I now understood Greenblatt's sister.

"Weissbaum, I know that when I tell you this, you're going to know, in your heart of hearts, that it is absolutely accurate, that I have solved the riddle of Greenblatt's sister, that it explains everything she has ever done or ever will do. You ready?"

"Yeah yeah yeah, what is it?" Weissbaum impatient, skeptical.

"The woman has a *screw loose.* "

Weissbaum is silent. I know my revelation of the truth has staggered him. Finally he speaks up:

"You're a fucking genius."

I bask in self-pleasure. I have solved the mystery of Green-blatt's sister. I can move on. Weissbaum and I can sleep in peace, except he pops out of bed, saying, "I have to get this on tape," and makes me repeat the entire conversation, verbatim, for his video camera. I later tell Greenblatt's sister about my discovery, and she responds by saying, "You mean you don't think I'm playing with a full deck?"

"Precisely."

"You think I'm some kind of nut?"

"Exactly."

"A fruitcake?"

"Bingo."

"And you're Mr. Normal. I'm crazy and you're a big shot normal person. So congratulations. *Kish mein tuchus.* "

***

Many vegetarians agree that if you eat enough hot pastrami sandwiches and honey-glazed donuts in your lifetime, you will wind up feeling like a sickly junk-heap, slowly dying from toxic waste. Some people insist that the only way to remedy this is through colonics, which is like an enema only much worse and much longer. It flushes out your entire colon, ridding you of all the old cold cuts which you never fully digested, but which instead still coat the lining of your intestines like Jewish wallpaper. Jerry Greenblatt once telephoned his mother, Flo, complaining that his colon hurt. Later Flo called her daughter:

"He says his colon hurts. How does he even know where it is? I don't know if I have a colon or I don't have a colon...he knows his hurts?"

Needless to say, Jerry Greenblatt tried colonics. He said afterwards that he felt "lighter." For Greenblatt, with no self, this was a huge testimony to the power of colonics. He once spent close to a thousand dollars doing an intensive holistic health program, which included fasting, acidophilus enemas, heavy doses of vitamins and herbs, raw foods, and so forth. The program lasted six months, and Greenblatt never looked or felt better in his entire life. When it was finally over, he celebrated by having a hot pastrami sandwich at the Carnegie Deli on 7th Avenue. If you have grown up in the home of Flo and Ed Greenblatt, your eating habits are stored in you forever.

Flo Greenblatt was actually a terrible cook. When I ate at her house, back when I was going out with her miserable daughter, she would stand over me as I tasted her soup; before I had even swallowed, she would demand to know,

"It's no good the soup? You don't like it?"

Greenblatt's sister picked up this negative way of speaking from her mother, and several times a day, when we were together, she would turn to me and say,

"I'm no good? You don't like me? I'm a lousy person?"

Her way of asking me to go to a movie was to say,

"We can't go to the movies?"

And quite often she would say,

"We can't get married?"

Now, as it turns out, we can't. And her mother's soup, by the way, *was* no good. And everybody knew it. Even her own sister, Aunt Dora, who I used to insist looked exactly like Moe from *The Three Stooges*, knew. Dora would evade the embarrassment of actually commenting on the quality of her sister's soup by instead commenting on all the different things she could find floating around *in* it:

"Look at this, Flo, you put little pieces of celery in it, too!"

Or,

"What do you know, Flo, you put some macaronis in the soup, too!"

Dora recently dropped her boyfriend of thirty-five years for a new man. "Between you and me," she informed Greenblatt's sister, "he don't like sex. But we go for rides." Dora was also famous for tricking telephone operators into free long-distance calls when phoning home after a trip, by saying, "I'd like to place a person-to-person, collect call to Arrived Safely."

Dinners at the Greenblatts were multi-layered affairs: There were always several main events going on simultaneously, of which eating was never one. Zeyde, the Grandfather, who was ninety-seven, would hobble around, hunched over and shaking, and say over and over again,

"The stick, Jerry, the stick."

This referred to the time he had seen Jerry watching a baseball game on TV, and after observing the peculiar activities of the men on the screen for a while, he had turned to Jerry and said,

"The stick, Jerry, the stick," which was apparently his final word on baseball.

And while Zeyde kept talking about "the stick," Jerry would be kneeling on a prayer rug in the corner chanting to Allah in the name of His Messenger, Mohammed, while at the same time making little bunny rabbits out of his handkerchief. Like an Islamic ventriloquist, he would often hold up the bunny and make it say "*La illaha il Allah*" in his high-pitched, falsetto bunny voice. Or sometimes, he would claim it was a Japanese bunny and make it say, "*Ra irraha ir Arrah*." Through all this activity, I would literally be the only person eating, and Flo would stand over me and demand a full report from me after every swallow:

"It's no good the brisket? You don't like the turkey? It's too dry?"

"No no no, I like it very much. I love the brisket, especially," I would reply.

"YOU HEAR THAT, DORA?" Flo would call out to the other room, "HE LIKES THE BRISKET!" and in the other room I would hear the reverberations of this, excited murmurings:

"The boy likes the brisket."

"He likes the brisket."

(And I should add that for some inexplicable reason, both of Flo's children agreed that something about their mother reminded them of a saltine cracker.)

Ed, still dead. Greenblatt's sister, still miserable. Jerry Greenblatt, has no self. And Flo? Perhaps her way of expressing love to her kids explains everything: "A mother loves her children, and *I'm* a mother."

CHAPTER FIVE

Bernstein

"Wilner?"

"Yeah?" I say sleepily, into the phone. It's six am.

"It's Jerry Greenblatt."

He always tells me his last name, like we haven't been friends for fifteen years, like if he just said, "It's Jerry," I might think it was Jerry Lewis.

"You're kidding? You sound exactly like Milton Berle."

"Last time you said Georgie Jessel."

"You know, there *is* a bit of Jessel in there, too—like Milton Berle doing his Georgie Jessel impression, but with a cold."

"Bernstein's in jail."

"Again?"

"Big-time. A mid-town high-rise, selling acid to a guy he met at the High Times New Year's party. A set-up."

"What's the bail?"

"What bail? He doesn't want bail; he likes it in there. It's free room and board, he can meditate and chant all day. He's a happy camper. Guess who his lawyer is?"

"Not Finkelstein...he hates Finkelstein!"

"Finkelstein hates him."

"So?"

"Friends are friends, he said. The trial's not for six months."

"That's a lot of meditating and chanting."

"Nah, piece of cake. Don't forget this is the guy who sat in a cave in Tibet for two years."

"So he says, but I have friends who saw him at the Holiday Inn in downtown Lhasa every weekend. I think he put in a forty-hour week in the cave, tops."

"Still..."

"All those drugs are destroying his brain cells."

"What does he need brain cells for? Is he writing a fucking thesis? Nuclear physics? With his lifestyle, he can afford to lose a few brain cells."

"So Jerry, if you don't mind my asking...he doesn't want bail, he's relatively happy..."

"Not relatively. Who said relatively? He's happy as a clam in the sand where nobody digs."

"So he's happy, the trial's not for six months...why the call at six am?"

"I'm up. I couldn't sleep."

"Oh, that explains it," I say, and hang up and roll over.

Bernstein. The guy was unbelievable with his drugs and his jail terms and he just kept going back because he liked it. He says he'd pay through the nose to get six months of retreat time in your basic monastic hermitage:

"Those guys at the monasteries get you coming and going," he tells me. "They hit you up for contributions every minute, and you can't say no to a guy in a white cowl with a cross around his neck. A room is a room, it's all I need. They let me bring my little statue of *Hanuman* and my tamboura and some incense. The guards know me already. 'Here comes the Holy Man,' they say when I show up. And don't think I don't catch them humming along with my chants under their breath. I tell you, I am single-handedly transforming the prison system from the inside out, all with the simple name of God, *Ram Ram.*"

I remember his last near-bust. He was out on the West Coast, at Disneyland, and got escorted out of Fantasyland for lighting up on "Alice in Wonderland"—he and his buddy Jake, the local Congressman. Jake was shaking in the parking lot, in fear for his reputation, though being expelled from the park was the extent of the punishment.

"Jake," Bernstein said, "Mellow out, buddy. Have a hit of this."

Jake was shocked, naturally, particularly when a police car pulled up in the parking lot and two guys got out, looking angry and tough. To make a long story short, they were not real cops, they were Disney security with a great show of bravado but no substantial clout— schoolteachers working part-time, moonlighting. Underneath all the tough talk they were essentially asking Bernstein and Jake to leave the parking lot. Bernstein, a street-smart druggie who can tell a cop from a security guard a mile away, pulled out of the lot still puffing on his joint, waving to the guys, telling a trembling, sweaty Jake,

"Jake, honey, relax. Listen to me...we are in *Disneyland*, Jake. *Disneyland.* Those were not police officers. That was Mickey and Goofy, Jake. We were just asked to leave Disneyland by Mickey and Goofy, and you're upset. Do me a favor, have some of this."

And then there were all the other busts: the time on the White House tour, the time on the airplane, the army induction center, on and on. Bernstein went out of his way to get arrested, and Finkelstein would usually get him off (along with the local judge he went to law school with, getting through it together by shar- ing lines of coke every night in graduate housing, B.U.). No jury could convict Bernstein anyway—he was too damned charming. People from all over the courthouse would stop into his trials— paralegals, aides, attorneys on their lunch breaks—just to hear his testimony, because in spite of numerous calls to order, the whole gallery would generally end up laughing, including Finkelstein's law school chum, Judge Klein, coughing to cover up his laughter as he banged his gavel.

Bernstein had a magic to him, and he'd wind up preaching to the jury about the vast mystery of the cosmos and the awesome power of Brahma the Creator, Vishnu the Preserver and Shiva the Great Destroyer. He had a knack. Listen to his last closing argument:

"Ladies and gentlemen of the jury, I submit that I, like every one of you, am nothing more than a walking chemistry experiment. Everything we put into our bodies and minds changes the mix and thus the outcome. The cafe lattes and cokes and M&Ms, the Merlots and Heinekens and the random shots of Tequila, the lamb chops rare and the t-bones medium-well, the heavy cream sauces smothering our fettuccines, plus the pesticides on our produce, the irradiation, the way we breathe first and second-hand smoke, and in my case, third-hand smoke which you don't even want to know about, the smog and the dust, the mildew we inhale, the vitamins we pop, the herbs and aspirins and cough syrups, your NyQuils, Mytols and Mylantas, the anti-depressants and the blood-thinners, your Rolaids and Tums, the Evening News and the Internet, the half-naked girl in the Coppertone ad on the back of the bus—*everything* we eat, smell, ingest, touch, hear and see sloshes around inside us and has an impact. And it's a long list—I'm just mentioning the tip of the iceberg—don't forget the electric power lines, the filthy public toilets, gummy bears, French fries, television telling us lies about who we are and what we need, cellular phones eating our brains, mercury in our teeth wreaking havoc with our nervous systems, I could go on and on, but you get the picture. Everything. Everyday. Shampoos and skin creams and soaps that enter our pores. Nasal sprays. Scented candles. Paint thinner and Super Glue. Valium. Add all these things together, shake, stir, boil, add in our individual genetic codes and social strata and possibly longer-term karmic tendencies from other lives, and all of it results in who we are—our present mood, attitude, physical health and vitality or lack thereof, and the concomitant mental states of either clarity or cloudiness, emotional freedom and joy or wild rage, utter terror or unfeelable grief.

"And yes, ladies and gentlemen, to this extraordinary and daunting list of influences on our psyches I add marijuana and psilocybin mushrooms. Listen to me: When I get up in the morning, I take a baby aspirin and Pravachol to keep my arteries unclogged, flax oil, vitamin E, glucosomine tablets and shark cartilage to keep my joints greased and flexible. I add a green powder to my juice that is composed of spirulina, chlorella, blue-green algae, wheat grass, lecithin, ginseng, bee pollen, and about 73 other things the Earth Rise company believes are good for me. To this I add a dropperful of echinacea, goldenseal, and astragalus. And saw palmetto for prostate health. Vitamin C powder goes without saying, plus Liquid Minerals containing 49 trace elements, some B-12 sublingual lozenges, garlic capsules, and zinc. Lysine for herpes simplex. Psyllium husks to clean out my colon and acidophilis to plant new bacteria in my colon. Bitter Chinese liver and kidney tonics. Ibuprofen.

"So we come to just one more naturally-occurring herb, the cannabis sativa, more commonly known as marijuana, and the state singles out this poor plant as wrong and arrests me for it? It's completely absurd! I would rather you arrested me for the Pepto-Bismol, the antihistamines. Give me 5-10, no parole, for possession of Listerine with intent to gargle. And odd, isn't it, that marijuana is the only one on that long, long list that I use for my *mental* well-being and general sanity. No wonder it's illegal—it actually helps me feel better about all the stuff that's killing me.

"Ladies and gentlemen of the jury, I implore you to take these words to heart: I am not a dysfunctional person. Nor am I a functional person. I am *a-functional*. I am a religious man. I have tasted the bliss, the Divine nectar of being in the ecstatic Presence of the Living God, and I am too obsessed with my craving to merge with Brahma to waste even a minute of my time here merely functioning. I turn to my herbal support system, the religious sacraments of my spiritual tribe—the sacred mushroom, the holy herb—and they help to relieve the deep, deep ache in my soul-ar plexus that is unbearably sensitive to the incomprehensible suffering and torment so many humans and creatures are undergoing at this very moment. So I say to you, please: Just say Know to drugs. I rest my case."

"Has the jury reached a verdict?"

"We have your Honor."

"What say you?"

"In the case of Arjuna nee Alan Bernstein vs. the State of New York, on charges of possession of an illegal substance, we find the defendant out of his mind, and therefore innocent."

I go down to see him—it's always fun visiting Bernstein in jail.

"Did you bring the stuff?" he says to me quietly, through the bars, looking around furtively. The guard's ears perk up.

"Yeah, I brought the stuff," I reply, and look around cautiously. It's our little game. I pull out a plain, brown paper bag and slip it through the bars. The guard jumps forward:

"Now wait just a minute."

Just in time, Bernstein pulls out from the bag a corned beef on rye and two kosher dills.

"Pickle?" he offers the guard.

"Kosher?" the guard says.

"Would my friend the Rebbe bring me *trayf*?"

"So how is it this time?" I ask.

"Good, good," Bernstein says, already with a mouthful, chewing and talking. "I should complain? God's good to me, knock wood, I don't talk back."

"You have a nice cell?"

"Nice? Compared to my cave in Nepal I'm in a penthouse suite on Central Park South. A little stuffy, though. They need better ventilation—a window would be nice for starters. Listen Reb Wilner, maybe you could do me a little favor..."

"What? Pastrami next time? I thought Hindus are vegetarian, anyway."

"I *am* vegetarian," he says indignantly, picking at a piece of corned beef stuck in his tooth, wiping mustard from his beard. "Okay, not strict, but for all intents and purposes...you begrudge a friend a little deli when he's behind bars? Anyway, could you call my mother—you know the number—and tell her I'm in India."

"She'll believe that?"

"Why not? It won't be the first time...and tell her I left a few things unfinished at home, she'll know what I mean."

"What *do* you mean?"

"Not your business. Is this too much to ask a friend when they've got me locked up in this hell-hole?"

"Come off it, Bernstein, everybody knows you like it in there. It's your home away from home."

"Yes, but that's only because I am a very strange and unusual person. But let's face it, the place is a pit. *Jai Ram.*" And he's off.

"Hey Mr....uh" the guard calls out as I'm leaving.

"Yes?"

"Maybe next time, if it wouldn't be too much trouble, a nice half pint of potato salad, only if it's convenient, don't go out of your way, I'll reimburse you."

***

I'm wandering Manhattan after seeing Bernstein. Bernstein likes God, and he really has no reason. I remember the story of his first trip to India, when his Swami instructed him to go out on the streets of Calcutta and find one of those beggars with no arms or legs who looked happy, and to figure out why. So he did it. Bernstein spent three months sitting on a trash-ridden, dusty, smelly sidewalk in Calcutta next to a guy with no arms or legs, and they became fast friends. He'd help feed the guy, light cigarettes and bowls of hashish for him, empty his begging bowl, count the rupees. The guy was ecstatic, Bernstein told me. Blissed out. A real God-intoxicant.

"That's when I figured out," Bernstein had told me, "that when you have God in your heart there's nothing in the world that can bring you down. If he could be happy with no arms or legs, I'm gonna let myself be miserable because my mother *hocks* me a *cheinik?* Or my bursitis aches a little? I can't be unhappy anymore—it's too embarrassing, I can't find any legitimate excuses for it."

So he's not so dumb, this Bernstein—for a drug dealer who lives in jail half the year the way other Jews winter in Miami, he was still no dummy. Who can argue with a person's happiness? Reb Miltie and Bernstein would get on famously: they both like God. Or forget like, they both love the bastard.

But the question is, do *I* like God? What does that mean? Don't we have to define our terms? I mean, God Who? Do I like the world God created? I love cats, beaches and magnolia trees. Giraffes and snow. It's manmade things I don't like: specifically, crematoriums and land mines. I hate those two in particular. And revolving tie racks. And just basically all the stuff people make and sell and buy, and also everything they do and say and feel. And I'm not nuts about myself, either—everyone knows that. But that's not God's problem. On the other hand, if God made people, He must have had His head up His ass to make us so capable of being royal first-class *shvantses*. Maybe free will was a bad idea. Maybe God fucked up and we have to live with it. Maybe *we* fucked up and *God* has to live with it.

So yes, I have some complaints against God, it doesn't mean I don't like Him. He wouldn't have been my first choice to design this carnival ride, though. My cousin Louie could have done a better job. "Leave out the free will and you're golden, Louie." Okay, bottom line, let's face it, I don't like God.

I stop at a phone booth, corner of 47th and 6th.
"Who's this?" a raspy woman's voice answers.
"What? You can't even say hello when you answer the phone, like a normal person?"
"Yeah yeah yeah hello to you mister, who is it?"
"It's Norbert Wilner, Mrs. Bernstein."
"Norbert? Why didn't you say so, you don't have to stand on ceremony with me, we're practically family—where are you Norbella?"

"Midtown."

"Midtown? You're at my front door! Hang up the phone right now and come up for a nice cup tea and we'll *shmooze* a little. You're such a busy man you can't stop the world a minute to visit an old lady?"

"But Mrs. Bernstein you live on..."

"Hang up Norbella, the water's boiling already...you take lemon?"

She had a way about her, not unlike Bernstein himself. How she figured midtown is "at her front door" on East 96th and First Avenue, I don't know, but she knows I don't work, she knows I'm a *kibitzer*-extraordinaire, and on top of everything else, she knows I'm a sucker for those German Linzer Tortes she buys on 86th Street. So I hop in a cab. (Okay, so I spend for cabs—I'm allowed. I don't always feel comfortable standing in crowded subways rubbing my *tuchus* against strange men of other races and creeds.)

"Norbella!" She greets me at the door with a wet kiss. She's wearing a pink, flannel housecoat—a real *shmateh*—and slippers. She's about half my size, and in her mid-seventies.

"I'm sorry I'm not dressed yet...what time is it?"

"Four thirty," I reply.

"So, it's not a crime to spend a day inside—look who I'm apologizing to! I knew you, Norbella, when your behind was the size of a tennis ball. To you I should apologize? Sit! Sit already, you're not a stranger. I have some nice Linzer Torte for you, the one you like. But you don't eat standing up in my house. Sit!"

I sat.

"You're looking good, Mrs. B."

"Thank God, I can't complain. Everything hurts but it could be worse—at least it hurts!" she laughs. "At least I don't have what Mrs. Ribikoff has with her legs—she's using a walker now, I knew her when her legs were something to look at on the beach. So? What do you do? You know the old saying, '*Az me vil nit alt vern, zol men zikh yungerheyt oyfhengen*...If you want to avoid old age, hang yourself when you're young.' So tell me Norbella, what do you hear from Bernstein? I have to ask you for news about my own son."

I always thought it peculiar that she called him Bernstein.

"He was here for dinner last week after the Lipschitz boy's funeral," she went on, "isn't that terrible Norbella, such a nice young man, I remember when he threw up on my new carpet...and not a word from Bernstein since. It's been at least two or three days, I can't imagine...God forbid nothing terrible happened to him, with those horrible people he knows..."

"He asked me to tell you he went to India."

"In jail again? That little *mamzer*, I'll kill him. He didn't even let me know. I could bring him some nice soup chicken he likes so much...you know what they say, '*Tsores mit zup iz gringer tsu fartogn vi tsores on zup*...Trouble with soup is better than trouble without soup.' He hates the food in there, they only give him frozen vegetables because they think he's a big-shot holy man who won't touch anything else—this is the son I've got. How long is he in for this time?"

"Looks like six months."

"Eh, not bad. He'll enjoy himself. He'll miss the Feinberg Bar Mitzvah, though."

"He told me to tell you he left some business unfinished."

"*Nu*? You had to tell me? The *shmendrik* doesn't think I check the books on my own? What am I, a little *pisher*? So I'm a nosy busy-body—he left me with three big deliveries and a few collections."

I stop short, my fork with Linzer Torte in mid-air.

"You mean..."

"What else should I mean? Your friend Bernstein and me, we're in business. I didn't know he sold to poor Freddy, I never would have allowed it, we keep it strictly professional, no personal friends...tomorrow, Norbella, you'll have to laugh, me, an old Jewish lady with varicose veins, I have to go to the docks on the East River and collect $5,000 from a longshoreman with a thick neck and a tattoo. I'm surprised Bernstein never told you. I have no secrets from you, Norbella, I knew you when you were a little *pishiker*. Listen, now that you're here, you can save me a trip."

She opens a kitchen drawer and hands me a small bag.

"Give this to Finkelstein, would you Norbella? You're gonna see him, yes?"

I nod and open the bag. Three grams of coke.

"It's his retainer," she says, "You know what everyone says, '*Di kats hot lib fish, nor zi vil di fu nit aynetsn...*The cat loves fish, but .doesn't want to wet its feet.'"

"Right."

***

Reb Miltie's assignments are getting to me. How to become the Baal Shem? How to act like him, sing like him? Or perhaps more to the point, how to love like him? I remember a story of a small Greek village enacting the yearly Passion Play, how each villager gradually transformed as they prepared for their parts, actually developed the qualities of the character they were to portray. I have been launched on a similar path, and it is a steep one. For what is there about me, within me, that I would have to let go of in order for me to properly portray an Ecstatic Joyful Mystic? Only everything. Only me. I read another poem from the Mordecai book:

> *Freedom of the spirit is not for the*
> *Rabbis and Scribes.*
> *They are too busy*
> *discussing the matter and*
> *writing everyone's good ideas down.*

> *No, to learn how to be with the*
> *Tender One now,*
> *spend more time in back alleys with*
> *stray cats and prostitutes;*
> *sometimes God spends the night there.*

Mordecai will tell you:
If you're looking for the answer,
you're much too late:
the Wild One you love is
asking all the questions.

CHAPTER SIX

Breshman

Damn Abe Breshman. His life doesn't add up, and it throws off all my thinking. First and last, he is basically a happy man, and he has no right to be. Breshman has no wife, no children, no career, no great accomplishments, no money to speak of, no house or condo, no particular goals or direction, ambition or drive. He skis and plays tennis, period. All of his worldly possessions fit into two cardboard boxes, which fit into his 1971 Chevy. Plus his skis. He has a two-box policy, and if you try to give him something—a birthday present—he'll mentally calculate the room in his boxes and either won't accept the present or he'll recycle something else out to make room for the new acquisition. He is not a man who likes to feel burdened.

The maddening thing about it all, for me, is that Breshman doesn't even have some fancy philosophy to explain himself—no raps about "voluntary simplicity," no great political stance about the materialistic society. On the contrary, he greatly enjoys the wealth of his friends, and swims laps in Finkelstein's pool regularly. No religious idea about giving up the temporal things of this world for the more lasting heavenly rewards. No hip New Age dictum about traveling light. Nothing. He is simply a happy, carefree person for no reason whatsoever.

And it bugs the shit out of me. If I thought that I could achieve a level of contentment by honing my possessions down to two boxes and going skiing, I would do it. But I know myself, and nothing I ever do externally alters the fundamental quality of my life. I would, I know, merely be a melancholic skier with two boxes, instead of a melancholic whatever-I-am, with more boxes of stuff than I know what to do with. Same same. And it also follows that if Breshman chose to change his style and began to acquire a bunch of junk, he'd simply become a happy man with a bunch of junk. We take ourselves with us.

I'm thinking about all this as I sit with Breshman at a greasy spoon counter on the Upper West Side. We're having coffee, and as usual, I bring the conversation around to his life, demanding an explanation. It's like pulling teeth. Finally, he utters the words I will never forget, revealing the source of his unusual disposition once and for all:

"Ever since I accepted the fact that I was never going to amount to anything, I've been really happy, just doing the things I like to do."

No no no no no—silent screams of protest well up inside me—this I didn't want to hear. Are you Jewish, Breshman? Or are you some sort of alien, a mutation? Jewish boys don't say things like that—it's a crime against their mothers and God. We all must amount to something—and not just something, but a great big something. We are the doctors and lawyers of the world, Breshman. Where did you come up with such thinking? If that's the price of your happiness, it's too much, you've sold your Jewish soul to the ski devil. You are an intelligent, capable man, you could have made something of yourself, you "couldda been a contenda," you're wasting your life, squandering your resources, frittering away your potential, your talent, your brains. Breshman, something is alive in you, what can it be?

Not amount to anything? God forbid! Blasphemy—get thee behind me, Breshman. The fucker is so damned happy. And really a kind, warm and good person, compassionate and generous of heart and spirit. Damn! Now what do I do? I collect myself. I had been vigorously stirring my coffee during all this internal warfare, and I now attempt to surface:

"Abe, Abe, be reasonable...think of Finkelstein..." (Now *I* wasn't being reasonable. My mental system—the way I had the world put together—was struggling for survival, clutching and grasping.) "Now he puts us all to shame. He did it right, he's an office supplies entrepreneur, a Jewish lawyer with a Jewish wife and a..."

"Finkelstein's an asshole."

"Completely."

"But he lets me use his pool."

"Ever consider humping Lilah?"

"Too fat."

"A blimp."

"But Abe, what do you mean you're never going to amount to anything?" I affect a slightly pleading tone, as if in pity he might reverse his statement and either admit that he wasn't happy after all, or that he *would* try to amount to something.

"What I mean is," he replies, "this is it."

"What's it?"

"This. Remember when you were a little boy and you wondered what you'd be when you grew up?"

"I'm still wondering...it's between rabbinical school and the doughnut business."

"I'd go for the doughnuts...you don't have to go to services."

"Yeah but everybody calls you Rabbi..."

"I can get everybody to call you Rabbi...waitress?" he calls, "could you give the rabbi here a little more coffee please? Anyway Norb...this is it. This is who I turned out to be when I grew up. The game's over, the votes are in. Little Abie's an amateur skier and tennis player. End of story. That's all she wrote."

"But..." My mind was giving up. I heard the faint echo of "something is alive in me" but it wasn't really alive in me. "But your mother?" I finally manage.

"Dead."

And that was that. Abe Breshman, my friend who's happy. Who never amounted to anything. But me? I still have to amount to something...after all, my mother is alive.

"Good-bye Rabbi," the waitress says as we leave. I make one last try on the street, just as Abe is pulling away.

"Hey Breshman, ever considered writing in your spare time? In the ski lodge maybe, with the hot chocolate and the girls in wool sweaters all over the place. You know, when the lift lines are too long, maybe write down this little philosophy of yours, tell your story, help others who struggle to find meaning." I was trying to give Abe one more shot at giving his life a purpose, for my own peace of mind.

"Nah," he says, "I did that already." And he drives off.

***

Breshman was a quiet kid. Painfully shy. Never raised his hand, even to go to the Boy's Room. He holds it in rather than have everyone watch him stand up and leave the room. Never went to parties, and later, didn't go to the prom. Not one date, until senior year. No eighth grade kisses. No freshman feels or sophomore sex. No junior jism.

But smart. A real head on his shoulders. Only A's, A+'s, nearly perfect SATs: 780s verbal, 800 math. Graduated with honors, first in a class of 2500, would go off to Harvard on a pre-med scholarship.

Nineteen sixty-eight was a good year in Cambridge Square, and a good year for Breshman, although his mother couldn't see it. It was the year he first tried LSD to let off steam after finals one spring day. And that was the day that Breshman became Breshman: burst out of his private mental chamber and actually danced and sang, in public, on the banks of the Charles. And decided, then and there, that he didn't have the time to become a doctor.

Medical school, if nothing else, would be time consuming, and he did not want to have his time consumed, suddenly seeing his time standing before him, clear as day, wrapped in red ribbons like a birthday present. In fact, he saw that this gift of time had been given him on his actual day of birth, and contained a finite number of days, each with a number on it, the seeing of which led him to laugh with delight and say aloud, "My days are numbered."

And so they were. That had been the 7,356th day of Breshman's life. The day we all met to say Kaddish for Freddy was his 17,543rd. Obsessed with not having his time consumed, Breshman became consumed with time, and was fond, in particular, of the notion of "free time." "I've got some free time!" he would think, happily, but unlike most people who struggle to carve out an hour or two of free time on the weekend, say, or after work, Breshman considered his entire life to be free time, awarded him as though he'd won a lottery for which first prize was one life span.

When Breshman said "Don't waste my time," he meant it quite literally, as if time was a tangible commodity, like fresh peaches, as if some people have more time than others, as if life itself is a God-operated hotel with an old, faded sign out front that reads "TRANSIENTS," and humanity flocks to the desk to try and get a room and Breshman is worried they will fling him out on his ear, throw his bags out after him, leave him on the street, homeless, all for not paying his bill—a life misspent. So he could not afford to waste any time.

(Or time tangible the way kids from a poor family might sneak a perfectly good potato from the kitchen to use for their Mr. Potato-Head game, and their mother comes home and says, "Don't waste my potatoes." Tangible like that.)

Now see him there, in third grade, a yellow puddle forming under his desk, leaking from his pants, the class giggling and whispering as Breshman, in horror, is told to get some paper towels and clean it up. Filled with shame, he refuses to speak to practically anyone at all for years.

But he had friends. Spokespeople. Greenblatt. Playing poker with the boys, for example, he would throw his cards on the table, and Greenblatt would say, "Mr. Breshman folds." Or playing hide and seek, Greenblatt would stick by him as traveling interpreter "Mr. Breshman says 'Anyone around his base is it.' Breshman says 'Olly olly in free.'"

Greenblatt liked the job, liked being the front man, the mouth-piece: "You want to talk to Breshman, you go through me." Even teachers made allowances: "Breshman's here," Greenblatt would say during roll call, or "Breshman says the homework is too extensive," and the teachers would change the assignment, "Breshman says" as authoritative as Simon, his lack of speech somehow commanding more and more respect.

He even brought Greenblatt along when he finally started dating: "Breshman requests a kiss good-night, and would like to see you again on Friday night."

And finally, it even penetrated the Breshman household, where his own mother would, in spite of herself, find herself calling Greenblatt on the phone: "Jerry, what would he like for his birthday." And Greenblatt would get back to her later that night, nobody knowing just when or how he had been debriefed: "Breshman says he wants cash. In tens and twenties. And he says goodnight."

By his senior year, Breshman was a living legend, and as valedic-torian, was asked to deliver the graduation address. He stood before thousands of people—friends and family—and simply looked out, in silence, as Greenblatt stood alongside on the podium and said into the microphone, "Breshman says the world is on fire." This was '67. "He says our generation must become firefighters or perish. Breshman says make love, not war, bring our boys home, save the planet. Make the world safe for little children. Breshman says and so forth."

Breshman, the mute genius, the silent kingpin, the Howard Hughes of Avenue D, the man behind the scenes. He didn't break his silence until the day, soon after his acid trip, when the Dean at Harvard called him in and said,

"Mr. Breshman, you're one of our top students, you're receiving substantial financial aid; what's this I hear about you discontinuing your course of study?"

To which Breshman had replied,

"My days are numbered, Sir. I'm afraid I don't have the time."

And ever since then—although his mother was sick about it, and his mother's neighbors thought it was a shame "what happened to the

Breshman boy," and there were even rumors that he had "cracked up on that LSD"—Breshman has been Breshman. That is, a happy man. And a great conversationalist. With lots of free time.

CHAPTER SEVEN

Gelberman

It's Sunday, and I amble over to Zabar's to pick up bagels for my breakfast with Reb Miltie, who in my mind I find myself privately thinking of as "Gelberman the Prophet." Standing in line, by the counter, this old man turns to me and says,

"You know, my wife, and my doctor, they tell me I shouldn't eat these foods, it's bad for my heart...but the brisket, and the salami, and the flanken...it's *so* delicious, I *have* to eat it."

I experience a deja vu, but I can't place it. The seemingly incidental things I see and hear every day affect me deeply. Sitting on the subway, I glance up and notice a headline in someone's *New York Times* Sunday magazine: "Foot Care Is A Year-Round Task." Are there really people, I wonder, who believe this? Even gardening is seasonal. Who are these year-round Foot People? Do they also have regular jobs and families, or do they only take care of their feet?

At Columbus Circle, someone leaves behind a Sunday *Post*, and I find this item: "The world's largest Ritz Cracker (three and a half feet in diameter, eight pounds) was on display at the Waldorf Astoria." How many packages of Philadelphia cream cheese would be needed to *shmeer* the entire Ritz giant, I wonder. And how do they really know it's the world's largest? How do they keep track?

Are there laws requiring people to register every cracker? Could they really be sure that, say, Bernstein hadn't once made a Ritz cracker so large that this imposter at the Waldorf was a dwarf-cracker by comparison?

An obituary grabs my eye: "Victor Dorman, 80, Altered the Packaging of Cheese Slices." The article explains that Mr. Dorman became famous for his slogan, "The cheese with the paper between the slices." *Famous.*

And from a human-interest story, a quote from a female senior at Great Neck High School: "I want to go to graduate school. I want to get married. I want to have children. I want to live in Great Neck. I just want a typical Great Neck life." The simple beauty of it, I think. She just stated the facts of her life as clearly as, in the board game "Clue," one might state, "It was done in the library, by Miss Scarlet, with the lead pipe."

For several days, I go around silently repeating the girl's words to myself, trying them on: "I want to have children. I want to live in Great Neck. I just want a typical Great Neck life, I just want a typical Great Neck life." But it's no use. I'm too far gone, it's too late for me to turn out normal. (Even my own mother, who once hoped I was merely going through a stage, now accepts the fact that she has unintentionally reared a nutcase.)

An hour later, finally, I'm knocking on #6H.

"Rabbi!" he greets me. Breshman works quick, I think.

"Reb Miltie!"

"Good *Shabbes*," he says.

"It's Sunday," I point out.

"Oy. You kill me. First of all, *Shabbes* is that moment out of time, right? So *any* time you step out of time, it's *Shabbes* for the soul, a rest for those who are caught up in fear as the clock tick tocks its way closer and closer to the tragic *denouement*," exaggerating the French with a terrible accent. "To be free of that story is *Shabbes*. And that's where I like to live.

"And secondly, do you really think that one day of rest is enough after creating a whole world? In the Talmud it explains that when it is said that God rested on the seventh day, they meant She took the whole weekend off. What, you think a day then was like now? It was two for one—that's why they lived so long. Divide by two and you find out their real age—you're no dummy. Though a genius you're not. Go, eat a bagel, try a nice cinnamon-raisin."

Should I accept this from a sixty-seven year old man with a toy propeller on his head and little bunny slippers on his feet? Yes, I should.

"You're not a genius *shopper*, because you brought such a tiny little package of cream cheese, like we're two babies who have to eat, two little *pishikers* with no appetite. But we're in luck, because I still have some from last week, but do me a favor...splurge! Buy the big package next time, the extra thirty-nine cents won't drain your trust fund. Can you imagine anything sadder than a bagel on a Sunday morning and no cream cheese? They could strip me of my ordination for that...so, *nu*? Let's start the lesson...you did your homework?" he asks.

I nod, wiping cream cheese away from my mouth and beard.

"See," he says, "it goes to waste in your beard, on top of everything else."

Okay, the guy was a cream cheese nut; I allowed him this fetish. He should only know what's going on at the Waldorf Astoria, I think, with their colossal cracker.

"So what do you have to say to my question?"

"No."

"No what?"

"My answer to your question is no, I don't like God."

What happens next is the single moment of my relationship with Reb Miltie that will remain etched in my memory forever, the moment that binds me to him, that wins my heart: he spontaneously starts weeping. For real. Earnest sobs. Genuine tears. From his pocket he withdraws a Flintstones hankie and blows his nose on Wilma, wipes his eyes with Barney Rubble. I stare, speechless, feeling vaguely responsible and guilty.

"I...didn't think you'd take it personally," I finally stammer.

"How could I not? She's my God! You put a knife in my heart. But I also cry for you."

"Me?" I didn't get it.

"You must live in a very frightening world."

Me? Have fear? Does *tzimmes* have raisins? Need I tell him about my E.M.D.S. —Early Morning Dread Syndrome—or the constant anxiety I live with, like there's only one bus in life and it's forever pulling away from the station just as I arrive?

"Yes," I say, simply.

"So tell me," he says through the tail end of his whimpering, "what's not to like?"

"What's not to like?" I repeat, in disbelief. He must be joking, or blind! "What's not to like?" I say again, indignant. "I don't like little four-year old boys getting run over by pick-up trucks in the Wal-Mart parking lot"— something I had just read about—"and I don't like heavy metal rock and roll bands with swastika tattoos singing 'Going Back To Birkenau.' I hate that all my parents' friends are getting chemo, quadruple bypasses, new hips and Alzheimer's. I really don't like that tidal wave in Papua, New Guinea washing away all those people —if that's an 'act of God' then I wish He were all talk and no action, like me."

"You sound angry," Reb Miltie, the Rogerian.

"And what about osteoarthritis, global warming, drug-resistant bacteria, Ebola, e coli, e pluribus unum..."

He reaches into the bag, fishes around, pulls out a cinnamon-raisin bagel and places it in front of me.

"Okay, this is not just a bagel. It's everything you don't like, yes?"

I nod.

"Now, I want you to watch the bagel very carefully, and while you observe the bagel—don't let your attention wander, or you might miss something very important—I want you to increase your dislike. Build it up inside, the anger, the outrage, let your blood boil with your righteous indignation, about all those things you don't like. Imagine yourself, if possible, not liking them even more."

He watches my face, my brow. I watch the bagel.

"Good," he says, "now even more. Maybe turn your dislike up a notch into all-out hatred, contempt, and watch the bagel. Good. Just a little more. Some real furious rage..."

I find that I am actually able to do it, to generate the emotions. I am about to explode and start breaking things. My face is red and bursting.

"Okay, now relax, and tell me."

I take a deep breath and let it out in a long sigh of tension-release.

"What did you notice happening to the bagel?"

Was this a trick question? It's a bagel. A bagel is a bagel. I didn't notice anything. I struggle for a moment to come up with something more insightful, but fail.

"Nothing," I say, irritably. "I didn't notice anything."

"Right!" Miltie exclaims. "The bagel didn't budge. It was totally indifferent to your feelings and your opinions and your preferences. You could scream at it 'til you're blue in the face, the bagel sits there, you should excuse the expression, like a man with his *tuchus* glued to the toilet seat."

"So?"

"So for now that's all I want to say. I want you to think about it for a week, because God is the bagel—a big, cinnamon-raisin bagel."

"But..."

"Sha!" he cuts me off, dismissing any further discussion. Now read me today's message from Mordecai—you know if you let just one page of that book really sink in fully, you'd never need anything else. You wouldn't hear another word out of me. Read!"

I flip it open to this:

There is nobody in this world,
and nobody in the next world,
who will say no to the Tender One.
Would a hungry newborn infant
refuse her mother's breast?
Or a minnow shy away from
the pond to flop around in a field?

When the soul is nursing on the Real Thing,
there is no window display in heaven or on earth
that can even lure you into the store.
For who goes buying and selling
when the One Great Pearl
is already dangling on a
silver chain around your neck?

Mordecai will tell you:
Your true heart is an empty hole that
only the sound of the
Tender One's whisper can fill.

It happens again. The poem stops me dead in my tracks. And Miltie knows it.

"Now let me tell you a little story," he says, "and then we say good-bye until next Sunday, when you bring the big box of cream cheese, for adults. So, there was once a very holy Rebbe—Reb Schloimela of Vitebsk in Poland—who had a huge following of Chassidim. They adored Reb Schloimela because no matter what went on in their lives, no matter how heavy their hearts with worry or grief, whenever they saw their holy Rebbe, they began to smile again, to laugh, and sing and dance. He was a man so filled with love for God and for the world and for every person he met, that his joy radiated out from his face like a shining sun.

"So, to make a long story short, one day it was time for Reb Schloimela to leave this world, and as he lay on his deathbed, his closest disciples crowded into the room, to be near their beloved Master, to experience his precious presence for the last time, and most of all, to hear his last words of teaching. For it is a well-known thing that when such a soul leaves this world, his final words contain a great and holy wisdom and hidden message.

"So *nu*, the time finally came, and Reb Schloimela called his disciples near. They listened so intently, no one should miss a word, a syllable, an intonation or an accent, a facial gesture—anything that might prove to contain hidden meanings later on, the very secrets of life and death. 'Now listen carefully, my friends,' the Rebbe said softly, the quiet voice of an old, dying man. The room was so silent and so still, you never heard such a silence. The Chassidim listened:

"'Di di, de de de, de di...'

"The Rebbe began to hum a *niggun*, a sacred melody.

"'Di di, de de de, de di.'

"It was one they never heard before—enchanting and lyrical, from the other world.

"'Di di, de de de, de di.

"He motioned with his hand for them to join him.

"'Di di, de de de, de di.

"Slowly, quietly, everyone began to sing, and then gradually increased their volume, ever so gently and slowly, until finally they were putting all their hearts and souls into this beautiful, mysterious melody from their dying Rebbe, and they sang full-voiced now, and a certain joy and ecstasy rose from within and lit up their faces, brought smiles and tears, eyes rolled upwards. 'Di di, de de de, de di' they sang, as their beloved teacher gently passed over to the other world. 'Di di, de de de, de di.'"

Reb Miltie was losing himself in his own story, his own song. In amazement I watch his face transform, brighten, I watch tears stream forth from his half-closed eyes. In spite of myself, I tentatively begin to sing along, and soon both of us are in Poland, centuries ago, with our holy Rebbe on his deathbed, singing in a sort of trance. I feel myself laugh inside at this strange sight, and I let go a little, and start to sing louder, and at the same time, yes, I feel a distinct shift in my mood. I can't help myself, my anger is gone, I'm feeling a certain, not quite joy, but lightness. Miltie stands up and still singing, takes me by the arm and leads me to the door. As I move past the table I grab the bagel and put it on my finger like a big ring...and before I know it, I find myself out on the street, smiling, humming, twirling a bagel, all for no apparent reason.

***

From the bio in the back of *Mordecai's Book*, I learn that Milton Gelberman lost everything to Hitler: mother, father, all four grandparents, seven aunts and uncles, fourteen cousins. He arrived in New York City in 1945 a broken man, dumb with grief and horror. He remained broken, and completely useless, until traveling back to Germany twenty years later to visit the graves of those few of his beloved family that had graves. Most of them didn't. Most were vanished smoke.

There, in the small cemetery, on a cold and damp day, he met a man named David Wise who would change his life forever. Milton saw him from a distance at first, and had to squint a few times, to make sure he was seeing correctly, for there was a man, many headstones down and to the right, *dancing*! And *singing*! Miltie approached quietly, not wanting to disturb the man, and not wanting to be seen. But David Wise saw him, smiled and waved, and shouted, "Come over here, don't be shy. Come meet my family."

Milton approached, hesitant.

"This is my father and mother; you're standing on my Uncle Friedrich, behind you is Aunt Sophie."

Milton just stared, not comprehending. What kind of man is this, dancing on his murdered parents' graves?

"Listen to me very carefully, young man: If we are sad and broken, then Hitler won. If we can dance and sing with joy and laughter, then we are alive, and Hitler lost. And who would be more appreciative of our joy and aliveness than our dear families? So it is for *them* I dance, and for the Jewish people, and for my own soul."

That night, after dark, Milton returned to the graves. And he sat in silent prayer, conversation really, for five hours, conversing with his parents, his grandparents, his aunts and uncles and cousins, most of whom weren't even buried there. He told them all about America, about the Diamond District on 47th Street in New York City where he was trying to make a few dollars to survive. About the subways and the big buildings, the shops and the synagogues, and all the Jews from Europe and Poland, the Chassidim in their black clothes. And he wept as he told his story, and laughed. And when he was talked out, and had said everything on his mind, he stood up, and slowly at first, then with increasing energy and animation, Milton Gelberman danced on the graves of his ancestors. And sang. In celebration. For hours, until dawn. By morning, he had become Reb Miltie, and from that day on he committed himself to a life of joy, a life of song and dance and laughter, his ultimate expression of utter loss and horror.

And now he carries the transmission of the Mad Ones, the Holy Rebbes and Mystics, the Whirling Dervishes and Hidden Saints. The ones who keep one foot planted in the center of human suffering while simultaneously reaching for the heavens with outstretched arms and ecstatic song, able to find the laughter of the Other Side, the joy of the Deathless, all the while keeping in heart and mind the Buddha's smile of Unbearable Compassion in the face of unfathomable human suffering. Beings so free as to stand before death and evil, and laugh in fearless awareness of the Undying Living Reality Of The Divine Presence, unalterable by even a single event.

(Or perhaps, the opposite is true: Every single event *does* alter God; pokes Him; God a writhing, twitching mass of pokes and bruises from each of our every actions. We pray to God; He should be praying to *us*.)

CHAPTER EIGHT

Wilner

Wilner's first day of school. See him there, posing on the porch, fresh crew cut hair gooed up straight, brand new striped polo shirt, and his very own briefcase, just like his Daddy's, containing a loose-leaf notebook. Inside the notebook, the best part: the zippered, blue plastic bag filled with hidden stash—unsharpened yellow pencils, a six-inch green plastic ruler, brand new pink erasers, a red sharpener. All the tools of the trade. The kid is equipped, ready for action.

His mother proud in the photo, bending down, her face next to his, never guessing that in his mind the scene is a bit different: It's an army uniform, a duffel bag, rations, firearms. He is being sent off to war, and who knows if he'll make it, if he'll ever come home again, ever see his mom, his family? (And in some sad way, the truth is, he didn't ever come home again, sending a kid off to school for the first time is as dangerous and unknown as setting Moses adrift in a basket. Let my people go.)

Kindergarten, to the little Wilner, is boot camp, recess is maneuvers. He is on his way to the front lines, and there are no atheists in foxholes. Grade school would make Wilner a religious man, praying to God he'd traverse the enemy territory safely and make it home for dinner. He feels out of sync with the other troops; the school nurse should have given him a 4F—unfit for duty, cannot serve in the first grade, honorable discharge from East Lake Elementary for security purposes. Assigned a civilian desk job, able to work out of his home.

The kid marches off to school that first day, and everyday thereafter, backward, *waving good-bye to his mom for as long as he can keep her in sight. And then turns the corner and gingerly enters the field of battle, furtively looking around, scouting out the terrain, sniffing out trouble. Wilner, the five-year-old draft-dodger, a miniature conscientious objector. And yet on the surface, he is all crayons and construction paper, wearing grade school's implements like camouflage, his white paste no-muss-no-fuss arts and crafts veneer, his multiplication table decoy, the Go Tell Aunt Rhody avoidance procedures, the Rise and Shine and Give God Your Glory Glory deflections.*

But this is wartime, and he sits in school drearily copying out spelling words, definitions, imagining his family back home sitting anxiously around a radio, listening for news from the front. He envisions returning home for lunch break and his whole family greeting him on the street with tearful hugs: The son is back, and he's okay.

But there are no purple hearts for Wilner, only the notes sent home: "Norbert is an excellent student but seems to withdraw into his own world a lot." And what about the other kids? Do they share his fear? Not Goldberg, that is clear. Philip is the guy who volunteers.

"We need someone to circle behind the Japs and get a message to the lieutenant and his men there. It's a dangerous job, we don't want anyone with a wife or kid."

"I'll do it, Sir."

Philip's the man for the job, risking his neck to serve his commanding officer, his country. In East Lake he is the Hall Monitor, the Safety Patrol, the A-V kid who knows how to load the filmstrips, set up the P.A. In gym he's the goalie, not afraid to get his face smashed in. Goldberg, the fire drill captain, the last one out of the building when it goes up in flames. The rep to Student Council. How could he ever understand a kid like Wilner? They were cut from a different cloth.

And what about little Jerry Greenblatt, growing up on the Lower East Side of Manhattan, in Alphabet City, Avenue D, surrounded by kids named José who carried blades, and pregnant black girls in the sixth grade? Jerry, the "Jew boy," who knew junkies by name and stepped over their nodding frames on his own stoop every night—was he scared? You bet, but he wore his fear in street-style, learning to walk with shoulders hunched, head down, hands in pockets, kicking pebbles like a young tough, the seven year-old Jewish ex-con look, talking hard-nosed stuff, swearing. It was his way, and it concealed a heart quivering in fear as much as Wilner's, though if Wilner had grown up in his neighborhood, Greenblatt would have steered clear of him, called him a mama's boy, maybe even grabbed his school books and thrown them in a big mud puddle—whatever he needed to do to distinguish himself from one such as Wilner, the worst sort, never guessing one day they'd be partners in dread, middle-aged men still terrified of "big kids."

And see little Weissbaum there, his first day of school like the first game of the season. Even then, a blown-out-of-proportion mythological sense of himself, approaching kindergarten as the Rookie of the Year, the promising young southpaw making his debut in the majors. The kid never changed his entire life, the passing of years for him a mere trick of time-lapse photography. You can see the aging process—he gets taller, he starts shaving—but the eyes of the five-year-old and the eyes of the forty-year-old remain constant, and they look out on life from a box seat on the third base line, or from the bleachers in center, behind Mays, behind Mantle, cheering and yelling, keeping a scorecard, engrossed in the game. Listen to him, in second grade, being chosen to hand out graded papers:

"And she chooses Weissbaum, all right, a popular favorite with the fans...and what's this? The first paper goes to Norbert Wilner who pulls in a solid and respectable B+, but normally an A student, a long-ball hitter, this Wilner...and who's up next? Ladles and Gentlespoons, the Sultan of Social Studies, Philip Goldberg, sliding home safe with an inside-the-park A+, the crowd is on its feet."

Weissbaum, the midget Mel Allen, the pygmy Howard Cosell, announcing his life from the time the bell rang to start Round One:

"And he's out of the womb, folks, suspended upside-down, not quite breathing yet..."

Weissbaum, always grinning ear-to-ear, gleeful day and night. Would he understand Wilner? Fear? Fear what? School as the American Pastime, for Weissbaum. The honor roll, for him, equivalent to being inducted in the East Lake Hall of Fame.

Only for Wilner are the bases forever loaded. Bottom of the ninth, two out, full count, the pitch is on its way...and Norbert Wilner is forever at the plate. Let's interview the kid, find out what's what:

"I love being sick because then my father brings the record player into my room and I can lie in my bed reading Hardy Boy books all day, listening to My Fair Lady and The Nutcracker Suite. And whenever I need anything, why, I just pick up this little bell here on my night table and ring it a few times and my mother shows up and finds out what I want. She brings me toast and jello and chicken soup. And when I had the measles, she brought me scrambled eggs and baked beans, Ummm-ummm. Whenever I get up to go to the bathroom, she sneaks into my room and freshens up my bed.

"In the mornings on sick days I watch I Love Lucy, December's Bride, Donna Reed, Pete and Gladys, Father Knows Best and Leave It To Beaver. I love all those families. I stay sick as long as I can, because I love staying home in my pajamas, and I hate going to school. And that's final."

Why? What's so terrible about school?

"Well, first of all, I saw some strange kids hanging around the playground after school. Catholic kids, from St. Anne's, and they're pretty tough. Up to no good. Suppose they get me one of these days?"

See Wilner running from the school building to his father's car every day after school, like he's running across an open field, dodging enemy artillery, his life at stake. He is a twelve-year-old baby who just wants to stay home, to sit at the kitchen table and play with his red and blue modeling clay, pretending to make an apple pie, smoothing clay-dough over a bowl like piecrust.

"And the best part, of course, is that my mother is just a few feet away, making a real cake, with a long, wooden spoon which I alone, Norbert Wilner, will get to lick in just a few minutes."

So you feel safe.

"Yeah."

What else do you do to keep yourself occupied?

"I like sitting on the living room floor, building big houses out of playing cards, or practicing my new magic tricks. Or setting up my soldiers all over the place: some hiding on the back of the couch, waiting for unsuspecting robbers to ride by, some in the main fort, keeping the Indians away, and some up on the bookshelf, scouting, peering across the plains with their binoculars."

There were clearly lots of things Wilner loved to do. They just didn't involve getting dressed and going out of the house. If Finkelstein wanted to come over after school, that was okay with Wilner. He never turned Finkelstein away. But he preferred to be alone, especially in October, when it started to get colder in northern New Jersey, and dark by five o'clock. Then Norbert's favorite activity was to lie on the rug in the den and watch Superman and The Three Stooges, all the while hearing the sounds of his mother just up the stairs in the kitchen, cooking his favorite dinner— browned chopped meat with macaroni.

And then the big moment comes: the sound of a car in the driveway, and Superman or no Superman, little Wilner races up the stairs and jumps on his Daddy, home at last, his beard rough and cold, smelling of October. And yes, now Wilner is happy. His parents are home. He is home. Everybody is safe and together. Only then does his fear subside momentarily, the panicky fear he has lived with ever since the first time he was separated from his mother in nursery school, the day those mean ladies locked him in the dark garage. The day he learned that to be home again was all that mattered, and that everything outside of home could be terrible and scary. (The Hitler, the Hitler; never forget the bitter.)

"When I grow up I want to be a baseball player, and second most I want to be a detective, and third of all I want to be a magician and a puppeteer."

And Wilner would, in fact, carry his Mattel Detective Badge in his wallet until his early twenties, along with a business card that he typed himself on three-by-five cards, cut down the middle. The card said simply, "Norbert Wilner, The Detective," followed by his address and phone number.

Finkelstein and Wilner had been partners in the private-eye business at one time. Together they had somehow deduced that several crossbeams of lumber nailed across the door of an old shack behind Temple B'nai Shalom were actually some sort of coded signal being transmitted by outlaws who were planning to rob the Mona Lisa, which was then on display in New York, on loan from the Louvre.

Clearly, the young sleuths felt, the increased incidence of auto thefts reported in their local paper were none other than the actions of this same group of bandits, melting down automobiles in order to make bullet-proof vests and a getaway jet...all this from two boards nailed to a shack!

And where was Philip during all this crime fighting? Campaigning. He was the new kid from Brooklyn, fighting against the odds to make a name for himself. Already he had invited Butch Taylor's antagonism, merely, we can only conjecture, through his attitude of fearlessness on Taylor's territory. Butch Taylor, the Numero Uno in Goy-land, the kid everyone deferred to, the East Lake Elementary School resident Godfather, way beyond mere bully. So who was this chubby little Jew boy coming in the middle of the school year and acting like he owned the place?

Butch's way of dealing with the threat? He called Philip "Basketball." Rotund Goldberg would not stand for this for very long, and he as much as told Taylor this, who only scoffed. Although he was uncertain of this newcomer, Butch couldn't even begin to consider that anyone would actually stand up to him. Philip's threats were vaguely unsettling to him, but he laughed them off, and continued to periodically call out, "Hey, here comes the Basketball!" when Philip walked past.

Now, what use would Wilner be to Philip if a showdown occurred, if push came to shove? None at all. Philip was only beginning to get an inkling of this, and he felt vaguely betrayed by Wilner, although he could not yet point to a particular act of betrayal. Perhaps he saw it coming from Wilner's behavior in team sports.

Whenever there was a dispute, no matter which team Wilner was on, he would suggest that the players "do it over." Philip's blood would boil—he wanted to see justice triumph, he was not a man of compromise. But he should have seen that Wilner was terrified of conflict of any sort. And yet, he was blind to it. He didn't see that Wilner would never, under any circumstances, choose fighting over arbitration, and failing arbitration, would choose retreat, embrace humiliation, back down and lose face rather than risk hurting himself in a physical fight. He was no Vince Grisatti—Butch Taylor's sidekick —no tough guy.

'Course the truth was, Grisatti may have been tough, but he couldn't fight for shit. See him there, leaning over the fence, blood dripping from his nose and forming a puddle on the blacktop, little Norbert Wilner staring in horror, terrified...it could have been his nose!

But Wilner was safe, for the moment, because he paid off the right people. It was a protection racket. Wilner shmeered Butch Taylor free bubble gum in exchange for not getting beaten up. But nevertheless, Wilner walked across the school yard with the same fear and caution that an American soldier would have walking across an open field in Vietnam, knowing not who lurked in the bushes, knowing not which step might trigger a land mine.

See, what we have here is a little kid who was supposed to be just an ordinary child going to school to learn how to subtract and divide, to draw maps of the seven continents in colored pencil, but in fact what must be faced is the plain, hard truth that in the boy's consciousness, each day at school was a dangerous, threatening matter of life and death.

If you don't believe it, just take a look at his face, watching Grisatti lean over the fence, big red drops of blood dripping onto the blacktop. All the kids are standing around in the circle that forms to watch the fight, everyone against Grisatti, Grisatti more unpopular than Sonny Liston. And why shouldn't they be happy to see Grisatti get beat? Hadn't he and Butch Taylor intimidated the entire playground? Wasn't everyone in bubble gum payments over their heads? And now Jimmy Holler—a fifth grader, for Pete's sake—was creaming Grisatti.

It would shift the entire political structure at East Lake Elementary School. It would shake Butch Taylor's empire. Holler would attract other dissidents and an underground would surely form. And yes, Phil

Goldberg was sure to play a key role in the resistance. Chubby Philip Goldberg, who Butch Taylor had tauntingly called "Basketball" just once too often.

Yes, Philip would surely get involved, and he would surely try to bring Wilner in with him. Wilner, the pacifist. Wilner, the chicken. It just would not be a fair request to ask a man like Wilner to come out publicly against the goyim, *against Taylor and Grisatti. He had too much to lose. He felt his life was at stake. He was running scared. The horror on his face as he watches Grisatti bleed is more than simply a sensitive child's reaction to violence. No, there were far greater, far-reaching implications.*

His terror is equally triggered by catching a glimpse of Phil Goldberg, across the circle, grinning and throwing his fist in the air, as if Grisatti's defeat is some sort of personal triumph. And Norbert is no dummy. He has felt the undercurrent of political unrest at East Lake; he can feel Philip's driving ambition, Phil beaming at him across the way; he can sense the inevitable crisis of special interest groups coming to blows, for which Grisatti's bloody nose is somehow paving the way; and he can see himself torn apart, standing in the middle, shmeering Taylor bubble gum in order to survive, yet presumably allied to Philip. A double agent by default, as a result of fear and fear alone. Something would have to give. Wilner would have to take a stand. If Taylor's people leaked the fact that Wilner was paying them off, and Philip got wind of that little piece of information, it would ruin Wilner and he would be left in no-man's land.

All this goes through the boy's mind as Mrs. McQuistan ("McQuicksand,") steps through the crowd and pulls Grisatti by the hair, blood spattering behind him and creating a red trail from the blacktop right up to the principal's office, Grisatti snarling, like a miniature Jimmy Cagney always in trouble with the "feds"—little, tough Grisatti, with his sharp, chiseled good looks. You could see—even then—that one day he'd have about eight kids, work hard on a construction site, drink hard with his buddies after work, slap his pretty wife around if she complained about his lying ways.

And yes, one look at Norbert Wilner in the sixth grade and you could just see—even then—that he would wind up spending thousands of dollars on therapists, never put in an honest day's work in his life, be plagued by depression throughout his days. You could really see it all; it's amazing nobody did.

But then again, Norbert covered up. He had to. He couldn't afford to let anyone—not Butch Taylor, not Grisatti, not even Phil Goldberg—see him for who he actually was: a sixth-grade baby, a scaredy-cat. The idea that Grisatti himself might have been afraid, that his toughness might have been a desperate over-compensation for his own terror, this never occurred to little Wilner, just as it never occurred to the adult Wilner that perhaps Grisatti really was tough and unafraid, for the older Wilner could not conceive of a human life without at least some degree of sheer terror patrolling the underground of consciousness at all times, a terror that is best friends with death.

The exception for Wilner, naturally, was Finkelstein. With Finkelstein, he was fearless. Finkelstein he would fight, and did fight, everyday. For one thing, Finkelstein posed no real physical threat to Wilner. But even if he had, Wilner would have fought him anyway, because Finkelstein made him so mad he wanted to kill him. It was only in his daily encounters with Finkelstein that Wilner's rage surpassed his fear, so that the thought of giving in to Finkelstein, of backing down, was unthinkable. And the best part about fighting Finkelstein was that no matter who was in the right, Finkelstein's father would make his son apologize to Wilner. Ten minutes after a major battle, Wilner would get a phone call:

"Listen, Norb, you need me and I need you, so whattaya say I come over and we play a little Monopoly, no questions asked?"

But fighting Finkelstein was never like a real fight. Not like Holler breaking Grisatti's nose and blood dripping all over the blacktop. Fighting Finkelstein, for Wilner, was like a pre-season exhibition match: it had all the appearances of regulation play, with none of the consequences. And yet Philip, blinded by his desire to create a resistance movement, overthrow Taylor and establish his own empire, didn't see Wilner's tragic weakness for what it was: mortal fear. And this oversight would cost him. This little bit of clouded vision on Philip's part would be a tragic one when the stakes got high, when Philip had his little Brooklyn tushie on the line.

CHAPTER NINE

Goldberg

Okay: Simply put, why doesn't Phil Goldberg worry about the things I worry about? Who is Phil Goldberg that he should be spared the agonies of the spiritual quest? Are atheists the real winners in the cosmic crap shoot? Left to fend for themselves and make their own rules, they're usually highly ethical chaps. Goldberg's no monkey in the ethics department. I'd sooner trust him to take charge of things than hand the world over to Moscowitz with his forces of light and *I-Ching* readings, his power spots and chakra balancings, aura cleansings and Kundalini risings, his energy meridians and shamanic tap-dancing, the old karmic one-potato two-potato routine, his eenie-meenie-miny-moe of New Age this and thats.

And give me Goldberg's sensibilities over Finkelstein's fanatical salvation business, which essentially boils down to, "Accept Jesus Christ as your Lord and Savior, or get the fuck out." No, to Goldberg alone would I entrust proprietorship of this precarious life—not that he's doing such a fantastic job running his own—but I'm convinced that at least he's got that singular quality which is no small thing: He *means well.* Goldberg means well. To give you an example of how much impact this quality can be on all of our well-being, consider: Hitler did *not mean well*. Makes all the difference.

Lately I've been keeping a journal, working on an essay, which has the working title, "Piercing Goldberg's Thick Skull with the Reality of the Divine." I hesitate to show it to Phil, because I recently mailed him an audiocassette, a lecture on romantic relationships that I thought would be useful to him and his haberdasher girlfriend. The tape discussed romance in Jungian terms, and put forth the idea that if a man were to look for the Eternal Feminine—"anima"—within his own psyche, he would discover there the internal spiritual union for which he longs, and for which he mistakenly seeks through romantic relationships with women; thus wreaking havoc and distorting what ought to be a simple, loving companionship, supportive of each other's passionate spiritual quest for union, but not responsible for fulfilling it. Goldberg's response to the tape?

"It was very interesting, but I still think it's more fun to look for the Eternal Feminine *outside* of myself."

I can never win with him. He has always been basically happy, enjoys life, and God has no part of it. Me? I'm basically miserable, depressed and anxious, and the Big Guy has me running around like a chicken without a head. Go figure.

When Phil and I were in our early twenties, we once spent a summer at the Twin Oaks Home for the Criminally Deranged, which is what we, the waiters and busboys, used to call it. It was actually a summer resort for mostly old and mostly Jewish people whose lives revolved around eating. I shared a bunk with Phil, who was then, and continues to be, a budding young composer. Apparently, he has explained, in this culture, at this time, it is virtually impossible for budding young composers of serious music ever to blossom into successful, old composers. Fortunately, Philip was only twenty-two that year, and would continue to be a budding young composer for a good deal longer.

But that summer at Twin Oaks, Philip was very upset that he was working seven days a week, fifteen hours a day, serving food to people who would most certainly not live long enough to even hear his music, had he had any time whatever to devote to it, which he did not. And for some, it would be the very food Philip would serve them—a simple cheese blintz—that would prove to be the final assault on their system that summer. (Or the near-final assault, as in the case of Mr. Liebowitz, who once had a heart attack at lunch, was carted away in an ambulance, and was back in time for dinner, because, as he put it, he was "entitled.")

In the meantime, Philip felt increasingly restless, and began to declare, angrily, defiantly, on a daily basis, "I'm going to have something to show for my summer." That is, being a budding young composer, he intended to compose. The first thing he needed in order to do this properly, in our little bunk, was a desk of some sort; something to compose *on*. A composer must write his compositions down in order to feel like he has something to show for himself. Philip could spend an entire day humming the most original and delightful melodies to himself as he served enormous platters of boiled beef flanken, imagining these same melodies surrounded and enriched by the most exquisite of dense harmonies, and none of it would mean anything to him if it wasn't written down. This is understandable: Once it is written down, there is something, which *isn't Philip* that will be left over when one day *Philip isn't*.

It is unlikely, however, that Philip ever heard any such melodies or harmonies in his head while serving meals at Twin Oaks—not when he was constantly being hounded by the likes of Mr. Schacter, who calls him aside after dinner one day:

"Philip," he begins, polite but firm, "You have ruined my entire summer." Philip is staggered.

"What? How?"

"I asked you for medium well, you gave me medium rare. Red meat, the sight of it, makes me nauseous, I'm sick to my stomach."

"Your entire summer?" Philip asks, incredulous.

It certainly never would have occurred to Schacter that in filling Philip's consciousness with remarks like that, he was, in effect, ruining *Philip's* entire summer, who, as it turned out, *would* find a piece of plywood and spend several days constructing a makeshift but certainly usable little desk in our bunk. But unfortunately, perhaps due to Schacter and his kind, the only thing Philip ever had to "show for his summer" was that same slab of plywood, crudely nailed into the wall, and supported by a two-by-four.

On my first day at Twin Oaks I was taken to the kitchen to meet the man who would eventually become known to us as "the schizophrenic general manager," and whose job it was, that first day, to determine whether I should be a waiter and make $2,300 for the summer—assuming Uncle Sid with the big nose and the cigar gave his usual hundred buck tip—or a busboy, and make $1,700, and be in charge of clearing away dirty plates instead of bringing out clean ones. He became known as the schizophrenic general manager because of what happened one day when I came into the kitchen during a meal:

"Side of herring for Mrs. Klein," I say, innocently. He explodes.

"I DON'T GIVE A SHIT WHO IT'S *FOR*, DON'T *EVER* TELL ME WHO IT'S *FOR!*"

Several minutes later, I return to the kitchen and order another side of herring, a piece of fish I intend to serve to Mrs. Goldberg— no relation to Phil—but, having learned my lesson, I say nothing of the herring's destination. Unfortunately, everybody at Twin Oaks—all the guests, the chambermaids, the chauffeur, the pool attendant—know that Mrs. Goldberg only eats the middle section of herring. Naturally, then, she sends the end piece of herring I had served her back into the kitchen, with me in the rather unenviable position of having to communicate the problem to the general manager, who was about to forever earn the title of schizophrenic:

"Ahem, Mrs. Goldberg won't accept this end piece, Sir," I offer meekly. He explodes again.

"I KNOW SHE WON'T EAT AN END PIECE, WHY THE HELL DIDN'T YOU TELL ME WHO IT WAS *FOR?*"

So this was the man I was taken to meet on my first day, and rather than discuss business right away—whether to make me a waiter or busboy—he kindly suggests I eat first, and hands me a plate containing a piece of broiled chicken, a few stalks of broccoli, and a small square segment of noodle pudding. These items I promptly juggle. The chicken slides off the plate as soon as he hands it to me, and bounces off my knee. I catch it in my other hand, just as the noodle pudding begins to make its descent, landing on the floor with an unceremonious "plop." The general manager, watching this performance, says,

"I think I'll make you a busboy."

But no account of that summer would be complete without at least a brief discussion of what has come to be known as "The Baked Potato Affair," another incident involving the infamous Mrs. Goldberg, who only ate the mid-section of herrings.

Mrs. Goldberg once saw that Mrs. Levy at the next table was eating a baked potato, and became enraged that Levy was receiving some kind of special treatment, which was being denied her, she being served mashed along with everyone else. She calls Philip over and demands an explanation. He explains that baked potatoes need to be ordered a day in advance, because they take longer to cook, and she, Mrs. Goldberg, can have one anytime she wants. To which Mrs. G., still peeved, firmly replies,

"From now on, Philip, I want a baked potato every night; I may not *eat* it, but I *want* it."

There was no problem in supplying Mrs. G. with a baked potato every night. The problem was that, as it turned out, she never, ever ate it. The reason this was a problem was because the baked potato was served in its own separate dish, and at the end of every meal, the house rule was to salvage any "live" food that had not been touched, and return it to the kitchen. This was a simple matter when it came to rolls and bread, because the insane, mean chef from France had nothing to do with rolls and bread. They just went back to the bread man, who pressed each individual slice of bread with his thumb to check for freshness, and then put them away until the next day. (In fact, for awhile, I *was* the bread man.)

But if the insane, mean chef from France should catch someone bringing back the baked potato which he had cooked *on special order from Philip*, there was no telling what he would do, waving his big meat cleaver around wildly, threatening to make salad of the kitchen help. There was only one solution, and that was for Philip to wolf down Mrs. Goldberg's baked potato every night, before the chef would have a chance to see it returning to the kitchen uneaten. Philip had to eat a baked potato, whether he wanted to or not, every night for the remainder of the summer.

***

Meanwhile, Goldberg and I are standing before my newest acquisition: a 1957 shiny white hearse. On it is written, "Happy Hearse Funeral Parlor: Going in Style." Red letters against a mural of a gurgling brook in a green meadow on a sunny, spring day. Plus the little happy-face/skull logo.

"I thought you were just kidding about that funeral parlor idea..."

"No, I have a new personal policy. I don't kid about brilliant inspirations or visionary strokes of genius. Get in."

He sits in the front and turns to admire the interior. His eyes come to rest on a plain, wooden coffin in the rear compartment.

"Floor model," I say, "It's empty. Want to try it? It's got the new padded feature for extra comfort."

"I don't think the dead need added comfort, Norb."

"We're not selling to the dead, Phil, we're selling to the living—walking, talking, flesh and blood creatures like you and me, only terminally ill...but who isn't, eh mate? Anyway, what do you know about death? Go die first, then I'll listen to your opinion. Let me tell you our angle: Most parlors deal with the bereaved family after the fact; it's good business because you can sell a weeping widow anything, but who wants to get rich off of other people's grief? It's inhuman. I want to revolutionize the death business, take it out of the grisly shroud of fear and avoidance into the light of day, honor it as the natural part of the life cycle as it was most assuredly designed to be. It was built into the plan, that's obvious. 'The Pro-Life Death People,' is a possible motto we're toying with, or 'Still Living? But Not For Long? Die With A Smile With Happy Hearse!' Anyway, you get the picture, we're still working on the precise words...I hired Moscowitz to do all our ad copy and brochure materials."

"No!"

"He's already come up with contemporary sympathy cards using Peanuts characters. You know, on the outside Charlie Brown is holding Snoopy, limp in his arms, Lucy saying, 'I feel so bad he died, Charlie Brown,' and inside is Lucy with one tear falling, saying, 'He was one of my best friends in the whole world.' It's not bad—touching, real, but not like those maudlin cards with the twenty-line scriptural quotes that make you feel guilty about throwing them away, the word of God and all that...take a look at this."

From my backpack I dig out the preliminary layout for one of Moscowitz's ad proposals:

> *Tired of all the grieving,*
> *Just because you're leaving?*
> *Somber faces by your bed,*
> *Make you wish that you were dead?*
> *Let Happy Hearse lighten the air,*
> *Go on your way with a little flair.*
> *Happy Hearse: The Only Way To Go*

"Well, what do you think?" I ask him.

"I think hiring Moscowitz was a mistake."

"Nah, I'll coach him along, he's open to feedback, he's got a good heart, underneath it all."

"What's left of it."

"Don't be silly, the doctor said he's got a good 40,000 miles left on the right ventricle alone."

"That's if he gets off the floor once in awhile—his idea of aerobics is daily breathing."

"Not an active person, I agree."

"The rhymes get to me, too."

Moscowitz had spent fifteen years writing copy for Hallmark cards, and it eventually did him in. He could no longer carry on a normal conversation. Everything with him was a greeting card, a rhyme. He's leaving your house, he won't just say "See you later," he'll come up with something like, "Though this day was lots of fun, the time has come for me to run."

"Yeah, take care, Moscowitz."

"Before you know it, I'll be back, but now I'm off to hit the sack."

"Okay Moscowitz, that's enough."

"You're a real swell friend, I gotta say, so I hope to see you another day."

"MOSCOWITZ!!" Many times, many people, have wanted to strangle Moscowitz for his poetry. Especially Goldberg, with his passion for literature, when he overhears someone asking Moscowitz what he does, and the reply is,

"I'm a poet, and don't know it."

And he was bi-lingual:

"We said *baruch ataw*, we said *p'ree ha-gawfen*, finally it's time, to go and get some *shlof'n*."

Still in the hearse with Phil, I flip on the stereo:

"Check this out. I'm wired for sound...for the New Age crowd we got your basic Zen koto music."

Ethereal sounds fill the car peacefully. I press a button.

"For the older Jews we got the Vishnitzer Rebbe Live at the Wailing Wall, with the Yeshiva Bochur Back-up Band. We have a huge selection for the client to choose from: "Homeward Bound," "Leavin' On A Jet Plane," "Never Can Say Good-Bye," and when little kids die..."

I press another button, and a little girl's voice sings,

"So long, farewell, aufweidersehn good-bye," from the *Sound of Music*.

"Uh, on that note, Norb, so long yourself, I gotta get out of this death mobile..."

I quickly hit another button:

"We Gotta Get Outta This Place" by Eric Burdon and the Animals. Phil hops out at the light, a few blocks from his place on Fort Washington. I pull away, chuckling to myself:

"Am I a funny guy or what? Huh? Answer me, somebody, and I'll shut up. Ah, you're all a bunch of deadheads."

***

"This funeral parlor business, it's not normal." announces Jerry Greenblatt, on the phone, "It' a little warped."

"Who made you the Emperor of Normal? No Jerry, *you* are warped, for buying into this culture's morbid handling of the death process...in the name of Allah, you should know better. With all your aches and pains and arthritic joints and your hernia and hemorrhoids, not to mention your occipital lobe problem..."

"What occipital..."

"You know what I'm talking about: your neural misfirings, your little dendrite explosions, the synaptic gaps in your consciousness. Don't play dumb Greenblatt. If anyone should realize that leaving this body might be a welcome release from the tortures of corporeal existence, it's you...*al salaam aleichem.* "

"*Aleichem al salaam.*"

"So I want you to come in with me on the business—partners, the death squad. You drive the hearse, I'll set up the refreshments; you cheer up the widows, I'll do the follow-up; you're the soft-shoe, I'm the hard sell...together we're the Last Stop One-Two, The End of the Line Dosie Doe, the Kiss-It-Good-Bye Bardo Brothers, the Abbot and Costello of Death, the Burns and Allen of So Long It's Been Nice To Know Ya, the buck stops here...are you with me or should I go on? I'm talking Moe, Larry and Curly on the River Styx, Buddy Hackett in Hades..."

"Whoa, wait a minute...who's Curly?"

"Weissbaum."

"Weissbaum?"

"You're missing the whole brilliant part right here, Mr. Greenblatt, which is why you are the warm-up act and I am the brains of the outfit...don't you see the perfection? Weissbaum, camcorder king of the wedding and the bar mitzvah...the next step is obvious, elementary: Our man Weissbaum starts video-taping funerals!"

"I don't know, Jesus, it's a little..."

"It's a stroke of genius. Were those the words you were grappling for in that tiny peashooter brain of yours? Think of it: The weeping family, the eulogy, and of course, the crux of the matter, the close-up of the beloved, that one, last tearful glance of the deceased, now available on video cassette for countless viewings. This could speed up the grieving process by months; people could cry their eyes out anytime they felt the urge, just by tuning their sets to Channel 3. Admit it, it's brilliant. And then, the climax, the casket gets lowered into the ground, Weissbuam dubs in "We've Only Just Begun" and the viewer is left sobbing, but inspired by the intimation of new beginnings, the immortality of the soul, Eternal Life. It's a sure thing, Greenblatt, I'm telling you, a can't miss. Are you in or what?"

"Can I do my Jewish James Cagney?"

"How does it go?"

"You *schmutzadika* rat..."

"We'll work it in."

"How about my Gestapo bit?"

"I don't think so, Jerry—not in good taste."

"Yeah...okay, I'm in. When do we start?"

"As soon as someone dies—I'll let you know. For now just brush up on your embalming, research formaldehyde prices..."

"Embalming? What..."

"See you Jer," And I hang up, leaving him guessing.

***

As for Goldberg and his miserable love life, I failed. In matters of the heart there was no listening to reason. Over a nice lasagna dinner at Gino's, I tell him:

"Listen, you let her go, and in a couple of weeks tops you'll be back to your old self—flirting with and seducing all sorts of new women who are equally if not more inappropriate for you than Dorothy, but at least you'll get a breather in between."

"I'm not like that anymore...I've really changed. I'm actually very insecure."

"No no no, hear me out. This is how you've changed: you used to be basically *happy*, and now you are basically *not happy*. It's not complicated."

He stayed with Dorothy, and convinced himself things were getting better: "She even lets me touch her sometimes now," he said.

"That's good. Touching is good."

"Oh Norb, I think it'll work out, we just have to hang in together a little longer."

"Maybe you should get married—it's good to get your first divorce out of the way."

"I don't feel you are being supportive of my relationship."

"Actually, I am. I think not being together would be very healing for your relationship."

"Let love be enough then, I'm bored with the rest." He was going on automatic quote mode. I had to fight fire with fire. I pulled out my Shaw:

"The fickleness of the women I love is equaled only by the infernal constancy of the women who love me."

"There's nothing more boring than a woman who's in love with someone who isn't me." he counters.

"No," I reply, "there's actually nothing more boring than a woman who's in love with someone who isn't *me*."

"No me," he says.

"Me."

"Me."

101

"Me."

"Me."

This goes on for a while.

***

Ah Goldberg, see him there diving for the ball on the pavement, ripping his knee open, blood everywhere, and not a tear. A man's man, even then. For Goldberg, it was never "how you play the game," it was always about winning or losing. He loved to win and usually did, unless he was stuck with wimps like Wilner or Moscowitz on his team, which would drive him crazy.

"You know what your problem is, Wilner?" he would say, as early as fifth grade, "You lack competitive edge." And Wilner, defensive, would respond, "Yeah, but you lack a spirit of detente." Talk like that, at 11 years old, shaping their friendship for life. Goldberg forever itching for opportunities to prove himself, to taste sweet victory, whatever the arena—from simple arm wrestling to the "who can throw the rock at the stop sign" game. And Wilner forever seeking out opportunities to back down, literally looking to lose as quickly as possible, and get back home. See little Phil Goldberg, the show-off, the winner, gloating. Goldberg, secure and unflappable, his built-in "I can and I will" forever parading itself over Wilner's "I can't and I won't."

Rotund, chubby little kid, round-cheeked and baby-faced, it was no wonder Taylor dubbed Goldberg "Basketball." And Goldberg overcompensated by being fearless. Unafraid, even, of fighting Butch Taylor if that's what it would take, which to Wilner looked like suicide, like an amateur stepping into the ring with Cassius Clay. Taylor, undefeated and confident, the reigning king of East Lake, was rarely if ever challenged anymore. He usually got just a polite nod of respect from the other big guns on the playground, dignitaries like Mareschi, 5'7" in sixth grade, tacitly acknowledged as the strongest guy in school. But Taylor was the toughest, Taylor the one to steer clear of, Taylor willing to punch the shit out of anyone with little or no provocation. A man like Mareschi, on the other hand, could quietly go about his business, not a fighting man, no need to prove himself. This was in those elementary school days when the mere fact of height itself brought with it a certain respect and prestige. By the time Wilner finally shot up a few inches the summer after tenth grade, it was too late. By then his being 5'10" or 5'11" bought him nothing. When the prettiest girl in school laughingly dismissed him as "a loser," his "but I'm nearly six feet tall" fell on deaf ears. At a certain point, height was no longer enough, and Wilner had to learn the hard way—by growing.

So Goldberg had his work cut out for him, to establish his terrain, to challenge Taylor's power structure, to rock the boat of the Establishment at East Lake, and to be—and this predates Sandy Koufax—one of the earliest Jewish athletes to make a name for himself in the big leagues, albeit, in this case, it was in the fierce lunch-hour dodge ball games on the playground. These were gritty contests that Wilner, for example, wouldn't dream of playing in, even had they let him into the game, which wouldn't have happened in a million years. Guys like Taylor and Grisatti and yes, Goldberg, could throw a dodge ball with such velocity and force that guys like Wilner would be sitting ducks, mere target practice. Someone could get hurt.

Now, to the girls: Already—even then—everything broke down along religious lines. The Jewish girls were familiar—you saw them in Hebrew School, they lived around the corner, their mothers ran into your mother at Loehmans, at Petak's. You sat together during the High Holy Day services, entertaining them with your famous "tallis/tzit-tzit slipknot trick," over and over again. You left the sanctuary during the solemn Yizkor service for the dead, all of you hanging together outside watching the Gentile kids walk past with their school books, the Jewish holiday the best perk of the religion.

So the girls were there too, munching on rugelachs in the synagogue basement after services. They too had Israeli bonds in their names, had mothers warning them everyday of all the possible ways they could break a leg or lose an eye. So they were sisters, right from the start: the Esthers and Hannas and Naomis, the Ruths, Sarahs and Rebeccas. It was the Stephanies and Tiffanys and Daphnes that fascinated the boys—the blonde Katherines and freckled Marys, the ones with the little up-turned noses. All the Catholic and Protestant girls in their Brownie uniforms, with their Confirmations and Ash Wednesdays and Friday night fish, something deliciously unkosher about the very way they smelled, as if a diet free of stuffed derma and kreplach caused a fundamental organic difference in the bloodstream itself. The body odors borne of bacon and shellfish to the unformed young Jewish olfactory sense was somehow an aphrodisiac, charged with an erotic otherness—even then.

*So the pattern was established early: The Jewish girls already loved us like sisters, and therefore needed no further attention—(Greenblatt's sister, case in point)—but were fun to have around as friends. But the Shikseh Goddess syndrome literally began in kindergarten or earlier, was built into the subconscious from the start. And so the boys' sexual identity could only be validated and affirmed by a member of the foreign tribe, and yes, in this arena like all others, Goldberg played all out to win, and did. An unending procession of Christian girlfriends from seventh grade on, each held up as living proof of his own masculine worth. See him there—even then—*kvelling *when Judy Hunt writes in his sixth grade graduation book:*

> *Roses are Red,*
> *Violets are Blue,*
> *Sugar is Sweet,*
> *and So are You!*

Compare that to her entry in Wilner's book, identical except for the last line,

> *"But why aren't you?"*

Goldberg's "Shiksehs-on-Parade" *confused people over time—to the casual onlooker, they were virtually indistinguishable. Bernstein called them all "Carol," and said things like, "I heard Goldberg got the new '98 model, and this one comes with a/c." But with a good-looking blonde girl at his side, it was as if the adult Goldberg was looking back over time into the eyes of Butch Taylor and saying, "Basketball, is it? Well look at me now—eat your heart out."*

And there was yet more Goldberg had to overcome: The kid played a mean accordion, and had an ear on him Yascha Heifetz would die for. Surrounded by murmurings of "such a gifted boy" and "what a talented young man," he had no choice: He had to excel at two-hand touch, he had to balance his musical abilities by being willing to go mano-a-mano with Taylor, lest he suffer the unhappy fate of the Moscowitz's of the world, toting a sissy violin to school where guys like Grisatti wouldn't think twice about smashing it to smithereens. And the really scary part was that Grisatti's father would smile and approve. The goyim played by a different set of rules, and to Wilner, the playground may as well have been Bergen Belsen; Grisatti and Taylor, the SS; and he, with his clandestine bubble-gum operation, a Sonderkommando.

And Goldberg? What else? A survivor.

***

From my journal: *Which is it, Mr. Big Stuff? Life as cause for ecstatic adoration or bottomless despair? It is how it is—Miltie's cinnamon bagel sits there like a bump on a Zen log. God is the Presence of Presence, the Primordial Capacity for Being, the isness of Is, the thisness of This. Given That, is our only choice how we respond to the facts? And is joy really a possible choice in every moment? Or is despair as natural and involuntary a response to our world as sneezing? Like a tickle in the nose, the existential reality we observe around us makes us spontaneously despair and thus robs us of all possibility to truly be alive, at least with any enthusiasm.*

Therefore, if we are not to collectively sleepwalk through life in a haze of vast resignation, we must be willing to take on as a hypothesis that we do have the choice of looking out on the horror and suffering of this world and—in spite of all our preferences about how we think things should be—use our God-given option to be, if not joyous, at least okay, no matter what the evidence. Yet the question must be asked, "How can a mother with dry and shriveled breasts, cradling her emaciated and starving child in her arms, possibly be okay?"

I wrote myself into a corner and couldn't get out. This was a job for Reb Miltie. I break our Sunday morning tradition and go banging on his door at midnight on Saturday.

"You're early," he greets me, sleepily, wearing a little night cap with the words "Hi-Ho" printed all over it, matching a long, colorful nightshirt depicting Snow White and the Seven Dwarfs, frolicking in the woods. "And no bagels?" he asks.

"How can a mother with dry and shriveled breasts, cradling her emaciated and starving child in her arms, possibly like God?" For I had come to the conclusion that this notion of "liking God" was equivalent to "choosing to be okay with things as they are."

"We might as well cover the Nazis while we're at it," he replied. "How can any Jew like God, after watching his baby tossed in the air and shot like a clay pigeon? And yet we have very clear reports that there were certain people whose ability to rejoice in the Aweful Presence and Wonder of God barely wavered in the face of the atrocities in the camps. I'm afraid, my sensitive friend, we have come to the proverbial 'problem of evil.' "

"And do you pretend to have the solution to this problem?"

"No, Reb Norbert Wilner, it's more like you pretend that you don't."

"Meaning?"

"Meaning *you* are the solution to the problem of evil."

"Huh?"

"Huh what?"

"Meaning I am the solution to the problem of evil?"

"Exactly right."

"Like I said, 'huh'?"

"Listen, do you love any living creature on this Earth?"

"Of course."

"Problem solved. I rest my case. I can say no more, and with that, I bid you a good-night, and I'll see you in the morning."

"Bbbut..." Too late. The door is closed. My mind whirling, I return to the New York night in the moonlight, wander the empty streets, head home more confused than before.

Back to my journal:

Okay, let's go back. What just happened? I was upset about starving babies in Africa and I went and knocked on a strange old man's door at midnight on a Saturday night in New York City and he answered the door wearing a ridiculous outfit and told me that I was the solution to the problem of evil in the world, and then he went back to sleep. He asked if I love anyone. There's a connection. Love...what is the message here? What am I not seeing that is right before my eyes? What am I blind to?

Okay, I got it; it's really very obvious and simple. It sounds like a platitude or a cliché. Except it isn't merely a platitude or a cliché. It could be the most powerful sequence of thoughts I have ever thought:

Evil is the absence of love;

I have the ability to choose to love;

Therefore, I am the solution to the problem of evil.

Sounds so stupidly simple. Yet who among us is capable of exercising our capacity to Love Fully, right now? "Something is alive in me, what can it be? Love? Love. Yes. Love is alive in me. Love is alive as me. Hence, I am a missionary of the Good Word, and I am the Way, the Truth and the Life, and so are you. Commandment Numero Uno: "Thou shalt love the Lord thy God with all Thy Heart and all Thy Soul and all Thy Mind."

(Or, as Weissbaum has often put it, after those times I have made the mistake of pouring my heart out to him, and telling him the intimate details of my world of inner suffering, "Cheer up.")

(Or perhaps, I'm just a "self-indulgent, narcissistic Jewish guy," as a new woman acquaintance was kind enough to point out to me recently after knowing me for about 8 1/2 seconds.)

***

My one-man show is developing, slowly. The only problem I'm having is *starting*; the very first scene. The opening appearance of the Holy Rebbe seems beyond my capacity to effectively portray as an actor. His world of joy—true joy—is foreign to me. I am committed to my identity as a suffering Jew. The joyous Jew is a mystery to me. A joyous *me* is a mystery to me. So how to proceed with Miltie's assignment? Only by becoming joyous. Short of that, my production will be a sham, and I, an imposter. The character must radiate true joy, and raise the hearts of the audience, with laughter and love, to a hopefulness about ourselves and our world. In short, it must be inspirational—in the spirit—containing the very breath of life, the long, deep life-affirming breath of living Spirit. The Rebbe must look out from the stage and peer into a world he recognizes as heartbroken, and the very essence of his Being, before he even utters a word, must embody the response, must say to this world of tears, in the tradition of Arnie Weissbaum, "Cheer up."

I decide I must start where I am, and work my way to joy through the action of the show itself. And so I will begin by walking out on a bare stage, as myself, in a plain piece of torn, white cloth. The ragged human. A spiritual beggar. Behind me, projected on a dismal gray backdrop, will be the words, "God is an unbearable wound at the very center of my Being, for which there is no cure."

After a pause and a frightened glance around the room, my first line will be to scream with intense terror at the top of my lungs:

"I'M SCARED."

That may be the end of Act One. For joy can only exist in the absence of fear, and so I present myself in Scene One as the enemy itself, portrayed as generic, fearful, human. And then I must consciously push against that fear, steadfastly, during the show, singing and dancing and story-telling my way forward, until I can burst through and become the Rebbe himself, the laughing minstrel in all his splendor, the Wise Fool, playing practical jokes on death itself, smiling at the enemy, dancing on graves.

"Once the Baal Shem Tov dreamed of a twisted tree, in the shape of a great Ram's horn—a living shofar, like that which is sounded majestically on the High Holy Days. The master gathered all his disciples in the dream, and asked which one among them had the power to blow through this great horn rising from the earth, and issue the proper sound. They all approached and put their lips to the sacred tree, but not one succeeded at causing even a muted whisper to emerge from its wide mouth, open to the Heavens. Finally, a certain Reb Wolf took his turn, and taking a deep breath, blew one, clear, sustained note that seemed to issue forth from the depths of the earth itself and call out directly to the Almighty with a clear, resonant brilliance.

"Upon awakening the next day, the Baal Shem called Reb Wolf to his private quarters and informed him that he wished to begin instructing him in the hidden secrets contained in the blasts of the shofar, the mysteries and powers that reside in the very tones themselves, when emitted by lips of understanding. Over the year, he dazzled Reb Wolf with the concealed teachings—how each sounding of the shofar is in fact a branch of the Tree of Life, and so all-encompassing is its potential for blessings and prayer that even a single note, blown correctly, can travel through time past and future to the Halls of Eternity, and reach the ears of the Great One.

"Reb Wolf listened raptly, and took copious notes, which he studied every night by candlelight. He prepared his heart and mind and soul for the High Holy Days, when all his learning would at last be put to the test. And then finally, the day arrived, and as he reverently approached the Ark to blow the shofar before God and man, he suddenly could remember nothing, and his heart constricted in panic and terror—it was the ultimate stage fright, in the theater of the soul. Weeping inconsolably, he nevertheless blew on the shofar with all his broken-hearted strength, praying for a miracle, forgetting all the secret teachings he had spent a year studying with such devotion.

"And the sound which Reb Wolf caused to come forth from the ram's horn on that day caused Abraham himself to stir and smile from

the Other Side; for the note was so pure and holy that its sound carried the prayers of all who were present directly to the Highest Place. And it even carried the prayers of some who were not present. Everyone recognized it as a triumphant blast of union, of heaven and earth coming together, the sound of shattered vessels mending and singing in full voice once again.

"*Afterward, it is said, the Baal Shem said this: 'In the palace of the Queen there are many rooms, and each one has its own lock. But the master key is a broken heart. When a person truly breaks his heart before the Holy One, he can enter each and every door.'*"

CHAPTER TEN

Finkelstein

You need a file folder? Talk to Finkelstein. The man's a stationery store—you name it: plastic binders, yellow-lined pads coming out his ears, erasers, push pins, clipboards. Ask if you can borrow a pen for a minute, he'll hand you a box of forty and insist you keep them all, and then never let you forget it. Completely generous with his supplies, but always with a hidden price. You're a friend of Finkelstein's? You'll never put money out for Korect-type again; he'll keep you in Liquid Paper and white-out for life; gallons of the stuff delivered to your door like milk. He was an office products *pusher*—he made you dependent on him for life, everyone strung out on paper clips and sheet protectors. And he wouldn't hesitate to cash in his marker, if push came to shove:

"So Mr. Wilner, need I remind you that because of my good nature you've been flush with address labels since about second grade? Now, perhaps you'd like to think this little matter through again…? Which "little matter?" It didn't matter. It could have been giving him the aisle seat on a shared plane ride, or letting him have the end piece—the *shpits*—of a fresh rye bread; all the little ways he made everyone pay him back. You had to hate him.

Yet to his credit, Finkelstein was a self-made man. After quitting the family law firm his father started with the Cohen brothers—Finkelstein, Finkelstein, Finkelstein, Cohen & Cohen, Inc.; their cousin, little Finkelstein, was never brought on board——he created a corporate empire of stationery supplies that became an international operation. Little Taiwanese school children used red plastic pencil-sharpeners made in Taiwan, exported to the U.S., and bought up in huge quantities by "Finkelstein's boys," as he called his buyers. These Italian guys from Queens would go right down to the docks and unload boxes and boxes of the stuff right from the cargo hold into their delivery trucks. Schools all over Taiwan ordered supplies from Finkelstein's online store and wound up paying less than if they had walked out the door to the factory at the end of the road where they were making the stuff. Congolese kids were getting their reinforcements from Finkelstein, Laotians their masking tape. In the emerging Global World Order, Finkelstein was Office Manager.

His personality got even more intolerable once he let the Lord and Savior into his heart. Then there were *two* things Finkelstein could go on about for hours: stationery and Jesus. Most of us had learned the trick over the years: If you wanted to avoid a Finkelstein hard sell on salvation, get him to sell you on a new line of paper cement. He'd wax enthusiastic about either topic, and it was much easier to listen to the dangers and pitfalls of using the wrong glue than it was to be reminded of the hazards of believing in the wrong God. If the choice for conversations was between Jesus and Elmer, gimme me dat ol' white goo anytime. I'd rather be warned of my sticky, crumpled papers than my sinning, damned soul. And it didn't seem to matter much to Finkelstein—he waxed eloquent about both, believed in both, and preached about both with an equally intense fervor. Listen to him speak at a trade convention to the other office supply people:

"Ladies and gentlemen, hear me, and hear me well, for verily I say unto you: Let those who have staplers, staple, but let the rest of us, the meek of the industry, turn our cheeks to that bastion of antiquity...for Finkelstein Products has not come to abolish all binding methods, but to fulfill their promise, with this new line of state-of-the-art auto-clips. They are to the stapler what a Lear jet is to the horse and buggy. Lo, I must go now, but spread this good news to all your brothers and sisters."

What was initially charming about Finkelstein, to those who hadn't had the misfortune of growing up with the guy, was his candor and self-awareness; he knew exactly who he was and how he came across.

"Norbert, let me explain something to you about me," he once said, "I am your basic fanatic. I have a Messianic complex, delusions of grandeur, and a megalomaniacal compulsion to save the world. Unfortunately, the only real medium for my mission are rubber bands and loose-leaf notebooks. So I make do. But you watch—the Lord works in mysterious ways."

"But Finkelstein, why Jesus? You're a New Jersey Jew, after all,"

"Correction: I'm a New Jersey Jew for Jesus. You know as well as I do that Jesus and all his followers were Jews—they called him Rabbi, for Christ's sake. As far as I'm concerned, all Gentiles are actually Jews-for-Jesus, and Jews are simply Jews-not-for-Jesus, but let's face it, Reb Wilner, it's a Jewish world through and through, praise Jesus, someone say Amen."

"Someone say 'Go fuck yourself,'" Bernstein would have said.

It was a common practice in New Age spiritual circles for people to change their names. Bernstein became Arjuna, Greenblatt, Kanaka-das. The new names generally translated to "The Blissful One," or something similar, and the purpose of taking on the new name was to remind you that even if you thought you were miserably unhappy, your real self was actually having a great time.

I never got a new name, but I once took a weekend workshop with Finkelstein's older brother Jake, and everyone was encouraged to try on a new name, just for the weekend. People picked names like "Joy," "Freedom," and "Gentle Soul." Jake chose "Jim." We once did a retreat together, where we learned that if you stand directly under a pine tree with a branch resting on your head, green healing energy would travel down through your crown chakra. I would periodically observe Jake standing under pine trees, and when I passed by he would say, "My body is filled with light."

But as it turned out, his body was filled with fear. Finkelstein's brother Jake would one day kill himself by doing a swan dive off a twenty-two-story building in Queens. We think it had to do with a bad LSD trip he took in the '60s, during which for hours and hours all he kept hearing was the voice of a train conductor he had once seen in an episode of *The Twilight Zone*, saying over and over again, "Next stop, Willoughby. Next stop, Willoughby." Maybe when Jake stepped off the twenty-second story of the building in Queens, he thought he was getting off in Willoughby. In *The Twilight Zone* episode, Willoughby was everything anybody who was filled with fear could ever want: It was a small, friendly, turn-of-the-century simple town. It was not at all like Queens.

Jake's suicide triggered an intense period of mourning which eventually led Finkelstein to his conversion experience in Washington Square Park, when he was "born again." It was one of those sunny Sundays in Washington Square Park, the place jammed with Frisbee throwers, skateboarders, jugglers and fire-eaters, NYU students reading Section Two of the Sunday *Times*, drug dealers hawking their wares at special spring clearance sale prices, conga drummers and harmonica players, Finkelstein standing around, looking lost. And the Hare Krishna folks were there, dressed in orange, red dots between their eyes, and white guck painted on their faces and shaved heads, hitting tambourines, chanting, and warning passers-by of the dangers of reincarnation: Eat a burger today, be born a cow tomorrow; karma is karma; you are what you eat; you get what you pay for.

And of course, there were the invisible ones, but perhaps the scariest, with the radiant smiles and the shining eyes and the Holy Scriptures: the Jesus freaks. The main thing they teach you in Jesus-Freak Recruitment School is to assign the prettiest and youngest women to do the street work, and to have them go after the loneliest looking, single young men. Finkelstein was a natural, an obvious target. The Training School should have hired him to serve as a guinea pig for beginners. I couldn't really blame him for falling for it. They probably could have gotten me, too. For sure, they would have gotten Greenblatt and Weissbaum, and probably Moscowitz. No way they could have cornered Breshman or Goldberg. Although both of them would have certainly at least tried to sleep with young Caitlin and Sara, the two "Children of God" who enabled Finkelstein to find Jesus in Washington Square Park.

"What's your name, brother?" they asked him.

"Howie Finkelstein, office supplies," handing them a ballpoint pen.

"Nice to meet you, Howie."

Lesson #2: create instant intimacy through use of familiarity.

"Thanks. Call me Finkelstein."

"But you sure look lonely...is something hurting in your heart, Finkelstein?" Said with such innocence, such child-like naiveté, what could Finkelstein do? Of course he'd confess. Of course he'd break down. Little Caitlin and sweet Sara seemed to offer new life, new possibility; all was not lost, love still reigned. Finkelstein found himself weeping in the park, being comforted and caressed by two strange and beautiful young girls, as he told the story of his brother Jake.

"Can we pray for you, Finkelstein?"

Sobbing, he nodded, and said, "Yes. Call me Howie."

"Oh Dear Jesus, Our Lord and Savior and Best Friend, Oh Father in Heaven Above, Our Eternal Comfort and Protection, please bless our brother Howie that he may return to You, that his soul can find peace, please Jesus, grace your child with your love and heal his wounded heart..."

Before long they had Finkelstein join them, coaxing him to let Jesus into his heart, into his life, to let Him soothe his soul and caress his pain. The combination of cathartic tears, beautiful women, and Jesus was a can't-miss, a conversion experience made in Heaven. Finkelstein let it all out, and Jesus filled the gap. By the time he left the park, Howie Finkelstein of New Jersey was praising the Lord and joyfully walking with his two new sisters, hand in hand, to meet some more of their friends at "the Center." And because of Jake, we all let him do it. Preaching the Gospel seemed a step up from his unbearable grief over Jake, and we figured it was just a stage. It wasn't. That was ten years ago.

A couple of years in, I confronted him about it:

"So Howie, let's get real for a minute. This Jesus thing—some part of you knows you've lost your fucking mind, right? You do see that being utterly humorless about your beliefs is a sure sign that your beliefs suck, right? I mean, that should be obvious."

"So you're suggesting that Jesus is *not* my Lord and Savior?"

"No, I'm suggesting that if He is, at least allow Him to lighten you up a little. I mean where is it written that to enter the Kingdom of Heaven you have to be a royal pain in the ass to your friends? Blessed are the *meek*, Finkelstein. You need to work on your meek. You have no meek."

"You're absolutely right. I'll change."

Which he never did. But that simple declaration was a real conversation-stopper, and he used it whenever he needed an out. Girlfriends would complain:

"Howie, you're so self-absorbed in your business dealings and your religious beliefs that you don't even truly see this goddess that is lying right next to you night after night."

Invariably, Finkelstein'd say,

"You're absolutely right. I'll change."

And he wouldn't. It was the living testimony to both the failure of his conversion and the power of his hypocrisy, but the problem now is that, in his own estimation, Finkelstein is a happy man, and try as we might, we can't persuade him otherwise. He eats well, swims laps in his pool, preaches, sells rulers and scissors, and makes cameos in the courtroom. And he says affirmations daily:

"I, Finkelstein, am free to express myself."

"It is now safe for me, Finkelstein, to be happy for no reason."

"I, Howard Finkelstein, can enjoy the pleasures of my body."

"Finkelstein," Bernstein once said, "How about you try this one on? 'I, Howie Finkelstein, am a complete asshole.'"

Actually, Finkelstein had been reciting affirmations long before he became a Christian. The first time I ran into him after the playground years was sometime after college, at a party. He walked up to me, stuck out his hand, and said,

"Hi, I'm Howard Finkelstein, and I am free to express myself."

"I know who you are. We went to East Lake together. I'm Norbert Wilner."

"No kidding? Something looks different."

"I'm no longer 4'2", and I've put on about 102 pounds since then."

"That's it."

***

Even then, Finkelstein was dealing supplies. Born for office products; it seemed innate—the eraser instinct, the glue stick drive. He ran a stationery black market, even then. McQuicksand would threaten, "Everyone must have a #2 pencil and a ball point pen with them everyday, or face prosecution." (The principal's office as Juvenile Court, McQuicksand pressing charges against some hapless kid—not Finkelstein: "He never remembers to bring a pencil, Your Honor." And the judge dismissing the case: "First offense, no priors? Go on, get out of here...just don't let me see your face in here again." "Yes Sir, thank you Sir, good day Sir," the kid dashing out of there a free man.)

But Quicksand's threats—"No pencee, no shirtee"—fall on fearless ears, because the kids are covered, insured; Finkelstein'd. He is the bail bondsman. He'll be there with the spare pen, the extra pencil, you name it. He'll put up the necessary loose-leaf paper—you want three-ring? Lined? He's got it in stock, he'll back you. He'll make the arrangements, strike a deal. A big macher, even then.

"How about some nice dividers today? I got a run on felt-tips. I got three manila folders left, closeout sale, clearance. Who needs a protractor?"

*Finkelstein, the tiny businessman, had his hand in, had a piece of the action. Watch him hanging around the school office on his lunch breaks, during recess, after school even—*shmoozing *with Tess, the school secretary, talking to the bookkeeper, the assistant principal, feeling them out, quizzing them:*

"How much you paying for those crayolas Mrs. Schmale uses in the art room? Who're you calling for your India ink? Where's your three-hole punch connection?"

In this way, gathering information, jotting down numbers, figuring percentages. Following Tess into the supplies closet on the pretense of continuing a conversation, but madly taking it all in, a spy snapping pictures with a miniature camera hidden in his key chain, way beyond the mere stock-boy's mentality, his was the stuff of Inventory Control, the laws of supply and demand. Even then.

And then finally, one day, when the timing is right—he checks the market prices, figures in the sales tax, shipping costs, returns—he makes his move, makes East Lake Elementary an offer they cannot refuse, undercuts the whole industry, undersells 'em—"We beat any prices"—and now young Finkelstein, at eight years old, at nine, is in business. He is a businessman.

So he can afford the freebie—the giveaways, handing out samples like calling cards, ballpoints with his name and address on them. Everyone knew that Finkelstein kept the East Lake student body supplied; that with his pencils, they kept on adding and subtracting; with his sharp and fresh #2s they kept on multiplying and dividing; on his paper they continued carrying their twos, bringing down their zeros. Finding their remainders. Without Finkelstein, there was a school, but no schooling—*he provided the hum in the circuitry, the raw materials of education itself.*

And because he dealt in numbers, in credit and billing, his chronological age seemed a mistake, a mismatch for his profession, and people began to add on years to him to eliminate the confusion they felt. Yes, he was a fifth grader, a nine-year-old, but he carried an attaché case, a calculator, wore a white shirt, jacket and tie to school when everyone else had their checkered cottons, their polos and plaids. He wore glasses and shook hands when other kids would slap five. So while the principal, assistant principal, the bookkeeper and Tess knew he was a kid, they unconsciously elevated him to peer status in their way of dealing with him. ("Kids," Finkelstein would say to them, knowingly, to explain why they were going through so many rubber bands.)

So it isn't nearly so shocking as it sounds that one day in the supplies closet, Tess is standing on a foot ladder to reach for a box of push pins as Finkelstein holds it steady, his face pressed lightly against her thigh, her skirt riding up as she reaches for the pins so that he finds himself face-to-face with the edges of a pair of yellow lace panties. And something comes over him, something gives him the courage—probably his fake ID, his beyond-his-years rep—to do what seems to be the natural thing to do: he goes for it. Reaches up, turns Tess's hips toward him, pulls her undergarment down to her ankles, and cupping one hand behind each of her buttocks, buries his face in her secret place. She squirms, pretending still to be searching for push pins, muttering, "Oh Mr. Finkelstein, Mr. Finkelstein!"

And thus, both Mr. Finkelstein's business and sex life began through fortuitous events in the East Lake Elementary School supplies closet.

(The imprinting of this happening, the juxtaposition of sex and supplies, would never leave him entirely, later bringing dates back to his office for a nightcap and then, "Could you help me with something? I need a stack of blank receipt books from the top shelf. Here, I'll hold the ladder, can you reach them?" Finkelstein's primal quirk. Finkelstein, the fifth grade executive, the fifth grade sex pervert. It didn't escape any of our attention that even after he married Lilah, they kept a little stepladder in their bedroom.)

When it came to the battle lines being drawn on the playground, while it goes without saying that Finkelstein would stand with the Semites against Taylor and his kind, for the sake of business, he initially did his best to appear unaffiliated. In his mind, Finkelstein was Switzerland. He was the house in Vegas—it didn't matter who won or lost or what the stakes were, he just kept on playing the percentages, raking it in, skimming off the top, the dealer always wins. Because on the level of office supplies, he supplied both camps—munitions to Israel, arms to the Arabs.

But while he may have been able to sweet talk the administrative staff, the kid made the rest of us want to scratch his eyes out, he was so maddening. Watch: Wilner and he are playing kickball in the street. Wilner throws the ball to him. Finkelstein misses it and it rolls all the way to the end of the block. He stands there with his hands on his hips and says, "Go fetch, Wilner," as if it is Wilner's fault that he missed the ball. As if it had been a lousy throw.

But what was so maddening was that it was Wilner's ball, and if Finkelstein refuses to retrieve it, and if Wilner doesn't want to leave his ball lying there at the end of the block, he has to obey Finkelstein's humiliating "Go fetch."

And if Wilner's rage gets the better of him and he attacks Finkelstein physically, no sooner is he about to slug the daylights out of him than Finkelstein whispers, "Fake fight! Fake fight!" as if the two boys have some previously-arranged deal to merely pretend to be fighting, for the amusement of the onlookers. (An idea which obviously appeals to Finkelstein when Wilner is sitting on his chest, pinning his arms and shoulders down with his knees, about to smash his face in.) There is no real advantage for Wilner in this situation to turn the bout into a "fake fight." And yet, Finkelstein somehow wins Wilner over with his furtive whispering. For some reason, he complies.

But the amazing thing about Finkelstein is that he somehow manages to pull off this maneuver even when the boys are alone, when there is absolutely nobody present to appreciate their little charade of combat. You'd think in such a situation Wilner would choose the route of pummeling Finkelstein senseless rather than play his little game of make-believe. But no, those words—"Fake fight! Fake fight!"—are like a spell under which Wilner has no ability to choose.

Now, imagine the same scene on another day, only this time put Finkelstein *on top of* Wilner. Have Wilner *whisper "Fake fight!" in an attempt at self-preservation, and watch what happens:*

"Nothing doing, Wilner, you little chicken, you little scaredy-cat, you baby, none of that fake fight crap this time," and he punches Wil-

ner senseless. The guy was a sadistic, disturbed child who stopped at nothing to win—whether it be kickball, fistfights, or the place where his true colors really came forth, around the Monopoly board.

The kid so loved the taste of victory that if Wilner was about to go bankrupt and lose the game, Finkelstein invented ways to keep him in so that he could prolong the enjoyment of the slaughter. His first method was to offer Wilner a $50 salary in exchange for the service of moving his piece around the board for him—Wilner becomes hired help, Finkelstein's servant. Next, he allows Wilner to sell his own piece back to the bank for $100, and he must use his finger as a marker from that point on. Wilner is Finkelstein's charity case; the Monopolized homeless.

When the tables are turned and Wilner is ahead, Finkelstein lies and cheats to avoid losing. Watch:

Finkelstein rolls a seven. He mentally counts off seven spaces and sees that he will land on Boardwalk on which Wilner has erected a first-class, luxury red hotel. This will cost Finkelstein an arm and a leg. So he takes his marker and counts off seven spaces, only he counts the space he is already stationed on as "one," a technique which lands him not on Boardwalk at all, but on the relatively innocuous space right beside it.

Now, here comes the really maddening part, the piece de resistance, *the peculiar sickness of Finkelstein, his perversity, Finkelstein at his very best: When Wilner accuses him of starting his count from the space he was on, he doesn't deny it at all! He simply declares that that is the way they've always played. And he says it with such earnest sincerity, as if he really believes it himself, as if, after playing Monopoly together nearly every day for five years, Wilner has somehow forgotten the rules, taken leave of his senses. Finkelstein seems genuinely concerned about Wilner's inexplicable lapse of memory, suggests he see somebody about it, seek out professional help. Wilner wants to kill him. The argument that ensues results in Finkelstein accidentally overturning the board, and then saying,*

"Well, what do you say we call it a draw?"

In this manner, Wilner was always robbed of the opportunity of officially winning, and Finkelstein the ignominy of finally losing. Okay, there you have it: Finkelstein was, plain and simple, a sore loser. How simple! How eloquent and precise! If only we could step back in time and point that out to little Norbert Wilner, sitting there exasperated, fuming, wanting to strangle Finkelstein.

And, in addition to being a sore loser, the kid was an out and out liar. Finkelstein simply would not tell the truth about anything. He didn't know how to ride a bicycle, for example. When the rest of the boys are out riding their bikes, see Finkelstein there, running along, trailing behind on foot. But does he confess that he's running because he can't ride a bike? Not a chance. He is running, he says, because it is healthier, because it is better exercise. Finkelstein, the eight-year-old health fanatic. Everyone wanted to beat the shit out of him.

When nobody could stand to have him around even one more minute, Operation Ditch Finkelstein was put into effect. Everyone—Wilner, Philip, Moscowitz, the others—begins to circulate the signal behind Finkelstein's back. The code is plain and to the point. Several minutes later one of the boys—Wilner himself, perhaps—suddenly says, "Well, I'll see you guys, I gotta go home. I told my father I'd help him with something." And then, one by one, the others chime in with similar excuses:

"Yeah, I got to go too, we're having relatives over."

"We're eating early."

"Homework."

Finally, nobody left to play with, Finkelstein goes home as well. Five minutes later everyone reconvenes, sans Finkelstein. Perhaps it was a bit cruel; but nobody would argue that it wasn't necessary. Even Wilner's parents were sick of Finkelstein. Every single night, right before dinner, Finkelstein would show up to play, and rather than leave and come back after dinner, he insisted on waiting downstairs until Wilner was through eating. And since Wilner's parents knew that Finkelstein had a mouth on him, they dared not speak about anything of importance at the dinner table. As it turned out, because of Finkelstein, Wilner's family ate in virtual silence for years.

When the boys went to the movies together, Finkelstein's mother would pack his favorite snack for him: a chocolate sandwich. A few pieces of Hershey's chocolate between two slices of Wonder bread. Now watch: They're in the movies, the theater is dark, and Finkelstein can't seem to find his little brown paper bag. He starts to pinch Wilner's thigh—he's wearing Bermudas—and whispering loudly,

"Where's my chocolate sandwich, Wilner?"

Wilner, of course, hasn't the foggiest idea.

"Let's have it, Wilner," pinching him harder and harder, haranguing him every few seconds for the duration of the film, knowing full well Wilner won't get violent with him in the middle of the theater.

Yet through it all—the fake fights, the cheating, the pinching—he and Wilner found themselves on the same team, politically. Like it or not, Finkelstein was one of Phil Goldberg's people. Obviously, because he was a Jew, but also because underneath it all, Philip had a soft heart, and took in all the misfits. His top cabinet people didn't like it. They advised him against the likes of Finkelstein, and of Wilner, whom they sensed could not be counted on in a true emergency. But Philip overruled his cabinet. He took in Finkelstein and Wilner, and he even took in little Moscowitz, the mama's boy.

"Listen," Philip says, addressing his advisors, "what we lack in strength and courage, we make up in chutzpah. Who's got more chutzpah than Finkelstein? He's the chutzpah king—he'll lie and cheat his way through Butch Taylor's empire, if it comes down to it. Or we could use the little bastard as a decoy. The advantage to having men like Finkelstein on your side is you can afford to use 'em and lose 'em. It gives you a certain sense of freedom and power. Finkelstein's our kamikaze pilot. Expendable but necessary."

"But the little asshole could be a double agent."

"No," Philip replies firmly, adamant. "Say what you want about Finkelstein—he's a sadistic, lying cheat, a pain in the butt, a borderline psychotic, all the rest—but listen to me, and listen good: Finkelstein is not a double agent. Underneath everything, I trust the guy. He's a staunch Zionist. He sticks with his people. He'll hide money under the Monopoly board and call it an emergency savings account, but he won't work for the goyim, *no way. Finkelstein may keep Taylor and Grisatti stocked in ballpoints, but at the end of the day, his loyalty is with us. That much I know. Case closed."*

As for the chocolate sandwich, Wilner really didn't have it. He really didn't know what happened to the chocolate sandwich. The chocolate sandwich was never found. To this day, Finkelstein holds Wilner responsible. And he's a lawyer now, for chrissake. Wilner still expects Finkelstein to serve him up a subpoena any day now. Finkelstein'll probably win the case, too. Wilner could get twenty years to life for carrying a concealed Hershey bar, sliced on white bread, melting in the summer heat.

***

It happens at 2:15, in the middle of Mrs. McQuicksand's geography lesson—with all her colored pencils and maps and capital cities designated by paste-on stars. Wilner receives a note, and he senses something terrible about it even before reading it. It is almost as if he feels the full weight of the event which the note will precipitate in that initial moment. His heart drops into his stomach and his face becomes as white as the little slip of lined paper he is handed under his desk while McQuicksand is looking the other way, talking about the natural resources of Juneau, Alaska—nickel and zinc.

There had been threats. He knew a showdown was coming and it had only been a matter of time before push would come to shove, and now, finally, as far as he could tell, his cook was goosed. Frank Grisatti had Wilner by the balls. He had observed Wilner off in one corner of the blacktop during lunch break one day, talking to none other than his boss, Butch Taylor himself!

"Now what's this?" Grisatti mused, puzzled. "One of Philip's main people in secret talks with Taylor...is Wilner a double-agent? Now he's slipping Butch a piece of Bazooka bubble gum. Hmmmm, very interesting...very interesting indeed."

It was true; Wilner was playing both ends against the middle, trying to save his own neck. If Philip's people ever came to blows with the Taylor empire, Wilner would be spared—he could step back and side with the victor. Philip would never know the difference. Grisatti allowed everything to simmer in his mind for a few days. He knew he was on to something red-hot, that he had stumbled onto some highly classified, top-secret information, and he didn't want to squander it. Suddenly, his loyalty to Taylor was no longer a fait accompli; eventually he saw what needed to be done. He created a plan that, successfully implemented, would be to his own political advantage, and his alone, and which hopefully would leave both opposition parties in a confused and depleted state, unaware of what was taking place until it was too late to stop it. Grisatti was a crafty son-of-a-bitch.

To simply reveal Wilner's shady dealings to Philip was not enough. That certainly would upset Philip's organization and hurt its morale, but it would only be a matter to be settled between Philip and Wilner, and definitely wouldn't create the kind of playground-wide disturbance that Grisatti needed in order to step in and seize power. So no, that would not be the way. His plan was far more ingenious, and, he felt, had a beautiful simplicity: He would go right for the juggler, hit on Wilner himself, create a media event that would leave everyone spinning.

Very casually, therefore, he had begun to drop hints to Wilner that perhaps he knew something; just perhaps he had seen Wilner in the company of a certain Butchibald Taylor. Grisatti savored the unfolding of his plan like a seduction, enjoyed watching Wilner's fear increase as the horrible truth gradually became clear: that Grisatti wasn't bluffing, he really did have something on Wilner; trouble was brewing.

Wilner was nervous. No, Wilner was terrified. He intuitively sensed, like an alley cat, that his survival was threatened, and yet he couldn't quite make out the nature of his adversary. Why was Grisatti playing with him like that, keeping him on hold? Why hadn't he leaked his information as soon as he got his little hands on it? What did the man have up his sleeve? These were all pressing questions, which Wilner had to ponder completely alone. The one person who he would ordinarily have turned to for advice—Philip—was likewise the very person from whom he most needed to conceal the whole affair.

What would Grisatti demand of Wilner in exchange for keeping silent? He didn't know. He suspected it would be something much bigger than a crummy piece of penny bubble gum. He was prepared to go to great lengths to appease Grisatti, to silence the bastard. But in the meantime, no demands had been made. Grisatti was just dancing around it. Until this note arrived, nothing overt had happened at all, just enough vague and suggestive remarks to put Wilner's stomach in knots and to cause him to live through each school day in a state of abject terror. He was expecting the worst, and to make matters worse, he didn't know what the worst could be. The kid was living on borrowed time.

CHAPTER ELEVEN

Weissbaum

I've told you he's a sports nut. The problem is much, much bigger than this. Because it's not just sports; lots of men like their Super Bowl Sundays with their beer. (Though not these men—how many Jewish men know from football? Just Weissbaum, and Goldberg. None of their mothers would let them play tackle, so they only played Mattel's Electric Football with those little plastic guys that run backwards all over the metallic field. And even that they had to fight for: "You could get electrocuted.") No, Weissbaum turned each and every moment of his day into a playoff, a rubber match, a Stanley Cup. A torment for anyone in his life. After dinner:

"Okay sports fans, he's going to wash the dishes and it looks like he'll finish them in under five, a very respectable time."

Doing laundry:

"Okay, the question on everyone's mind is, 'will Weissbaum throw the whole load into one machine, or will he separate the colors from the whites?'"

"Weissbaum," someone invariably says. "WHO THE FUCK CARES?" He is not phased and keeps right on talking:

"...and folks, it ain't over 'til it's over, 'til the fat lady sings, 'til I've selected warm/cold, medium load and dropped my two-bit piece in the proverbial slot. And off we go," as he exits the apartment with his dirty laundry, imaginary crowds murmuring, Weissbaum looking up and tipping his cap as he waits for the elevator down to the laundry room. Other people have mystical · experiences in which they hear prophetic voices inside their heads; Weissbaum hears only "Beer here! Get your ice cold beer here."

And just as a game is not a game without rules and regulations, your foul lines and goalposts, so too, the sport which was Weissbaum's daily life was confined and prescribed by specific guidelines and bylaws. He took immense pleasure in explaining them to newcomers with a sense of benevolent pedagogy, like an old Master, twinkle in his eye, teaching the initiate:

"Well, Norbert, young man, I too remember the days when I might have just left my shoes in the living room, but I learned the hard way, and well, I guess you will too." He stoops and picks up my shoes. "See? They go right over here in this little nook by the door? Okay? Clear? Simple? Very good."

One of the rules in Weissbaum's house was that you were only allowed to drink milk or orange juice straight out of the carton if nobody saw you. If someone was watching, you had to use a glass. And this was when there were only two of us living there. Perhaps his most eccentric notion was this: When you finished showering in Weissbaum's bathroom, he asked that you turn the water off and remain standing there for a minimum of three minutes before toweling off. He claimed it made all the difference in terms of his "shower-per-towel stats." Poor Sally married this nut; I always imagine her standing naked in the shower, shivering for three minutes. No wonder he had gone through three or four wives in rapid succession: once they got the picture, they got the hell out.

Weissbaum never seemed particularly broken up about it. The guy perpetually lived only on the surface of life, never felt deeply about anything or anyone, and yet a happier man you will never meet. When his first wife tried to get him to take one of those Men's Weekends to "get in touch with your feelings," he said,

"What are you talking about? I have plenty of feelings. Right now, I feel cold." He tried to appease his wife by pointing out his feelings more often. When they sat down to dinner, he'd say, "Honey, I feel hungry." When it was over, "I feel full." Late at night, it was "I feel tired." When at last his wife couldn't take it anymore, she exploded:

"I'M TALKING ABOUT EMOTIONS, YOU CRAZY IDIOT! EMOTIONS!! YOU JUST DON'T GET IT."

And out the door she went. When Wilner asked him how he was doing soon after she left, Arnie said, "I feel sad."

"What are you going to do?"

"Have to train a new one."

So, a real creature of habit, this Weissbaum character. A man of prescribed, unshakeable routines. A drawer of t-shirts, a stack of blue jeans: He always wears whichever one is on top of the pile, and clean laundry goes to the bottom to keep it circulating. He never decides what to wear—his system covers it.

Now, you'd think that perhaps a high-powered executive with IBM might need such a system, to save time and leave the mind free to attend to more important matters at hand. But Weissbaum was not a busy man. He had time to spare. (A kindred spirit to Breshman, he could match Abe's *free* time with his *spare* time, moment for moment, like the opposite of the race *against* time that Wilner was perpetually losing.)

Weissbaum had lots and lots of time to watch television—more than a diversion or entertainment for him, a disturbing obsession. When Weissbaum spent several years of his life in North Carolina, in a remote mountainous area with no TV reception, he had people all over the country shipping him videotapes of television programs.

Okay, you think, that might be understandable if they were sending the occasional special from PBS, the award-winners, the Emmy material. But no, Weissbaum acquired stacks and stacks of reruns: episodes of *My Three Sons; The Price Is Right;* random installments of *As The World Turns.*

And he considers it his duty, like a job, to watch everything he accumulates. Like the shirts and jeans, he watches
them in the order they appear at the top of the stack. He is
the same with his record collection: Whichever disk is next
gets played, regardless of the mood of the moment. We'd get
the *1812 Overture* for dinner music, his girlfriends would find
themselves making love by candlelight to the Andrews Sisters,
the soundtrack to *Apocalypse Now.*

"Weissbaum, Arnie, please," I try to reason with him, "Normal
people *choose* the music they want to hear, they *choose* the videos
they want to watch."

"Damn," he says, ignoring me, looking at the top of his stack,
"it looks like *Cheers* and an '86 *Johnny Carson Show* tonight...oh
well, just have to make the best of it."

He was a professional, and he got his job done. Even now that
he has reception again, he's never got time to watch live, present
programming—he's far too backed up as it is, in way over his head.
So while attending to the demands of his accumulated stack of videos, he always has two additional VCRs hooked up, taping current
programming which he won't get around to viewing for at least six
months. And this includes timely events as well—the Academy
Awards, election returns. The rest of us were supposed to shield
him from hearing the outcome of such events. For six months into
Bush's presidency, it was like Weissbaum had his fingers in his ears,
shouting, "Don't tell me, don't tell me," singing to himself. Then
six months later he calls me:

"Do you believe it?"

"What?"

"Bush won."

"Really?"

"Yeah—the inauguration's coming up in mid-July or so."

"Did they resolve that Bay of Pigs thing yet?"

"Go ahead, make fun. Do I do that to you?"

"I don't eat Crackerjacks every night at 9 o'clock, whether I
want to or not."

The whole time I kept wondering why Gillian insisted that I had to go with him. I guess in spite of it all, he thought I was good police, even if I didn't buy his theory. Then again, maybe he just wanted company for the drive.

This was all before our initial arrival. Before angled chairs and two killer theories. It could have been the point I just surrendered to the cause. Instead, it just meant more waiting.

Gillian and I barely spoke a word for the first two hours of the trip. I just listened to the wheels riding over grey ribbon. They couldn't keep me from thinking it through.

I let my mind drift back to Adams. I had found Janelle sitting in the cafeteria. She was studying for Bio. An unremarkable girl in every way. I would have forgotten her if not for Carl. I warned her about my questions. They might not be the sort of thing she wanted to share.

"I'm told you went to some college parties with Eric." She tensed from my words but declined to comment. "Would you like to tell me about them?" I asked. "Not really." I told her it wasn't a choice and I needed more details. I already knew the basics. She seemed truly embarrassed. Ashamed, in fact, at many of the things she had done. "It's OK. I'm not here about any of that. I'm here about Eric." If my words reassured her, it was difficult to tell. She still seemed caught out and humiliated.

I got her to keep talking. I heard more stories of drugs and anonymous sex. I was a little surprised girls were into such things but I couldn't afford to get distracted. I needed names of Eric's partners and pals. I planned on talking with them all. Someone must know what happened. She gave me a few but most she didn't know. "They were all just kids in college."

I promised Janelle I wouldn't tell a soul. Nobody needed to know about her experimentation. She thanked me twice and said she would do what she could. "Eric was a shit but he didn't deserve to die." She came up with some names shortly after.

As I walked down the hall, I heard the voices. Someone teaching a class. It was hard not to laugh when I realized who it was. It was Mr. Just Say No talking overly loudly as if it was all so important. Every one of his words filled with wisdom. I kept on walking and was just about out the door when I saw someone I wanted to avoid. It was Miss Kamden herself, still looking fresh-faced and appealing. There was an awkward exchange of greetings. All I kept thinking as I walked to my car was how she had no right to be embarrassed. No right to be like that at all. I was the one who had been rejected.

"Did you hear that he was a lobbyist?" I was snapped out of my moment by Gillian's question. I asked him to repeat what he had said. "Did you hear that he was a lobbyist?" "Who was?" "Radovich." "I thought he was an accountant or something?" "Turns out he was a tax lawyer. Beats me what the difference is. Anyway, the reason it's important is he was involved in the big casino thing on the South Waterfront." My brain was having trouble graduating from High School. None of this was clicking yet.

"Maybe that's why they killed him" Gillian said. "Why? Was he one of the people pushing for it?" "No, the opposite. He was one of the people working behind the scenes against it. Maybe that's why they whacked him." I shook my head in amazement. I'm not sure Gillian bought his own theory but at least it was conversation. "I think you've been watching "Casino" too much" I said. "I love that movie." "You remember the end? The new Vegas customers?" "Yeah." "Family entertainment isn't like Vegas of old. I strongly doubt a publicly traded corporation would have someone executed on their behalf." "Hey, you never know. Where there's money to be made..."

I should have left it there. Gillian was trying. He was trying to thaw things between us. But I couldn't let it go. The way my case was being treated. This serial killer thing was taking up valuable time. I had to let it out. I had to explain why I thought this foray was so misguided. Gillian snapped and took issue with my protest. He'd had enough of my lack of support. I told him I would be professional and treat every angle with seriousness. This, even though I thought the theory was crap.

Silence invaded. It was a long drive up. We didn't say another word until after Olympia. It left me plenty of time to reflect on the case. Too much time to remember that awkward smile. Miss Kamden would have been fun. Just what I needed. But it wasn't meant to be. There were others to think about. To obsess over and desire. I just needed to find the right one.

"I've got to piss" Gillian said. "What are you telling me for? You want me to hold it for you?" I said. It was meant as a joke. As a way to break the ice. It didn't come off quite right. "Jesus, you're a prick." He slammed the door and left me in the car. As I sat wondering how to make it all work, I studied my fellow travelers. A few looked excited but most were just exhausted. The trip wasn't as fun as they had hoped.

CHAPTER THIRTY-SEVEN:

Nirvana soundtrack returned once again. Savaged by its guitars, I floated down the hallway. A tracking shot memory of John Adams. Lockers and tiles. Glass and false ceilings. It was all empty now, except for me.

The vocal kicked in as the shots continued. A ballet of imagery in the style of Antonioni. A cold, modernist world. An uncaring God. All we needed was some subtitles for clarity.

Through the double-doors like we were entering the E.R. The cafeteria was filled with kids. Patterns emerged as we weaved through the traffic. Groups, tribes and clicks. Conversations in snippets. All the latest gossip shared. The camera kept moving like a fish through the sea. Beware of the sharks in the tank.

A crowd stood before me, watching a show. All I saw was their backs. Faces were hidden from view. They clapped and they cheered as they encircled the table. I couldn't quite see the attraction.

Then the camera took off. A bird to the sky. It looked down on the scene below. The lyrics taunted as the crowd surrounded the stage. Figures atop a table. Naked and bare. A couple going at it, right there. They seemed oblivious to all the rest.

The merciless lens revealed their identities. Projected the image for all to see. It was me. Fucking a woman beneath me. I couldn't make out who she was.

The crowd cheered us on as the climax neared. A porn show for their public pleasure. But it was about to change up. An art house revival. Bright white and orange. Temporary blindness. My ears rung as the music ended.

"Are you the Worm?" I asked. "That's what my friends call me." "Was Eric your friend?" "Eric didn't have friends." I wasn't sure I understood what he meant. "I heard he was popular." "He was. Everybody loved him." "So, why didn't he have any friends?"

A switch up in suspects. The interrogation continued. Allison was now asking the questions. "Why don't you, Detective Dudek?" "What do you want from me?" I asked. "I already know what you want from me" she said.

The Worm returned. The questions went on. "What do you want from me?" he asked. "Did you go to parties with Eric at Carl Kraft's?" "Yeah, why? Are you pissed you never got invited?" I asked the obvious question. "Aren't you a little old to be hanging out with high school kids?"

I was back in the classroom. It was efficient and functional. I was being interviewed by my favorite teacher. "I didn't realize you were that into her" Dom said. "I'm not" I replied. "Be honest." "I can't." "Tell me something" she said. "What?" "Why don't you have any friends?" "I do." "Right. Emily." "Tell me about Eric" I said. "Bright, charismatic, disenchanted, clever. "How is he clever?" I asked. She replied with a smirk. "Just look what he's doing to you."

CHAPTER THIRTY-EIGHT:

I sat alone in a room with an extraordinary view. One wall was largely glass. Outside they skated, backwards and forwards. Rollergirls perfecting their drills. No fishnets or skirts. No outrageous costumes. These were athletes training hard.

There she was, the object of my attention. The one I had come to see. She was skating fast and kicking ass completely, even though it was all just practice. Cruel approached her and pointed inside. She said something about me waiting.

Julie entered the office with a glare. Maybe that was just her way. "Can this wait?" she asked. She was sweating and panting. It had apparently been quite a workout. "No." She took a seat. "Your alibi checked out." "Did you think it wouldn't?" She started to undo her laces. "Tell me about Carl Kraft." She didn't like my question. I had her playing defense instead of her normal position.

"Well?" I prodded. "What do you want to know?" she said. "He was an ass." "Why?" "Because he thought he was really hip and the reality is he is a total loser." "So, you've met him?" "Yes, once or twice." "At one of his special parties?" "I don't know how special they were. He served Bud Light and had a bag of chips." "I heard they were a bit more extreme than that." "Really? Why don't you tell me about it?"

I didn't like her attitude which must have shown. She realized she was playing it wrong. She corrected the oversight and became cooperative. It was a startling adjustment to witness. She turned on a dime and adjusted her attitude. She wanted me to be the object in play.

She told me about the parties, filled with drugs and sex. She said it wasn't her scene at all. She argued with Eric about why he wanted to be there but eventually let him do what he wanted. She declined to attend any further events or mingle with Kraft. Eric continued to go. "Can you give me some names of people he paired off with? I'm trying to come up with the people he might have met with the night he died." It was a harsh question but it needed to be asked. I was getting desperate to move things forward.

I explained how I still needed to understand that night. Was he with someone from the party or had he made a new friend? I still didn't have any leads. "What about the Worm?" I asked. She claimed not to remember the little prick with a nickname but then it all started to come back. "Yeah, I remember him. He and Eric talked about football all night. I don't think they were very close, though."

It was an awkward conversation but I asked about their arrangement. It made me more uncomfortable than her. "I didn't like the idea of Eric with other people but it was his decision." "Why didn't you break up with him?" "Because it wasn't that sort of relationship." "What sort was it?"

She thought about it a second and formulated her answer. She pulled off her skates with a tug. She looked me in the eyes, face covered in sweat. "When he wasn't with me, he could do what he wanted." It was an ordinary statement but something else was implied. Something about their time together. I should have left it alone but I fell for the trap. I asked the question I shouldn't have asked. "And when he was with you?" Her confidence grew and her expression changed. She was a girl who liked to be in control.

I moved on from the details of Eric and Dom. Instead, I focused on Kraft. "Did Eric see anyone from those parties on a regular basis?" I asked. "I never asked." "Would they have been male or female?" "To hang out with or to sleep with?" "Both." To hang out with, it could have been anyone. But Eric wasn't into guys for sex." "Are you sure?" "Yes, I'm sure. I know everything about him when it comes to that."

I asked for more names of women he might have been with. Julie only knew of a couple. She seemed perfectly calm but it must have upset her. To have him be hers so completely in some ways but to have no real stake in ownership. "Did it make you jealous?" "I already told you I didn't like it." "But you put up with it?" "I wasn't about to give up the rest of it because Eric wanted to be with other people." "What rest of it?" I asked. I was met with a smirk. "Are you asking me specifically what Eric and I did with each other during sex?" "No." "Then what are you asking?"

I could feel it all getting away. I changed tracks and switched up the questions. "Can you tell me some of the bars or other places Eric liked to go?" "Screen Door. Green Dragon. Kontrol. Roadside Attraction. I'd have to think about it some more." "What about Allison?" "What about her?" "Tell me more about her relationship with Eric."

She weighed her words carefully. She felt bad telling tales. All the same, the story came through. Eric was the older and wiser of the twins. He was born just eight minutes earlier. Starting very young, he played the big brother. Allison was his to adore and protect. But adoration became awkward as both entered adolescence. Their relationship had grown very strained. Allison loved her brother but became tired of her role. The good twin never had as much fun as the other.

Her choice in schools, the chance to go private, was about Eric more than education. Allison wanted to be her own girl. Big brother didn't like it and let her know that she would still always be his. It freaked her out and drove a wedge between them. Something that got worse with time. "I can understand both sides of it" Julie said. "Allison wanted to be left alone and thought of as her own person, which is hard to do around someone like Eric." "What do you mean?" "He was always really popular and surrounded by people. Allison needed to step out of his shadow." "Do you think he was a good brother to her?" "I think he tried. I went through the same thing with my sister." "You're the older one?" "No, I was the one always in the shadows."

I looked at her now. It was hard to imagine. Dom wasn't the doormat type. A looker and a leader, Julie wasn't someone who passed unnoticed. Adolescence had treated her well.

"Why so many questions about Allison?" she asked. "I'm just trying to get some answers." "About Allison?" "About who killed Eric and why." "She's pretty, isn't she?" "Yeah, I guess." "It's OK to agree that she's pretty. No need to get all bent out of shape over it." "I'm not. It was a brief exchange but one I didn't care for. I wouldn't let this get all twisted around. "Tell me about Dave."

Her opinion of Dave was none too high, even though she barely knew him. Most of her information was from conversations with Eric. Tirades of disdain and frustration.

"He would get really fed up and just say the meanest things to me about him. I actually felt sorry for Dave." "Why?" "He had the same problems Allison had but worse. He wasn't in Eric's shadow so much as he didn't exist without him." I tried to get it right in my brain and to understand their friendship. It sounded cruel and one-sided but Dave was a constant. A kicked dog coming back for more.

"Anything else?" she asked. There was but it could wait. I needed to get some better answers from Kraft. "No, thanks. That's it for now." She got up from her seat, carrying her skates. She came very close and then stopped for just a second. "If you want to talk to me more, it's OK. Just call me." It was a throw-away line. A sign of cooperation. But the delivery had changed the timbre. An offer had been made. An opportunity to investigate. It was a risk that might be worth taking.

CHAPTER THIRTY-NINE:

For dessert we went to the isle of the dead. A chilly ice cream palace of bodies. The variety was almost endless. Any flavor you might like. Murder, accidental and natural. Seattle had some money. The morgue was even nice. Functional and attractive, marble floors. It was such a pleasant setting that we both wondered who it was all for. The corpse of Ronaldo was pulled out of the drawer. He had been kept at the perfect temperature. He seemed small and shriveled in spite of his youth. A man who didn't have much presence. "You ever wonder what it would be like to be dead?" Gillian asked. "Cold" is all that I said. Gillian left it alone and farted bad burger gas. Dinner was not sitting well.

"So, what's your theory?" I asked. "On death?" "On his death. One killer or two?" "Would you like fries with that?" he joked. It didn't make any sense but we needed the humor. It was all that kept us from fighting. We both looked at his neck. Ronaldo had small, straight marks from where the tape had been wrapped. The killer had been none too gentle.

"Four out of five" he said. His gallery of victims had several winners. Three out of four had been executed in exactly the same way. Electrical tape and plastic bag. Death by asphyxiation in every case.

"What about ours?" I asked. "Maybe they ran out of tape. Beats the hell out of me." At least he acknowledged that Eric was different. He had been strangled in a more classic way. Somebody held the bag against his neck with their hands. They felt him kick, struggle and gasp. Heard the funny noises come from his throat. It was a different type of experience.

Ronaldo and the others had been covered and taped. The killer probably enjoying the more detached method. They would have convulsed and twitched as the killer kept his distance. A more visual than tactile method.

I started humming a tune. Gillian didn't get it. In fact, he was a little bit pissed. "Quit that. What's wrong with you?" he asked. "You don't recognize the song? It's a tune from a kid's show. "Which One Doesn't Belong." "Very funny, asshole" he said. "Seriously, how can you fit Eric Thurman into this group, even if all the rest are connected?" I asked.

He launched into a lecture how I only looked to tear down and had nothing to offer in its place. I pointed out that the difference between tape and not was bigger than he was giving credit. It was a different thrill for the killer. A different high. Pre-planned death rituals were very specific. I admitted that four of the vics were possibly connected. But I refused to back down on Eric.

"Maybe the killer planned on using tape but somehow got interrupted." Gillian threw out some scenarios, a few of which made sense in explaining the tape discrepancy. "Why didn't we find any records of Eric booking a motel?" "Maybe there was somewhere private he used that time. I don't know, Dudek. I don't know, OK?. But I will. Don't shoot me down before I've even had a chance."

We closed the door and let Ronaldo sleep. Happy dreams, sad little bastard. Gillian's words had hit home. I felt like a shit. Investigations take time. Gillian's theory was worth pursuing. I fessed up to my wrongs and was all apologies. All was forgiven. At least for now. As long as I promised to fight for the cause. Until proven otherwise, Eric was a star in the making. Serial Killer Victim Number Five.

CHAPTER FORTY:

Working the bars defeated their purpose. They were places I would rather not be unless I could drink. This was official. I was making the rounds. More haunts of Eric and his pals.

I started with Roadside Attraction. It was small inside but had a nice yard. It was littered with quaint tables and aging hipsters. I had made my appearance too early. The wrong crowd was in court. It was too old and mellow for the kids. I talked to the staff. The doorman and bartender. I flashed a photo of Eric. I started nicely, showing a gleaming portrait. Something I had finally gotten from his mother.

The bartender on duty barely looked old enough to drink. Manhattan's were out of his depth. He kept looking up recipes in a black leather book for anything other than beer. I asked him about Eric, his look said he couldn't be bothered. I made sure he looked again. He denied seeing the kid or anyone that young. Roadside Attraction wasn't that sort of place.

It started to rain as I walked through the yard. The drops pounded on the plastic awnings. The crowd started to go inside. There was a traffic jam at the door. There was one couple I envied a little. A guy and gal of maybe thirty. They were far too into each other to be inconvenienced by the weather.

Green Dragon was annoying but in a very different way. I really wanted to just sit and have a couple beers. It was a fine place with good brews, even if the food was a scam. Overpriced and overcooked but few people ever complained. The buzz numbed them from the tragedy.

I spoke to a bartender. Her face was familiar. She had once taken care of me elsewhere. She had moved on from there and was happy with her new home. Both the crowd and tips were superior. I asked her about Eric. She said she had seen him. She wondered if they were in trouble because of his age. I told her that wasn't my concern. The kid was dead. I was just trying to figure out why.

"Yeah, I remember him because his friends were total assholes" she said. "What were his friends like? Can you describe them?" "There were a bunch of them here that night. I had just gotten in. So, that would have been a Thursday." "What did his friends look like?" "I don't know. The usual type. You know, the kind that were t-shirts and ski hats even though they're inside or it's summer."

She tried to remember them one by one. The names didn't sound remotely familiar. I had been hoping for a link. Maybe something to Carl Kraft. But her descriptions didn't help me out much at the time. I asked the other staff if they could confirm the list of Eric's friends that night. Their memories were blurry. They really didn't remember. All I had was the word of my bartender.

I sat down at a wood table and had an iced tea. I wasn't about to drink on the job. I took out a notepad and scrawled an arrow. The timeline as much as I knew. From left to right, "Eric home," "Eric at School," "Eric at Green Dragon," each with an approximate time. There was even one part over to the side. The final notation. "Eric Found Dead at 3:25 AM."

I returned to Adams the very next day. This time it was the principal that I needed to see. The Green Dragon crowd didn't sound like Kraft's. They seemed younger. The sort with fake IDs. I sat in the office with notebook in hand and read of my descriptions to Mr. Williams. He identified two of them right away. "Ashley Berger and Donald McCormick."

A decision was made to not call in parents. At least not until it was necessary. Instead he summoned them one by one to his office. Ashley was the first to appear. The room was crowded and uncomfortable. Ashley looked nervous. Williams began the preamble.

"Ashley, this man is a detective from the Portland Police Department. He has a few questions for you." "Am I in trouble?" "Probably not, I'm just looking for information" I said.

I told her she had been seen at a bar even though she was underage. She denied it. I explained how lying to me could get her in serious trouble. She mentioned calling her parents. Williams was frustrated. Maybe even more than I. He laid into her hard and heavy. "Ashley, if I find out you're lying about this there will be very, very serious repercussions. Do you understand?" She looked at him from the catbird seat, sure she couldn't be touched. An attitude from a position of power. At least that was her perception.

I told Ashley she could leave but I might need to speak with her again. I would let it go for now. I would show her photo to the bartender and get a confirmation. If she was lying, she would be taken to The Cube and questioned more harshly. She hadn't earned an easy ride.

When Donald appeared, it was a whole different thing. Breaking the law didn't seem to matter. "Yeah, we were there" he said. Williams started to lecture about the legal drinking age. I cut him off impolitely. "Who was with you, that night?" He named names without resistance and rolled on his friends, as if it were no big thing. Among the names were Ashley as well as Eric Thurman. "We went for happy hour and had burgers. A few of us stayed and had a few more beers."

Williams look of disapproval wasn't helping the mood. I almost asked him to leave. "And Eric was with you?" "Yeah." "What time did he leave?" "Way before the rest of us. Like seven" Donald said. "That early?" "Yeah, he said he had someone to meet." "Did he say who?" "No, he never did. He just said he had to bolt and did."

Williams was tempted to start in with a lecture. I couldn't afford to let him get going. I asked Donald for more details of his socializing with Eric. He just said Eric was always a good time. "The guy knew everyone. It was crazy. You couldn't walk into a place without him running into someone he knew."

I kept pressing for clues on where Eric might have gone. He had driven his car alone to the bar. Donald said it was probably a girl, just from the way Eric was acting, but Eric hadn't said a word. Whoever it was they were his little secret and he wasn't about to share.

CHAPTER FORTY-ONE:

REWIND

CUE TAPE

Carl Kraft appeared on the screen. Date-stamped and time-coded. A relic in binary. It was fun to watch him sweat. He sat with his lawyer in silence. He was just a PD. The room was small and hot. HVAC haywire the norm for The Cube. An interrogation cell that was none too pleasant, even as far as it went. Sweat you little bastard. Let your lies drip out.

I just sat and watched the scene on the monitor. I was appreciating the silence. The Public Defender went through the case file, too busy to look at it earlier. Campus Police had come through for me big. Kraft had been caught with marijuana and coke. If intent could be proven, he was looking at five years in prison.

He physically squirmed. The fear built on his face. The sinful braggart was gone long ago. Caligula had fallen. His insides were overwhelmed with terror. His heart raced. He was short of breath. Anxiety was the least of his problems. Talk to me, young Carl, and save yourself. I'm your only hope of survival.

I walked into the room with pad and pen. I tossed them in front of the suspect. "Names and phone numbers of everyone who went to one of your "parties" in the last six-months." "Detective..." whispered the young Public Defender. He seemed afraid to even speak. "I'd like to discuss a possible deal for my client." I resisted the pun and cut to the chase. Or maybe more to the quick. "We can talk about that after he demonstrates his cooperation. I'll call the DA myself. Get writing."

Carl seemed eager to please and got right to it. The names started filling the pad. I waited for a bit and then hit him with more. "Don't forget all the under-aged ones." That stopped him in his tracks. He looked at his attorney. Self-incrimination didn't seem very smart. "I don't think..." "Carl, it's up to you. I can't make you do a thing. If your counsel advises you against it. All I can tell you is we already know everything about your parties. What you didn't bother to tell me before, I've found out from others. I'm just asking you to make it easy on both of us." "Detective, once again, I strongly..." "Eric was there. Now he's dead. Where do you think this is all going to lead?"

That worked well. It certainly had its effect. You could see Carl falling off the cliff. The floor was gone, he was tumbling to his end. He would grasp at anyone and anything to save him.

The Public Defender had it right but his client didn't really care. He was too terrified for logic. He looked for his savior and I was it. Do as I say and I can make it all stop.

The PD's inexperience showed not through his arguments but through his lack of understanding. Carl was done before he even walked in. He would do anything I damn well pleased. Nobody can understand, unless they've been through it, what an interrogation really is. Everybody breaks, or at least most, if you can transport them to a world of your creation. A place where logic is out and rights are abandoned freely out of fear and desperation. Carl was no street punk and jail would destroy him, even if it was only for a year. It was enough to make him sob. If I told him to put his hand around his counsel's neck and strangle the last bit of breath out of him, Carl would have done it. Anything to avoid going to jail.

The PD shook his head in disbelief as Carl kept writing even though there was no official deal. He was implicating himself in further crimes. Writing down things that would be used against him. He was drowning in adrenaline horror and this was his answer. The only window out of the cell.

Twenty minutes passed as Carl kept writing. Putting his guilt down in ink. I looked at the names. Most were unfamiliar. "Which ones are in high school?" I asked. "Only the first ones." I glanced at his list. It looked pretty thorough. He had even written "Eric Thurman." There was another name that was familiar right at the top. It took me a minute to place it. "Janelle Richardson." A face from high school. John Adams to be exact. I had spoken to her once before. She was one of Eric's playmates. A girlfriend, of sorts. She hadn't been completely honest.

"What about my deal?" he asked, feeling he had earned it. I wasn't ready to let up. "What deal?" I walked out of the room and left him consumed. I wouldn't be surprised if he puked. Truth be told, I would ask the DA to let him off lightly. He was just a stupid kid, still being stupid. Even though the law called him an adult.

Gillian approached me. He had been watching the whole thing. I swear he was about to laugh. "What a pussy." He meant Carl, I think, not me. At least that's what I choose to believe. I still thought it was harsh. I thought back to his kid, the one amused by the iPhone and the domino cars. I wondered what Gillian would do. How he would react if his kid ever ended up in the box. Would his kid do anything for a chance to breathe?

CHAPTER FOURTY-TWO:

Teenagers fucking. Perfect couplets of copulation. Images in my brain like some cheap web site that keeps linking me to other sites. Down the rabbit whole to places I don't want to go. Just $19.99 a month. New girls every week.

Eros took an arrow to his own heart. I'm in love with myself as Johnny Rotten had predicted. Fear inside keeps me from investigating further. Details and names. Vulgar descriptions. I tell myself it's just part of the job. I drink more Bitter. Enjoy the body. It's all a bit of indulgence.

Hiss. Crackle. Pop. Time to up the poison. Emily stands pretty in white. Perfect dress on a perfect day. Her smile beams eternal. "What are you thinking about?" she asked. I was back in the bar. I'd been there far too long. Even then the company was getting old. "You don't want to know" I replied. "Sure I do or I wouldn't have asked." I looked up from my pint and answered her question. "You in a wedding dress" I said. "Really?" "Yeah, really." "How did I look?" she asked. "Radiant." "Nice answer. The next one is on me."

I should have just ended it there. But me being me I just had to continue. The urge to be self-destructive. "And teenagers fucking." "You lost me" she said. "That's what I was thinking of before you in the wedding dress." "Please don't tell me the two are connected." "No. We're not teenagers." "Be nice" she scolded.

"Would you want to be a teenager again?" "I don't know. Maybe. You?" "Never" was my one word reply. "That bad, huh?" "I drank a lot." "You still drink a lot." "No, a whole lot. Not just beer. Vodka, Gin, Scotch." "In high school?" she asked. "I was bored." "What made you finally stop?" "I was bored."

She looked at me with sympathy, understanding too well. "Didn't your parents know?" she asked. "Parents don't see what they don't want to see. "Mine did. I got the shit smacked out of me for coming home fifteen minutes after curfew." "They beat you?" "No, not literally. My Mom slapped me though. That was her thing." I couldn't help but make a crack. "Sounds kinky." "Don't be gross."

Emily went about her business as I sat there alone. There was something else I wanted to tell her. When she returned I did just that. I told her about my talk with Dom. "I asked out the rollergirl." "The dominatrix?" "She's not really a dominatrix. I'll leave the leather and whips to you, thanks." "Not my thing. Sorry. So, when do you go out?" "Saturday. Assuming I don't have to run up to Seattle again."

She took a moment to clean something up. Then she returned to her many questions. "Where are you taking her?"

"Heaven" I joked. Emily wasn't amused. "No, really." "Dinner at Lincoln. Somewhere to get her drunk. My place." "Be careful. She can probably drink you under the table." "That's fine as long as she takes advantage of me."

If only memories could be boxed and contained. But my mind went back where it wanted. A few lines in a half-empty bar. A few lines I couldn't get out of my brain. "Thank you" Emily said. "For what?" I asked. "For being such a good friend."

CHAPTER FORTY-THREE:

We got back to SPD and their slick looking offices. We were guided to two other detectives. Harriman and Woodgate were their names. Both were young, barely in their thirties. It made Gillian and I both feel old. They'd just returned from Ronaldo's apartment, a dump on Capital Hill. Items had been boxed and tagged. Things were being logged but they had found their Holy Grail. A very used IBM, at least six years old. It was filled with chat logs and emails.

Gillian and I had to take a back seat as the tech scrolled through all the info. There it was in perfect Helvetica, an invitation to an early grave.

"How about we skip the drinks and just meet at a motel? If you're really good, I'll buy you a whole bottle." The reply was filled with poor puns and jokes. Ronaldo's attempt at seduction. The back and forth went on far longer than it should have as details were sorted through. "See you at The Emerald Inn tomorrow night. Rest up. You'll need it." It was signed by our serial killer with an initial. "N."

"N. What the fuck does that stand for?" Gillian asked. "It's probably fake anyway" Harriman replied. "I know but I want to know if this poor sap was led there thinking he was going to find a man or a woman." The tech mumbled under his breath, clearly not pleased. Everybody wanted instant answers. He scrolled through more emails. Dozens had been exchanged. They had started over three months earlier.

This wasn't a quick hook-up but an email romance. It was love from afar in ones and zeros. They had discovered each other on some free dating site. One used when people didn't like the high-price of communication of the more well-known options. It had started slow. No promises of sex. Lots of silly details. Favorite foods and favorite music. They acted sixteen not in their twenties.

Given the background and build up, the motel meeting seemed odd. In fact, Ronaldo had resisted. He had pushed for a real date with dinner and the rest but had been rebuffed for "a more private first meeting." All the suspect's emails were signed with just the letter N except for those at the very beginning. There was a name. Probably just another lie. But it was enough to get us started.

"Natasha Burnham Kruger."

CHAPTER FORTY-FOUR:

Noveau American wasn't my thing but Julie seemed to enjoy the variety. Classic pairings with a twist. Everything fresh. It seemed worth the exorbitant price.

"How's the case going?" she asked. "Lousy. But I can't really talk about it." "I understand" she said. I replied in kind and asked her about her job. It's a question I rarely bothered to ask. Her answer surprised me. She was a paralegal. A staffer at one of the city's biggest firms. I asked about the tattoos in the conservative environment. She said she just kept them covered. I was happy that her dress for the evening didn't do any such thing. There was plenty of skin and ink.

She gave me the details of how this profession had come to be. More precisely how she had gotten into it. She had been at law school, Syracuse no less, and dropped out at the end of year one. It was expensive and dull and she hated the school. Syracuse really was an awful city. Nothing there but snow and crime. Even the concerts were lacking in quality.

I asked her about transferring. She said it was considered but by then it was too late. She was already disenchanted and thousands in debt. The desire just wasn't there to go on.

She asked about my history and why I became a cop. My answer wasn't all that different from hers. It wasn't a passion or even a destiny. Just a job I happened to take. That was long ago and since then things had changed. Now, it would be hard to imagine life without. The darkness appealed not for its thrill but for its insight into human nature. At least that's the point I was trying to make.

It was then that she threw me a flirtatious prompt. A homerun to my softball pitch. "So, you like exploring the dark side?" It was said with a smile. Just another one of her throw-away lines. This girl was having her fun.

I ignored the obvious answer but kept to the spirit of the game. Besides, I really wanted to know. "So, why do you keep teasing me about Allison?" I asked. "Because of the way you are around her." "How's that?" "Nervous. Like you're ashamed you think of her sexually." "She's a kid." "She's eighteen in four months. Will you stop being embarrassed then?"

"The t-shirt was a bit heavy handed, don't you think?" I asked. "What t-shirt?" "Joy Division. Unknown Pleasures." Dom laughed into her wine. "I didn't even realize. I swear. A total coincidence. I just knew Allison was looking for it." "I don't believe you." She wiped the wine from her lips. "Seriously. I really didn't know. Hilarious."

We laughed through dinner. Most of it was real. The usual banter about siblings and childhoods. We covered goals and how long we had lived in Portland. It would have been a perfect evening except for the fact that I knew it was all a mistake. She was no longer a suspect but she could still end up a witness. Someone called to testify about the facts of the crime.

As we walked across the street for some more wine and dessert, I told her some of my doubts. "You realize I could get in some trouble for this." "For what? Eating Black Forest Tort?" "Seeing you." "Then why did you do it?" It was the perfect cue for some romantic declaration but I decided to pass up the chance. The point had been made that I was taking a risk. That was already more than I should have said.

As I watched her get up from the table and walk across the overly-cute café, I knew that I was in trouble. Perfect legs and perfect ass. A curvy delight. Lust was driving logic out the window.

We sat in the café for hours, talking over home-baked crumbs. I preferred a good pint to the overpriced grapes but I was too afraid to move. The conversation was on a roll. Interruptions weren't called for. Better to just go with the flow.

They threw us out of the cafe and into the streets. It was still fairly early. I suggested we go to a bar right next door. She declined. She said that she didn't want to get too drunk to drive. I applauded her maturity and made my play. I invited her back to my place. I stood there and waited for what seemed like hours as she contemplated my offer. To say I was disappointed when she demurred wouldn't nearly sum it up. It had been a night of anticipation. Now there was no pay off. It wasn't the sort of teasing I enjoyed.

We kissed goodnight with sugar-coated tongues, warm from alcohol and yearning. It was quite a kiss. Soft and romantic. Nothing at all like what I had imagined.

CHAPTER FORTY-FIVE:

"Natural Born Killers. Don't these fucking people have any taste?" "What are you going on about, Dudek?" "Natasha Burnham Kruger. Natural Born Killers."

How a crap movie became the signature reference of every killer is beyond explanation. At least "Catcher in the Rye" had some literary merit. Which was probably the issue. It takes at least a certain amount of intelligence and maturity to actually read a novel. Any moron can watch a movie. At least a piece of candy-colored violence like NBK.

"I guess it could be that" Gillian admitted. "Look, we tried every permutation of "Natasha," "Burnham" and "Kruger." None of them tie back to our victim." "I guess. They are pretty unusual names. Even one by one." "I'm telling you it's Natural Born Killers."

The investigation hadn't been going well. The NBK emails were traced from Ronaldo's computer which was all well and good. Unfortunately, it lead back to the Seattle Central Library. A brilliant building of sharp edges and steel which was visited and used by thousands.

There was CCTV tape which we tried to make sense of. The times the emails were sent were matched to the times people were in the library. None of it had gotten us anywhere.

It could have been anyone, young, old, male or female. There was still no telling who "Natasha" really was.

"If you had to make a guess and stick by it, one killer or two?" Gillian asked. I was surprised by his level of trust. "Two. Especially with this NBK thing." "You know, I never saw that movie" He said. "You're not missing much. You should probably watch it though, in case these idiots really are inspired." "You're not a fan?" "I'm more of a Decalogue sort of guy, myself." "Whatever the fuck that is. Can't you even watch movies like a normal person?"

"Basic Instinct" he said. "There's one I thought would be more of a trend setter." "I didn't think you were that old." "I saw it on cable after Sharon Stone got her Oscar. Wait. Did she win? I don't remember. Anyway, I wonder why that didn't influence more people on the whole bondage/death thing" he asked. "It only works if your murderer looks like Sharon Stone." "No, I think it's the ice pick. Who the hell uses an ice pick these days?"

And so it went, the friendly banter. I was once again on Gillian's side. I suppose it was a good thing, at least as long as it lasted. My interpersonal skills were showing improvement.

There was a problem though that quelled Gillian's thrill that he was onto something big. The tipping point had been reached. The case had gotten too major for minor law enforcement officials. It was going over to the FBI.

Promises were made that Gillian could stay on in Seattle. A member of the Special Task Force. Remembering his days on a previous beast, Gillian wasn't feeling very hopeful. But there was no way he was going to let his case be stolen. He agreed to put up with the FBI and all the condescension that came with it. He would miss his wife. He would miss his kids. But something like this was a rare opportunity

As for me, I was asked what I wanted to do. There was room for me on the task force, if I was so inclined. I said I wanted to be apprised and would be happy to help but I preferred to return to Portland. Gillian seemed a little upset that I had left him up there alone but I wasn't about to be swayed.

The Chief gave me shit for letting an opportunity pass but he confessed that he would have done the same. Once the Bureau moves in there's little room for locals. It's usually a frustrating time.

I had another problem, though, about what to do next. The boss thought I should get going on some other cases. I presented my arguments that there was still another angle to be played on the death of Eric Thurman. Since things were slow, he said it was Ok but only until I was needed elsewhere. Once the rain cleared and the warm weather returned, I would have no choice. Crime would ramp up as it always did. Most of the criminals stayed inside during the winter months. They preferred a good climate for violence.

CHAPTER FORTY-SIX:

Ashley Berger was asked to come down to the station. It wasn't just a request. She came to The Cube with mother, father and lawyers. It wasn't going to be much of a conversation.

"Ashley, we know you were drinking alcohol at The Green Dragon even though you were underage." Her parents gazed at her with stony disapproval but nobody said a word. "We're willing to let that go as long as you surrender your fake ID and fully cooperate with the investigation." The lawyer whispered into Ashley's ear. She nodded very slowly. "So, does that mean you're willing to cooperate?" "Yes, but they can't be here." The parents protested and told Ashley they had every right. She reminded them that she was now an adult. The law was the law and it was in her powers to have her parents dismissed. I would have done it myself but Ashley beat me to the punch. She clearly had things to say.

The parents got up from the room muttering a few more words of condescension. Ashley had really let them down. The door slammed behind them. Freedom for Ashley in a locked interrogation room, at least as far as speaking her mind. "So, do we have a deal? I asked. The lawyer piped in. "Yes, detective, she will surrender her fake ID and cooperate fully." "Is that right, Ashley? You're going to be cooperative now?" She nodded again and gave in to her circumstance.

"Were you with Eric Thurman the night that he died?" "Yes." "Until how late?" "I don't really remember." I couldn't tell if she was resisting or really unaware. Either way I let her know I expected better. "Try." She picked up the edge in my voice, as did her lawyer. They both seemed to get a feel for my mood. "Seven or seven-thirty, I guess." "Which one? Seven or seven-thirty?" "Closer to seven-thirty, I think." "What time did you meet him?"

And so it began, Eric's last night in more detail. At least up until seven-thirty. He had met them at the bar around five. The gang was already there. Present were Ashley, Donald, Janelle, Dave and five others I had never heard about before. Ashley said they were kids from PSU. I describe Carl Kraft to her. She said he wasn't one of them. She tried to recall their names but couldn't remember them at all. She said she rarely remembered such things when she was introduced to a lot of people at once. I asked her how she knew they went to Portland State. "They were complaining about tuition increases and one had a Vikings t-shirt on."

"Did you talk to Eric much?" "Not really. He was too busy talking to everybody else." "Anyone in particular?" "No, just whoever was around him. He was making fun of Dave for something. But that's all I remember." "Do you remember for what?" "No. Not really. He was always making fun of Dave. It was this thing they had."

I asked her to try to remember what else Eric might have said. She claimed she couldn't come up with a single thing more. He was usually too far away. I asked her to describe him. What was he wearing. What mood he was in. At least I got a few answers. His clothes were expensive but casual. The sort that would be home in LA. As far as his mood, she described it as buoyant. A word she had learned for the SAT. She said he seemed happy and energetic. He was looking forward to something big.

It hadn't been like that before. It was a recent change. Eric had been quite down. "That thing about his parents and NYU really got to him. He said he felt trapped" Ashley said. How not going to NYU meant the end of his world was something I still found elusive. I wanted to write it off and dismiss it, as adults usually do. Teenagers are just prone to drama. But I knew it been a turning point for Eric. It had set him spiraling into something I didn't yet understand. Something that ended in darkness. But then there was this sudden uptick in mood. It was an unusual aberration.

"Do you have any idea why he suddenly broke out of his gloom?" "Gloom?" "You know what I mean." She shook her head "no" but I asked her to guess. "He just seemed really excited about something but he wouldn't tell anybody what." "Do you think it was a girl?" She didn't answer my question. "Ashley, do you think Eric met someone new and that's why he was feeling so much better about life?" Her eyes looked down at the table and then over to her counsel. It wasn't to look for guidance. "Does he have to be here?" she asked.

I explained to her that having a lawyer present was for her own benefit but she was free to ask him to leave. He stammered and blustered how inappropriate it was that I would condone such a foolish action. I reminded him that Ashley had that right. She was free to make her own decisions. He left with a hostile glare.

"I think he was. Seeing someone" she said. The story came out in between tears and self-loathing. It was a nasty portrait that she drew. Eric and she had slept together more than a few times. It wasn't a boyfriend/girlfriend thing. Just a good time. At least that's the way it was explained. The thing about it was that the sex was always good and Eric never refused an invitation for more. But that night at the bar he did. In fact, he was very cruel.

As Eric left the bar, Ashley started to follow. She asked him to come back to her place. He said thanks but no thanks he had somewhere to be. But Ashley kept trying to convince. She offered to go back to his car and give him a blow job. Just a little way of saying goodbye. He didn't just decline. He went for the kill. What he said was incredibly vicious.

"What did he say to you exactly?" I asked. Her sadness turned to hate. Tears turned to malice. She couldn't bring herself to say it. "Ashley, what did he say to you?" Her answer was a whisper but the words were clear enough. "That he didn't want to waste his cum on an ugly slut like me."

CHAPTER FORTY-SEVEN:

Fantasy images failed to materialize. There were no whips or chains or strange devices. It was all very straight-forward but far from average. Sleeping with Julie was damn near spectacular.

Between her Betty Grable body and her willingness to please, I was one satisfied customer. It had happened slowly, not for five dates. But finally, we went back to her place. She had heavy wood furniture, Spanish in style. Candles littered the entire place. There was a lot of teasing, both verbal and physical. It made the ending that much more rewarding. She was a girl who knew sex and was confident in her abilities to make even the strongest man weak at the knees.

We lay there, that first night, naked and entwined. The two of us in her four-poster bed. A storm raged. Dogs barked at the thunder. None of it mattered in the least. As I kissed her shoulder I tried to tell her. I told this woman of fantasy that she was a remarkable girl. She said that was sweet but she didn't want to hear it. It wasn't the time for talk.

I woke up alone in an empty bed. For a moment I couldn't place where I was. The clank of pans from the kitchen put an end to the confusion. In fact, it was annoyingly loud. I threw on my clothes and took a piss. It was dark and still raining. I looked at a clock. It wasn't even seven. I couldn't believe she was up so early. I walked into the kitchen, eyes wide-shut, to see her at the stove. There was smoke rising from the pan, a minor cooking accident. She struggled to keep something from burning.

"Sorry, I was going to make you some eggs and surprise you. I don't think you're going to want these though." I walked over to her and gave her a kiss. I looked down in the pan she was holding. Eggs over easy, black and crisp, it didn't look very appealing. "Sorry" she said again. "It was a nice thought. Thanks." I thought about making some crack how she could really apologize. Something physical to make me less hungry. But the moment had passed, she was pressed for time. She had to be getting off for work.

"They make you get in this early?" I asked. "If you're not at your desk working by eight, you really hear it from one of the partners." I shook my head in disbelief. I never understood the Portland obsession with starting early. We were no longer farmers but the hours were the same. Get to the computer to feed the chickens. It made no sense but most work issues don't. I kept my thoughts to myself and returned to memories of the night. It was such a shame she had to go.

CHAPTER FORTY-EIGHT:

Another drive up the 5. Traffic at the bridge as it crossed over Vancouver, Washington. It was like Hoboken to Manhattan. Not a place that most found enticing. British Columbia's version was more of an inspiration. I'd only been there once but wanted to get back. Once I'd even tried to convince her. I told Emily she'd love all the great food on Robson. Stanley Park was also a treat. I almost had her going but then she thought it through. My offer was dismissed and the thought abandoned. Another fantasy history that would never be written.

Maybe a trip with my rollergirl friend would ease the pain of regret. A nice weekend away. A vacation for the senses. Could be just the ticket. I slammed on the horn as I decided to wait. It was too early to bring up such things. For all I know, this was a one off deal. Maybe Dom had other plans. Either way, one thing was for sure. My desperation was shining brightly.

I wasn't pleased to be stuck. This should have been my day off. But Gillian had called and sounded in need of rescue. The Task Force was as horrible as predicted. He was shut out and ignored. Dismissed as unqualified. The FBI had it all under control. If they could stop terrorist plots to blow up airports and malls, they could certainly handle a few murderers.

According to Gillian they had made a hash of it all. They were set on lazy answers. Profiler's fallbacks. A killer that fit the norm. He was white and well-educated, probably in his mid-thirties or forties and he had snuffed out chipmunks when he was a child. No matter how many letters followed the experts' names, the conclusions were constant. Serial killers were all the same.

I wasn't surprised that Gillian had turned to me, even after his bitching and whining. As much as we disagreed about the case, there was at least camaraderie and respect. He thought I was misguided and I thought the same. It was frustrating but not usually personal.

We met half-way at that British place he had earlier sought out. He was disappointed when he finally arrived. We sat at a booth. The walls were covered in kitsch. Endless photos of the king and queen. The food was disgusting. The beer was even worse. It did nothing to lighten the mood.

"So, why do you think they have it wrong?" I asked. Gillian looked exhausted. He mumbled his answer. "I keep thinking of your table thing and the idea of a person watching. We pulled a partial print off our scene in Seattle." Gillian was grasping at straws. I was the one who came up with the original theory and even I knew prints in a motel meant little.

"How many prints were pulled from that location?" "Thirty-seven." "Jesus, don't these places ever clean?" Gillian continued to go on about how this print was so significant but how it was being undervalued by the Feds. "A partial print means almost nothing unless it's found at more than one crime scene" I said. "What the fuck do you think I've been saying? They did match! The partial we found up in Seattle matched one taken at a crime scene in Chicago back in '04. And it was female."

Either he had misspoken or I had misheard. No wonder he was so put out and agitated. "So why aren't they convinced?" "Because the prints are just partials and it goes against the expert's theory. They insist it's a lone white guy. No accomplice. The usual clichéd crap you hear on TV." I let it sink in. It still didn't sound right. I wondered if Gillian was stretching things too far. "Are the partials really bad?" "They're not good but they're enough. The tech told me if she had to guess, they were a match. She also thought they were probably female but that was less conclusive." "So, the Feds just ignored her findings?" "She recanted when they asked her about it. She told them I had misunderstood."

"The NBK thing also fits. A guy and a gal who get off on killing people" he said. "You know how unusual that would be?" "It was your fucking theory, Dudek!" "I know. I'm just playing Devil's advocate." "Well, don't. Help me make these jack asses see what's right in front of them. Two people. A man and a woman. Premeditated, thrill-kill fucks."

We each had a pint of below average ale as we mulled over the details. It was pretty ironic how far Gillian had come. He had completely embraced my theory.

"So, let's put aside what type of killers they are. How many bodies are they trying to pin on these people?" I asked. "Seven, maybe eight." "That many?" "All those earlier cases that I showed you have been vetted by the Bureau. They reached the same conclusion. They were murdered by the same killer or killers." "Even Eric Thurman?" I asked, as if on cue. "Even Eric Thurman."

"Why would the C of Ds let me keep investigating then?" I asked. "Because you're a stubborn bastard and usually when you insist you're right, you are." It was a flattering statement but one that worried me. "But not this time?" I asked. "Nobody thinks you're going to come up with dick interviewing high school kids and roller derby girls, including the C of Ds." I wanted to argue but bit my tongue. It still tasted greasy from lunch.

CHAPTER FORTY-NINE:

I got a call out of the blue. I was already home and feeling a little bit drunk. I'd been to The Pig for a few. It was none other than my Labrador and victim, the rookie known as Johanson. He said he had been asked to call. He was trying to do me a favor. A friend of mine was in serious trouble. He went on to paint an ugly picture.

I ate something quickly and even took a shower but I was still too drunk to drive. I called a cab and waited far too long for what was only a ten-minute ride.

I arrived in Old Town not far from the office of Mrs. Vivian Thurman. It wasn't her who had reached out to me. She wasn't the type. It was someone with which I had more of a history.

The stairs to the SRO were crowded with people. Cops and techs I recognized on sight. I got to Johansen at the top of the landing. He told me in more detail what had happened. I felt sick for being such a bastard and making his life hell. He had been severely punished for his indiscretion. I made a mental note to make good with Tim Gage. Johanson wasn't a bad kid, just stupid.

I walked into the room, it was packed to the gills. People just trying to get done. There on the bed I saw my friend from way back. Reggie, the street kid who loved the Clash. He was covered in blood but it wasn't his. He was cuffed and sitting quietly. As he saw me walk over, relief showed on his face. He knew something had gone terribly wrong.

"What happened?" I asked. "I stabbed him." "Don't say anything until you get a PD. It looks like he's going to make it." "Too bad." "Shut up. Just keep your mouth shut and don't say a word to anyone unless your lawyer says it's OK." He nods his head in understanding but it's already too late. Reggie was in serious trouble. His victim had bled a lot and was close to death. Only some quick work by the paramedics had given him a shot.

"Don't you want to know why?" he asked. "Does it matter?" I responded. "You fucked up, Reggie. Just keep quiet before you make it worse." "He killed Dorothy." "What?" "Yeah, Dudek. That asshole killed Dorothy and then bragged about it too everyone." "Why would he do that?" "He said he got sick of the barking."

I told Reggie, one last time, not to say a word. I would try to meet him down at The Cube. I called the Nightshift Commander and told them about the incident. I did what I could to put in a good word. It wouldn't help much. Every detective had his job. It was obvious that Reggie had done the deed. I tried my best to get him a good public defender. As luck would have it, I was familiar with his assigned counsel. It was the incompetent fool that had sold Carl Kraft down the river. I pleaded for a new public defender. With a good defense, Reggie might have half a chance. With that guy, he was already done.

After much lecturing on procedures and how my conduct was inappropriate, I got the office to get Reggie a veteran. A man who'd been a public defender for years and knew the system inside and out. As detectives, we always hated him.

As I stood in the darkness unable to do much of anything, I reconsidered my promise. I was still a little drunk and none too put together. Going into The Cube might be a mistake. As long as Reggie took my advice and he got the PD I was promised, it was as good as it was going to get.

I called a cab and waited about a block from the scene. It was cold but not really raining. The cab finally arrived. The car smelled of chemicals. An air freshener smell that almost made me nauseous.

Sleep wasn't an option so I just stayed up for a while. I'd go into The Cube bright and early. I sat back in my chair and listened to some music. I had made my selection carefully.

Too late for Punk. Too early for Grunge. It felt more like a Thom York night.

CHAPTER FIFTY:

Julie's fingers worked me over. Black polished nails had turned blood red. I kissed her deeply as she continued to tease. I took my moment and pinned her to the bed. I tasted all that I could. She was mine for the taking and take her I did. It was sweaty fucking, Trent Reznor style. Pure animal sex and instinct.

We laid there afterward in purifying candle-light glow. Her place, with all the dark furniture. It felt like a painting. A Spanish Renaissance piece. Restored and displayed in a gallery.

She asked more about my past but I only told her a little. I was too busy admiring the gift I had been given. She was already unwrapped and I was ready for more. The conversation would have to wait.

There was no thinking of crimes or murders committed. No longing for girls soon to be married. It was a blissful vacation from all that had tormented. A fantasy theme park to roam through and explore. We only took breaks to eat.

It was during one of our rides that Dom had gently tied me to her bed. It was all just for a laugh and pretty harmless. In context, I enjoyed it quite thoroughly. She rode me to contentment but she said I wasn't through. She insisted that I stay tethered and bound. I didn't see the point in resisting. I was comfortable enough. Soon after, I fell asleep exhausted and happy.

I woke up in a flash or maybe to one. I wasn't sure what was happening for a while. I was still tied to the bed and on full display. I looked down at my grinning audience. The smile was so wide it covered her whole face. This girl appreciated humiliation. It was Allison looking none too merciful. "Good Morning, Sunshine."

I tugged my arms and slipped out of my bindings. They weren't tied very tightly. I was pissed off as could be and covered myself. Allison was laughing hysterically.

"What the fuck are you doing here?! Get out" I yelled. She fed off my outrage. Just more fun. She slowly walked toward the door. She stopped for a second to deliver her line. It didn't seem very fun at the time. "Yes, detective. By the way, that's a pretty nice gun you have." She laughed at her own humor as Julie came in. She appeared angry and perplexed by the whole scene.

"What the hell are you doing? Get out of here." She shoved Allison out the door, none too gently. I heard her yelling as I pulled on my clothes. "I told you to wait in the kitchen" Julie yelled. "I know. I just wanted to see." "Why would you do something like that?" "Just lighten up. It's not like I haven't seen naked men before."

And so it went, back and forth. I felt the urge to go out there and slap her. Young Allison Thurman had been a problem. A thorn in my side. She needed someone to keep her in line.

As I started to leave the room, a different thought struck me. What if that had been the plan all along? Maybe Julie and Allison just thought it would be a kick to make an old man confused and embarrassed. It was highly unlikely but I couldn't write it off. It's a possibility I had to entertain.

By the time I walked into the living room, Allison had left. More precisely, been thrown out and cursed. Julie apologized again and again. If her anger was false she was an incredible actress. Allison had gone too far.

"I'm so sorry" she said. "What was she even doing here?" "She came by to get an insurance form for the league. I told her to wait in the kitchen while I got one off my desk." I was too angry for words. Maybe I was just afraid I would say them. This whole thing was far from OK.

I gathered my things. Put myself together. I exited as quickly as I could. There were no kisses goodbye or promises to meet later. I needed to get away to think. Maybe I was overreacting but right then I didn't care. I just knew that I needed to get out.

CHAPTER FIFTY-ONE:

"Talk to me Dave." Just another day at The Cube. He had come with both parents and his lawyer. An expensive guy from a small firm in Lake Oswego. He was sure to gum up the works. "About what?" Dave looked nervous and tired which didn't mean a thing. Being brought in for questioning again wasn't easy on the nerves.

"We have people that put you with Eric the night he was killed. When I asked you about it before you said you hadn't seen him that night" Dave shifts in his chair. "Dave, honey, just tell the detective the truth." Words from a reassuring mother who should have kept quiet. "I didn't want to get in trouble." "So, you lied to me, Dave? Is that what you're saying?" "Yes, sir."

The father was fuming. He was a sales guy at Tektronics. A firm that made electronic equipment that could measure small electronic movements and changes. "David, you heard your mother. Tell this man the truth." Dave looked over to his lawyer. He got the nod to answer.

"Yeah, I was with him. I didn't want to get in trouble." "Did you think lying to a police detective wouldn't get you into trouble?" He just shrugged. I gave him the benefit of doubt that he really was that stupid. The logic of teenagers always seems to defy.

"Why don't you tell me about that night without lying to me this time. If you would feel more comfortable, I'm sure your parents wouldn't mind stepping out of the room for a few moments." The father gave me a look of hate. He was fighting the urge to contradict me. It turned out not to matter. Dave said he didn't mind them staying.

The story came out. All the details matched. A night out drinking and hanging out with friends. Janelle and Ashley were named along with Daniel. He confirmed the times they were at the Green Dragon. "How did you get a fake ID?" his mother asked. He blew off her question as the father intervened. They would talk about all that later.

"Dave, I want to make sure you realize that you've already committed a crime. Did your lawyer explain to you that you can't lie to me the way you did? It's against the law." That hit home. The fear was awakened. "Am I going to jail?" "Nobody wants to put you in jail. I just want to find out what happened to Eric."

He gave me details about the conversation that night. Most were about sex and who was fucking who. Sports was a close second. The Trailblazers were looking good. I kept pushing for more on what Eric had said. "Who was he meeting?" He told me about Ashley and how she had followed him out. "But he was meeting someone, right? Another girl?" Dave just shrugged.

"What do you know about Eric's relationship with Julie?" I asked. It was a grey area question. Probably not relevant to the case. All the same, I needed to make certain.

"Who?" he asked. It seemed sincere. "His rollergirl friend. She goes by the derby name of Dom." "I never heard of her." "Who was he seeing, lately? Who were some of his girlfriends?" "I don't know. He didn't tell me much about that stuff unless he wanted to give me a hard time." "Did he give you a hard time a lot?" "Yeah. You know. We were friends."

I decided to forgo a lecture on the meaning of friendship. I probably wasn't the most credible source. I kept pushing and pulling for information. Dave had given me nothing new.

"Was Eric giving you a hard time about something that night at The Green Dragon?" "Probably." "Do you remember what?" "Not really." A small tremor in his expression. He was holding something back. I wondered if it was on par with Eric's line to Ashley. "Think about it a minute. What was he giving you a hard time for." I knew that he remembered but didn't want to say it. "Dave, answer his questions" his mother prompted. Micro-expression magic. The gestures betrayed. He tried to deny it again but the signals all contradicted. His body language cried out liar.

I turned to his counsel and laid it on the line. "If your client won't cooperate, I think its time to call the ADA." Murmurs and a huddle. Urges for Dave to come clean. They didn't understand his resistance. All I could think of was that it was something painful. Something so cutting the memory alone made him bleed.

"He was making fun of me for getting lost." Internal oscilloscope readings indicated the truth. His honesty made less sense than the lie. "Getting lost? On your way to the Green Dragon?" "At Home Depot. I spent like an hour in there trying to find something but couldn't."

I pushed him to elaborate. The story seemed irrelevant but mildly funny. Dave had driven out to Home Depot by Mall 205. He was looking for electrical wire and couldn't find it. He left never getting it because he was too shy to ask for assistance.

When I asked him about the wire and why he would need such a thing. I finally learned a bit more. It seemed Dave was quite the hobbyist. Model trains were his love. He had a rather extensive layout. Miles of scale track. Buildings with detailed interiors. Even lights in the buildings and on the streets. "That sounds pretty impressive. Is the town just a town or is it somewhere real?"

It was not a place that existed, he explained. But it was kind of European. The building kits were made in Germany. The locomotives too. They were built to exact specification. The way he talked, I could almost see him with his precision engineering. Banks, homes and plastic people. He was the king of his world. A god who controlled every detail. It was no wonder he spent so much time alone.

CHAPTER FIFTY-TWO:

Gillian called. Things were finally breaking. You could hear the glee in his voice. A young man had been approached by an internet "friend," a woman calling herself Natasha. She had asked him to meet her in a cheap motel, somewhere down in Salem. Oregon's capital, it wasn't much of a place, but a man will travel far for sex.

His name was Mike Fuer, he was only nineteen. He said he often used the internet to try to get laid. He'd had a lot of success with a particular site, "Playdates" which is where he had encountered Natasha. Over the course of three weeks they had exchanged flirtations and photos. She looked pretty enough for a fuck. She was thirty-three with dark brown hair. Her eyes made her look like forty.

Mike had driven down to Salem from Tacoma, where he lived. He booked the room, checked into the motel and waited patiently for Natasha to arrive.

She was an hour late but she eventually showed. The thing is, he saw her get out of a truck. A black SUV with another person inside. He was sure it was another guy. It was enough to raise his suspicions. Natasha clearly had an agenda a little different from his own. He liked the way she looked. In fact, he was pleasantly surprised. But there was something wrong about her from the start.

She didn't want to talk. She didn't even want a drink. She just told him to take off his clothes. As suspicious as he was, Mike did as instructed. He wanted to see where all this went. It's when she told him that she liked her men tied up that Mike finally said no. He wasn't comfortable being put in that position. He refused her request and they both started to yell. Mike told her that she had to leave.

She called him a pussy and stormed out of the room. He watched her as she returned to the SUV. Natasha and the man argued. He couldn't be sure what it was about but it sounded like they weren't sure what to do. She wanted to go but he was insisting they stay. Something about it being too late to turn back. Mike grew increasingly uneasy and felt a surge of panic that he couldn't explain. He ran out the door at full speed.

They started to chase him, at least for a few minutes. It was faster than he had run in his life. Mike made it to the coffee shop next door. He sat in the booth filling up on soda trying to calm his nerves. He watched the SUV drive off and remembered the headlines. Something about a serial killer on the loose. As embarrassed as he was, he made the call. He told the police that he had almost gotten killed.

"We have a really good description now" Gillian said. "Of both of them or just the woman?" "Just the chick but that's something. Between that and the description of the vehicle..." "Did he get the plates?" "No, we didn't get that lucky. Fuer had other things on his mind at the time." "Like getting laid?" "Like not having his head wrapped in a plastic bag."

Gillian was downright jubilant. The break had been huge. Moreover it had been down in Oregon. He was coming down tonight and checking in at The Cube. He said he missed the stench of decay.

CHAPTER FIFTY-THREE:

Serial killer excitement had taken center stage. The Radovich case had almost been forgotten. It was the actions of a lone young detective who kept it alive. Hersh was an industrious little worker. While others moved on, he remained focused on why someone would kill a not-so-nice family from Seattle. He came to me one day. He looked like hell. "I was wondering if I could just bounce some things off of you." "Sure. But I don't know much of anything about your case." "Good. That's what I want."

He took me around to his own little space. The cubicle he called his home. There were personal photos of his wife and kid. She was young but not very attractive. "I've been driving everyone else nuts with all this and nobody wants to hear it anymore" he said. I guess that meant I was the only one left. I let it slide and tried to focus. Hersh laid out photos across a desk.

The first was a photo of Radovich. "So, we have Radovich. He was a lawyer and a lobbyist." I nodded. "I got a list of his clients and they all seem legit." "Who were they?" Hersh pulls out a sheet of paper and reads off of it. "A craft soda company, a real estate firm..." "Firm or developer?" I asked. He looked. "Residential real estate. Houses for sale.

Why?" "Nothing. Just wanted to make sure I had it right in my head."

He went back to his list. Started from the top. "A craft soda company, a real estate firm, an athletic apparel company, an association of tech start-ups, some sort of Native American business alliance, a hospital, a chain of campsites, a Lutheran church and six private individuals." "What did they do?" "Who?" "The private individuals? What would they be hiring him to lobby for?" I asked. "I don't know. Residential zoning restrictions keeping them from expanding their McMansions?" "Well, that's the first thing I would check. Who are these people and what did they want? Try to find out what Radovich promised to do for them all." "I did. At least I started to. But, yeah, I can find out more about the individuals. Thanks." I nodded. The veteran detective helping out the youngster. It was hard not to get caught up in the role.

"How's your own case going? Sounds like you guys caught a real break with your suspect being ID'd in that liquor store." "Yeah. Too bad they won't let Gillian or I near her. They have two FBI guys leading the interrogation." "So, what are you and Gillian doing?" "Gillian mostly" I corrected. "I'm sure he's just sitting pretty and representing the face of local law enforcement." Thinking of The Cube's way of juggling case loads and fucking up everybody, I thought I'd prepare

Hersh. "Listen, if this Thurman thing gets wrapped up, you might get some more company again on Radovich" I said. "I know. I'm OK with that. It beats being pulled off the case altogether."

He thanked me again and I returned to my own space. I appreciated the moment of human interaction. I was too stuck in my thoughts. I was still going in circles. NBK killings were not what they seemed. I was sure there was more. My mind popped with a thought. Not for me but for Hersh. One more piece of sage advice.

"Hersh." He looked up from his desk. "Did you take a good look at the wife and the kids?" I asked. "What do you mean?" "Maybe Mr. wasn't the target. Maybe somebody was after the wife or something." Hersh nodded. "Yeah, I thought of that. Maybe she was cheating on her marriage with somebody. I checked. Nothing." "What about the kid?" "One was seven the other fifteen." "Check on the fifteen-year-old." He gave me a look. He was trying to understand why I would say such a thing. "You really think somebody went after a fifteen-year-old and took out his whole family." "You'd be surprised what kids get into these days."

CHAPTER FIFTY-FOUR:

He took the plea and got a sweetheart deal. Reggie had been reduced to Assault. He would still do six years in a cell. Maybe more. They weren't going to be good times.

Julie delivered her own confession. Apologies and lies. I was feeling battered and bruised by the breach of trust. Allison shouldn't have been involved. There was no excuse. But I let Julie make her case. Just a series of mistakes. Nothing had been committed with intent.

The story went on how Allison was out of control. She was determined to test the limits. It had been bad before Eric had died but now she was more extreme. Acting up and acting out, Julie was beginning to get concerned. That last trick Allison pulled by walking in was just one in an escalating series. Julie was done. The friendship was over. Allison might even transfer to another team.

"I'm not sure I should give you this. Maybe I should have just destroyed it." She handed me a phone. "What are you handing that to me for?" I asked. "It's Allison's iPhone." I was confused all the way around. "I took it from her." "She must have been pissed. But I'm still not getting it? Is that your payback? Stealing her phone?"

She grabbed the phone and touched her finger to the screen. A simple swipe. Menus selected. She showed me the cause of her concern. An image appeared on the high-resolution screen. An unflattering portrait. Saint Dudek on the rack in his fully exposed glory. Allison had taken it that morning before I had awakened. That morning she had intruded. The morning of panic flooding my brain.

"How do I erase this?" She took it out of my hands. Seconds later she returned the device. "Just hit that" she said. I pushed on a button and the photo disappeared. History that never happened. "Does that fully erase it or do I have to do something else?" She took the phone back and finished the job. My portrait was deaccessioned from the collection.

I thought about asking if she had more than one. Maybe Allison had made copies. It seemed a paranoid question but one I asked anyway. I was assured that was there were no more to be found. The next part was awkward. Julie expected thanks. It hadn't occurred to her that she was the cause. The situation was of her making and Allison her responsibility. I wasn't inclined to forgive.

Delusion kicked in full speed as I thought of the glass and how my fingerprints were all over Allison's phone. I debated whipping it clean. A criminal covering his tracks. I eventually decided that was going too far.

"I don't know what else to say. I'm sorry." Her words seemed sincere. There were no coy phrases about how she could make it up to me. No drama in the least. It was an exercise in careful restraint.

She started to leave but I told her she could stay as long as she answered my questions. "About what?" she asked. I knew she wouldn't like my response. "Eric" I said. "I want to know more about your relationship." I thought she would be offended. Maybe even disgusted. If she was, her curiosity overruled. She knew what I was asking. What I wanted to know. I told her it was part of my investigation.

At first she resisted, saying that it was all private. Something between just the two of them. I played on her guilt for Allison's intrusion. I was the one who had claim to violation of privacy. She still wasn't convinced until I admitted that it was personal. It had nothing to do with police business. I'd been thinking some pretty perverse things. She asked me what things and I promised to share. But only if she told me what I wanted to hear.

I think I saw her smile. Fish back on the hook. I had almost gotten away. She sat in a chair and told me calmly what things had been like. All those nights between her and Eric. I made it clear I wanted details. She already knew. She promised to describe every sordid moment.

I sat on the sofa as she began to tell her stories. The words poured from her mouth. Oral pornography. The tales polished to tease. Her relationship with Eric had been purely sex. Emotions were reduced to fetish. They each had their role to play. It was more extreme than I had expected. Adventures in pain and humiliation. Eric just couldn't get enough. He was hers to do with as she pleased. At least when they were playing their games.

I had a difficult time sorting through how much Dom there was in Julie. I couldn't take my eyes off her. This changeling creature sitting pretty in blue jeans. A trickier task was how it made me feel. I was both excited and abhorred. A conflict of interest. Since I had insisted on the information it would be unfair to judge.

Julie was expert at detecting those small moments. Those moments that warned of the quake. She was able to tell, even from across the room, which of them had the most effect. I insisted I needed to hear it all. I didn't want her holding back. Positions were described. Punishments laid out. She had really put Eric through the ringer. I asked her if she liked it. She said "Very much. Otherwise what would have been the point?"

We went at it right there on the living room floor. It was basic and primeval. There was no time for games or costumes. No psychological ploys. The time for words had come to an end. I just needed to get inside her.

CHAPTER FIFTY-FIVE:

"How's the sex?" she asked. "Don't answer that, I don't really want to know." I told her anyway. I wanted to tell Emily I had found happiness of a sort. "It's amazing" I said. "Really?" She claimed she didn't want to hear but of course she did. I just explained that Julie liked variety and was into experimentation. She had a real comfort with her sexuality. More than anyone else I had ever known.

Emily smiled, keeping her thoughts unspoken. I was annoyed she was afraid of the discussion. "What?" I asked. "Nothing. I'm just jealous." "Of me?" I asked. "I'll hook you up with Julie as long as I can watch." "Pervert." She tried to use the laugh to move on. I decided not to let it go. "What are you jealous of? You and Billy not getting along in that way?" Part of me hoped for malicious confirmation that the Indie Star Stud has fallen flat. An icon on the stage but a dud in the sack. "No, actually, he's amazing. Really. It's just..." she refused to finish. "Just what?" I prodded. "Sometimes I still get really self-conscious and I hate it. I wish I was as comfortable as Julie sounds."

I resisted the urge to make further jokes. Probably at her expense. Instead I sympathized and preached profound words of wisdom. A self-proclaimed expert on the psychology of sex. Along the way, somewhere south of the punch lines, I told Emily I thought she was beautiful. She didn't say a word. She never did. But I could see the smile in her eyes.

"How is Billy anyway? I mean, in general?" "Not too good, actually." She went on with a story about Billy's foray into fame. He and his band had been paired up with a big producer. Billy didn't take kindly to this Hollywood hack telling him how to make music. It wasn't Billy's call, the producer was expensive and the label backed him in every argument. They told Billy they could fire the guy but that it would be a real mistake. A threat was more than implied. Do it our way or go back to singing in coffee shops. Welcome to the big time, kid.

Billy swallowed his pride and laid down his tracks. He just wanted to make good music. The songs weren't to his liking. They were over-processed and overly slick. But the producer thought they were brilliant.

"I still don't get it. Why didn't he just quit?" I asked naively. Emily explained to me it was a no win situation. Anyone could record music these days. The equipment was cheap. Computers changed everything. But the actual recording wasn't the point. The hard part was getting it heard. The world was now awash in music. Recognition was far more important than quality.

"Maybe he just sucks." I said. It was meant as a joke. Emily didn't think it was funny. She was really concerned about Billy. He had become very difficult to be around since the recording sessions began. He was a constant ass but she said she understood. I wasn't sure I bought her story. I hesitated to say it but I had to bring it up. At least part of me was still invested in the idea of friendship.

"Is it possible he's just nervous about the wedding? I mean, that's a big step for a guy like that. Maybe it has nothing to do with his music." She said of course that was part of it but their future plans seemed to please him. He swore she was his queen forever. It was the whole weird process of coming so close. Of finally getting what you spent years and years wanting. "How could that not flip him out just a little?"

I had so many comments. So much to say. But I knew better than to utter a word. I knew what Billy needed. I had the perfect girl for the trick. Julie would relieve every stress. I self-censored the joke. Clearly a smart move. I didn't even add the part about arranging the trade.

At Emily's behest, we made tentative plans to see a movie. Gus Van Sant was speaking at Cinema Twenty-One. It was probably already sold out. Such things usually were. I was actually hoping we missed the chance. I wasn't looking forward to the pretension. Not the movie but the questions after the screening.

We had a fine night in a restaurant that did Indian vegan. Emily loved the food. I thought it was alright. It tasted good and was different, even if it was a little too light. She asked me more about Julie. Not the details of sex. More about what she was like. I told her she was a study in contrasts. Paralegal by day. Derby Vixen by night. She asked where Julie worked for her day job. Emily had a friend who was a lawyer at one of the big downtown firms. I told her the name as best I could remember. Something that ended in "and Partners." She said that wasn't it, which was too bad. She thought Julie might know her friend.

I explained how much I had learned a lot about derby. Pivots, Blockers and Jammers. It was all second nature now. Just a few more words in the master lexicon. "See, aren't you glad you went that night?" she asked, looking for some credit. I saw her point. I could trace it back to that evening when we went to the bout. The after-party near Grand. She seemed to have forgotten all about the rest.

CHAPTER FIFTY-SIX:

Gillian and I sat in The Cube. The search for Natasha was already in full swing. The C of Ds gestured over. Gillian thought it was for him. The C of Ds corrected him. His summons was for me.

I stepped into the office wondering if it was about Gillian and I. A cursory check on my interpersonal development. I sat in the chair and waited for him to unload. I was prepared for death by verbal firing squad. Exactly, what for, I wasn't quite sure. I just sensed impending doom.

"Mr. and Mrs. Thurman are coming in." he said. "They want an update on the case." "Well, at least Gillian has something to tell them." "What about you?" he asked. I wasn't sure what he meant. "What do you have to tell them?" I ran down the details I had discovered about Eric. The drugs, sex and parties. The cruel parting line to Ashley. "And what does any of that have to do with him being killed?" I said that it probably didn't except to help establish a timeline. A breakdown of who Eric was with when and what he was doing. "If it's not relevant, leave it out" I was told. Mr. and Mrs. Thurman didn't need their image of the good son shattered.

As the Thurmans walked in under pale florescent lights, my heart began to race. Allison. What would I say about

Allison? It was probably just as the C of Ds said, they were just looking for news. All the same my head went dizzy. "Are you alright, Detective Dudek? You look a little flush." "Fine" I said, as I stood up for the greeting.

Smiles and small talk were briefly exchanged. The Thurmans were a polished act. Praise was offered for the fine efforts of the department. I kept wondering why Gillian wasn't with us.

Images of Allison and that tormenting gaze. It was hard to focus on the formalities. I waited for the questions. Rebuke for my inappropriate behavior. Instead there was just talk of Natasha. The woman who had murdered their child.

Gillian walked in and joined us. He excused himself for his delay. He praised the task force to high heaven. A team of all-stars from the region. Federal resources and reach. The Thurmans were suitably impressed. Especially Richard. He was glad his son was receiving so much attention. Vivian's concerns were more about Eric's last hours. She kept asking Gillian questions that were poised so delicately, he didn't know what she was after.

"If you're asking if he was tortured or held prisoner for any length of time, we're pretty sure he wasn't." They were comforted by Gillian's words. A version of the old lie. "He died peacefully and didn't suffer." Death is rarely painless but nobody wanted to hear that.

Gillian rhapsodized poetic about the manhunt going on. Natasha would be caught. It was only a matter of time. Once they had her, they would get her partner. Then it would be all wrapped up.

None of this would bring Eric back but it would provide "closure." Another of the standard lies. It was one thing if you didn't know if your child were dead or alive. Then, answers mattered. But if someone was dead, there was rarely "closure" to be found. Only the numbing of grief over time. It would never disappear. Especially if it involved a child. Even a child like Eric. The sorrow just became part of breathing.

"What about you, Detective Dudek? Do you have anything to add?" Mr. Thurman asked. "No, Sir. I think Detective Gillian has brought you up to speed." He nodded graciously, apparently fulfilled. Mrs. Thurman was looking at me oddly. My heart skipped a beat. I could feel it coming. Something about Allison. Sure enough she hit me with the question. "I heard you saw my daughter, recently" she said. I wasn't sure how to answer. How much had she told them? How much truth and how many lies? Mr. Thurman looked curious. So did my boss.

"You've seen my daughter again, detective?" Mr. Thurman asked. "Sure he has" Mrs. Thurman added. There wasn't a trace of hostility in her voice. "He's apparently become a big roller derby fan and saw our little baby skate." I fumbled for words. I think I got them right. "Yes, I did. She was in the warm up bout at the Coliseum. A friend of mine took me. It was my first time. How does she like it?" "She loves it" Mrs. Thurman said. Mr. looked perplexed. I'm not sure Richard Thurman was even aware his daughter was in the league. "I worry about her though" Vivian Thurman added. "Those girls seem to always get hurt."

I offered words of reassurance that the younger girls were well looked after. The older girls made sure they didn't get pushed too hard. Mr. Thurman seemed bored. Even annoyed. I'm not sure he approved of any of it. The Thurmans thanked us again and excused themselves from the office. They hoped the case would be resolved soon. Gillian assured him it would be.

I escaped a lecture from the C of Ds. I guess he was happy at the way things went. As I walked back to my desk I felt Gillian following. He was trying not to let out a laugh. "Nicely done, Dudek" he said. I looked at him both angry and curious about what he had to say. "You looked ready to piss yourself when Mrs. Thurman brought up the derby." "What are you talking about?" "Dude, I don't blame you. I'm sure the boss wouldn't approve of your relationship." I assumed he meant with Julie but I wanted to be sure. "Why?" "Come on. You know you shouldn't be fucking a chick you met on the job. Especially one named "Dom.""

I put up with his ribbing. The routine brought comfort. At least I didn't have to suffer through another lecture on questioning young girls.

CHAPTER FIFTY-SEVEN:

REWIND

TIME CODE BLURS

Denis sat in the interrogation cell. Denis. The Worm. Friend of Kraft. Friend of Eric. He knew what was waiting in store. "Your buddy Carl gave you up" I told him. "Gave me up for what?" "Dealing drugs and having sex with a minor, for starters." He scoffed. "Bullshit." "That you did it or that he gave you up?" "Both. There's nothing to give up." "We'll see about that. I looked at your juvie record." "You can't do that" he protested. "Like I said, I looked at your juvie record. You're quite the fuck-up, aren't you Denis?" "Whatever."

He was annoyed but still far too confident. "Tell me about Eric" I said. "What about him?" "Were you friends?" "Yeah, I guess." "What sorts of things did you do together?" I asked. "You know. Get drunk and pick up girls." "Were you with him the night he died?" "No, I hadn't seen him in a couple of weeks." I stared at him for a second. "A couple of weeks? Are you sure about that? We have statements from several other people that you were both at Carl's on the night of the fourteenth." "Right. Yeah. I forgot about that. I was distracted, if you know what I mean." "You mean fucked up on drugs and banging underage girls? Yeah, I know what you mean."

"It wasn't like that" he mumbled. "What was it like? Describe it for me." "What do you mean? What are you asking me?" "Forget it. Let's move on. What about the time before? What did you and Eric do?" "I don't know. Stuff."

I sat back in my chair and just looked at him for a moment. I needed to be clear where this was headed. "I gotta tell you, Denis, right now I like you a lot. You know what it means when a detective says "I like you." It doesn't mean we're going to become buddies. What it means is I like you for the crime. You did it and I'm going to prove you did it. Now, quit being a shit and talk to me." He shifted in his chair. "We went on a trip the weekend before." "Who?" I asked. "Me, Eric, and Dave." "Where did you go?" "The Dalles." "Why?" Denis didn't answer. "Why did the three of you go to Eastern Oregon?!" Denis shook his head to himself. "You better tell me. This is only going to get worse" I demanded. "I'd like to get a lawyer now. That's my right, isn't it?" "Why? Are you guilty? Only guilty people need lawyers." He wasn't to be swayed. "I want a lawyer."

END TAPE

You clever bastard. I should have known it was you. The puppet master pulling the strings. Your vampire image didn't bother to appear but I already saw you in their eyes. You watched the mistakes made. The tragedy unfold. And you thought it was funny as hell.

CHAPTER FIFTY-EIGHT

"Why are you here?" I asked. My visitor was uninvited and unwelcome. "Well?." She looked down at the floor searching for an answer. "I just wanted to say I'm sorry." It was young Allison Thurman, confused little girl, come to make her apology. "Alright, accepted. Now, please leave."

I thought about asking how she even knew my address. I assumed she had gotten it from Julie. She played the innocent well. There were tears in her eyes. Not too much to make it seem forced. "Really. I don't know what I was thinking. I guess I thought it would be funny." "It wasn't" I responded. "But it's already over and done. How about we both just move on?"

Given the things that had transpired and the things I had heard from Julie, it all seemed a little absurd. So much importance placed on such a trivial prank. I started to wonder if I had been over-reacting.

"Can I come in for a second?" she asked. "Why?" "Please" she pleaded softly. It was almost too perfectly played to be convincing. Against my better judgment I showed her in. Her eyes scanned my cluttered apartment. "It's not like I thought it would be" she said. I ignored her statement. I was growing increasingly impatient. "Allison, why are you here?

You said you were sorry. I believe you. There's nothing more to be said." She nodded her head in agreement but didn't want to leave. "Shouldn't you be in school?"

She explained to me how second period was open. They called it Study Hall but that meant nothing. It was time for students to do whatever they liked. They didn't even bother to take attendance.

"I erased them" she said. "I made copies and was going to send your photo to my friends. But I erased them instead." My heart starting racing and the embarrassment that would have caused. I can only imagine the ridicule. Julie had assured me there were not others. Maybe that's what she meant. Allison had made copies but erased them.

I needed to be sure. This was trivial but not. I grabbed Allison roughly by the arm. "Are there more copies of that photo or not?" "NO! That's what I just said. Now let me go." I looked in her eyes. I chose to believe her. It was preferable to worrying about things I couldn't control. "You should go" I said. But Allison didn't move. She took a seat at the table.

"Fine. Then maybe I'll go and just leave you here" I said. She seemed to like that idea and then explained why. "That would be fun. I could go through all your things. I can only imagine what I might find." That did the trick. My anger took over. I grabbed her and shoved her to the door. "Alright, alright. I'm going" she said. I made sure and pushed her along.

I was done playing games. At least of that sort. Allison was a dangerous little child. Apologies were threats. Promises were lies. She was an exercise in sexual terrorism. But I defused the incident and reduced the charges. Just a simple assault on my quiet morning.

"Get the fuck out of here, Allison, and don't ever come here again. If you want to talk more, we do it at the station." "It was Julie's idea" she said. "What was?" "That I come by and apologize." "It was a bad one. I'll tell her so later." She grinned that grin. An all knowing smile. "You guys are good together" she said.

CHAPTER FIFTY-NINE:

I told Julie about Allison's guest appearance. She apologized for her involvement. She kept telling me how Allison wasn't a bad girl. She was just going through a lot, right then. I didn't want to hear it and turned the conversation toward the issue at hand. Julie and I had gone a long way together during our nights of sex and candles. We had reached a delicate point where trust had been developed. But it only applied in bed. When it came to knowing one another, we had both been protective. Getting too personal might confuse the issue.

I picked up little details, here and there, about this woman who brought me so much pleasure. She had grown up in Long Island. The "Five Towns" as she called them. I guess they weren't that far from Manhattan. She was a lousy student in school and always got into trouble. Minor stuff. Nothing involving the police. Only later did she straighten out and get her act together. Law school was just a default choice. She said again and again how she didn't really like it but it just sounded so logical. A well-respected woman with a lucrative career. It certainly sounded better than waitressing.

When it came to boyfriends, she made a point of saying she had only been in love once. She was only sixteen and he was the same. They had gone out until the end of high school. She went to Syracuse and he went to Pomona. A long-distance thing would never have worked out. They called it quits and stayed in touch. Then he got married. His new wife forbid him to talk to his ex's.

"That must have pissed you off" I said. "It did. I thought that was really lame. I'm pissed that he went along with it." "You can understand it though. How his wife would be threatened by someone like you." "Someone like me, meaning what?" "Someone that her husband had once been in love with." "We were kids." "That makes it worse. "That's ridiculous. How can people be so damn stupid?"

She asked about my girlfriends past. I think it was more out of politeness than real interest. I told her the names and how long I had gone out with each. I even told her about my years with Liz. "Five years?" she said with surprise. "So, why didn't you marry her?" "I didn't think I was ready." "Guys are never ready." She had a point and I admitted guilt. She hit me with another theory. "Was she boring in bed?" she asked. "No, she was great." "So, why didn't you marry her again?" She was just giving me grief but it was a question I had asked myself on many a drunken occasion. "Because it didn't feel right."

It's then I learned that Julie had been married once. It was when she was twenty-four. "I thought I wanted the whole house and kids fantasy." Incongruous images pulsed through my brain. I tried to picture her pushing a stroller or making home-baked cookies. It was too much of a mismatch with the woman I knew.

"What made you finally realize you made a mistake?" I asked. "I got pregnant." "You have a kid?" I asked. My shock couldn't have been greater. "No, I miscarried." She trailed off into silence. The memories still haunted her of all that she had lost. A reminder of things better forgotten. She left the story incomplete and retreated into bad jokes about the weather.

CHAPTER SIXTY:

"Percy Kindle got arrested. He got too close to the playground. They sent him back inside." Gillian was gloating. "I hated that creep. I don't know why they ever let those perverts walk the streets." I was sure it was just information. Gillian's Longview suspect arrested for a different crime. All the same, I couldn't help feeling that Gillian was harassing me.

We were headed to the hospital. We got the doctor's Ok. Natasha was fit for questioning. The harder part was getting the task force's permission. As we stepped into the hospital my senses were assaulted. Chemicals and illness. Human decay. The false ceiling hallways reminded me of the morgue. The resting place of John Doe/Adonis, more formally known as Eric Thurman. How far we'd all come from those happy vampire days. How much more still lay in store.

Natasha was awake. Her lawyer was present. A man wearing a suit from J.C. Penny. Her prints had been taken. Her identity confirmed. Her name wasn't Natasha but Natalie Holt. She had a long history of abuse. Mostly receiving. She'd been beaten and molested as a child. She'd been without real parents since age thirteen. Foster homes and shelters were juggled until she was released at eighteen. An adult who had been seriously damaged.

After her independence, there was no record of activity for many years. Just a change of address to Seattle. She'd worked retail for a living. Mostly men's furnishings. Her employers thought she was a hard worker. "How are you feeling, Natalie" Gillian asked. "My name's Natasha." "Alright, Natasha. We understand you've been read your rights and understand the charges against you. Is that true?" She nodded. "Good. Why don't you tell us what happened that night at the motel?" She looked at him with hate. "Why don't you shove your badge and gun up your ass?"

Gillian kept dancing. She was already done. This was just normal routine. The truth would soon win out. "Natasha, you've already been identified by the man you lured to the hotel. He also saw you in an SUV that fits the description of a vehicle at another crime scene." Natalie remained quiet. Mr. J.C. Penny soon stepped in. "It seems to me, detectives, you don't have proof of anything here. What exactly is Natalie's crime supposed to be? Meeting a man in a motel?"

"It must have hurt" I said. "Cutting your wrists like that? Why did you do it?" "I was frightened" "Why? If you're innocent then you have nothing to fear." A strange moment passed. I swear she laughed. "Do you really believe that?"

Gillian moved the conversation on and told her to help herself. We had more on the case than she knew. Her prints had been lifted at two murder scenes. Emails had been traced to three of the victims. It was all forensic evidence but it all added up. All the same, a confession was required. Anything less would be accepting defeat.

"Natasha" Gillian said. "Now is the time to help yourself out. If you make our lives easier, we'll go easier on you. But if you wait until we prove the case without your cooperation, you'll probably get the needle." Threatening someone with death who had tried to commit suicide wasn't the best of strategies. I think Gillian said it out of habit. "I'll take that chance." "Yeah, so, if it doesn't matter. Why don't you tell us who you were talking with in that SUV?"

"Detectives, my client has already answered these questions, many times over. Your colleagues have already been through all this with her." "Well she hasn't been through it with me." Gillian kept at it. The full court press. Natalie's lawyer shut him down at every turn. Natasha remained uncooperative.

As we left the hospital Gillian fumed. "If those assholes had let me have first crack at her, she would have talked." "You really believe that?" I asked. "Yeah, I fucking believe that! Those FBI pussies treated her with kid gloves. Like they expected her to just be really nice about everything and spill because they said please." He was probably right, I didn't really know. In spite of trying otherwise, I didn't feel very invested.

Natalie was never mine. She was something created to fill space on a TV screen. Even if she confessed it wouldn't bring any peace. There was something underneath. Something horrible and grey. Flesh from a rotting corpse.

CHAPTER SIXTY-ONE:

Hiss. Crackle. Pop. The mind was playing tricks.

REWIND

"Where are the guns, Dave?" I asked. "What guns?" "Your pal, Worm, told us about your trip to the gun show. What did you do with the guns?" "I don't know what you're talking about" he insisted. "Where are the goddamn guns?!" "There aren't any." "Where are they, Dave?" "I really don't know what you're talking about. What guns? I don't have any guns."

I suddenly got very quiet. "So, the Worm lied? We're going to find them anyway. At this very second, there's police at your house with a warrant to search it. So, why don't you just tell me?" "You can't do that" he protested. "Yes, we can. We are." "Whatever. You're not going to find anything." He seemed far too sure of himself. "Yeah? You certain about that? You better be." Dave just grinned.

A change-up in moments. Recall blur. Emily appeared before me. "What's so funny?" she asked. "Nothing. Nothing at all" I said. "Have a pint of the double IPA. The world will be a happier place." "No, I can't" I said. "Gillian was right."

"About what?" "Me." A horrible admission but one that needed to me made. It felt right to finally say it. "No, he wasn't" she said. I wanted to believe her but wasn't sure that I could. All the same I was glad she had disagreed.

REWIND. CUE TAPE.

Hiss. Crackle. Crackle. The fires already burned. I was returned to The Cube. The Time of the Worm. Interrogation on a Friday afternoon. "Did Eric tell you what it was all for?" I asked. "No. I kept asking. He just said he thought it would be cool to have them." "And why did you help him?" "Because I'm his friend." "That's it? Nothing else motivated you? He didn't pay you or give your drugs or anything?" "No." "You're lying" I said. The Worm reconsidered. "He did promise he would try to hook me up with someone." "Who?" "Some slut named Janelle. He said she could be a really good time."

Pop. Crackle. Crackle.

FREEZE FRAME:

Allison.

Allison.

Allison.

Cue shot. Slow motion smile. "You have his eyes" I told her. "I'm not my brother" Allison said. "How can I be sure?" The question hung there unanswered.

END SEQUENCE.
DRINK MORE.
ENGAGE IN SELF-PITY.
PASS OUT.

CHAPTER SIXY-TWO:

Gillian and I went back to The Cube. Natasha's resistance had soured his mood. We walked off the elevator into the familiar swamp heat. H/VAC doing its usual thing.

Gillian went to the break room and got a soda. I returned to my desk. Hersh was there working diligently. The kid just never gave up. "How'd it go?" he asked. "Shitty. She's not going to give it up easily" I said. "You'll still make the case though, right?" "Oh, yeah, there's probably enough already to get her convicted on a couple of the bodies." "So, what's the problem then?" "Gillian wants it all. Full confession to thirteen or more dead. There is no other ending for him." Hersh just shook his head as I watched Gillian pout in the break room.

"How's your day going?" I asked. He seemed shocked that I asked. "Alright. I checked into kids like you said." "Anything?" "Nothing." "Sorry I sent you down the rabbit hole." "No, it was a good thing to have checked into. I should have thought of it myself." I admired Hersh's attitude.

"I did get some more information on Radovich that was interesting." "Yeah, what's that?" "He had a reputation for playing hard ball. A real nasty character when it came to influencing people." "What do you mean?" "His lobbying efforts included flat-out bribes, blackmail, visits from prostitutes, drugs, whatever it took." "And you're just learning this now?" "Well, yeah. It's not the kind of thing people talk about voluntarily. You know?"

I walked away trying to hide my disgust. I was dumbfounded. Hersh couldn't be that incompetent. I entered the break room and found Gillian sitting alone. I told him what I had just heard. Went on about how disgusted I was that it took them this long to get a take on Radovich. Gillian didn't seem to care. "Do you have any idea what sort of enemies that could have made Radovich?" I asked. "Of course I do. So what?" he said. "Look, it's not your case and it's not mine anymore, either. Let Hersh and whoever figure it out. We have our own problems." He went on complaining about how frustrated he was that he hadn't been able to break Natasha.

I told him something about it all still didn't feel right. Eric's death didn't fit the bill. Gillian let loose. "What is it with you? You're on every case and none at all. You've spent months digging around into everybody's business and haven't come up with one substantial thing." I was too shocked to respond. Gillian wasn't through.

"I know you're a good detective. But you've been a fucking mess on this Thurman thing from the beginning. Every time I get us pointed in the right direction you just go off on some weird tangent involving high school kids or something. It's just fucked and I'm sick of it, OK? The C of Ds was ready to yank you a month ago. The only reason he hasn't is that I keep telling him how helpful you've been building the case on our NBK pair. But I'm done covering your ass. Get your shit together and help me build a case on Natalie or just fuck off and leave it alone." I could tell from his expression that he wasn't lying. In anger there is honesty.

"Why did it take this long for you to talk to me if that's the way you feel?" He laughed a laugh that couldn't be less kind. "You don't think I've been trying, Dudek? How many times have I told you something and you needed me to say it again and again before you finally realized what I meant? It's like talking to an Alzheimers patient or something." I remembered that time in the nasty English place off the 5. The discussion that seemed to have gaps. I wondered how many other times it had occurred. A failure to process language as the brain struggled for balance.

"I can't believe I'm saying this" Gillian said. "But maybe you should see a shrink. If you pay cash and keep it off your insurance, it would never get back to the Department." "A shrink?" "Yeah, a shrink. See a counselor or something to talk about whatever weird shit it is you've been dealing with." I felt myself blinking. A spastic reaction. "And watch the drinking. I know it's just beer but it's not helping you any to be downing so many pints."

He left it at that and walked back toward his desk. I sat at the table as electric hum haunted the room. Grief overcame me as I mourned my loss. The death of my identity as skilled detective.

CHAPTER SIXTY-THREE:

White, rectangular tower, thrust high into the tiny Portland skyline. Crowds gathered impatiently for the MAX and busses along Pioneer Square. I walked into the pink granite lobby. Took the elevator up to the twelfth floor. Cleary, Thompkins and Partners.

The waiting room was filled with Le Corbusier. Not the cheap kind but those with full pedigree. Authentic reproductions of furniture for the masses. A receptionist sat behind a huge desk. Dark wood veneer and brass letters remind the forgetful of the place they have come to visit. The receptionist asked me politely to state my business. I told him I was there to see Julie.

"She's not answering her phone at the moment, would you like to take a seat?" Black leather and chrome surrounded my tired body. I mindlessly picked up a heavy brochure from the coffee table. An award winning piece of marketing material from one of the town's many design firms. Baker. Bartley. Barking. I tried to remember the name of Dom's boss. Barting. I found her profile. An unflattering photo included. Overweight and over-worked. A University of Oregon Grad. She probably wore an "O" on her fat ass.

Specialties listed were too confusing to clarify. It had something to do with the public good.

"You're early" Julie said. I was taken aback by her ability to blend in. A total chameleon in perfect attire. Not a trace of the woman I enjoyed so thoroughly. "Sorry." "Wait a few more minutes, I have to finish something up." As she walked away I stared for a little too long. The black pants she was wearing couldn't make her body disappear.

I turned my attention out the floor to ceiling windows. Grey skies had parted for a bit of sun before the dark set in. Mt. Hood could be seen in the distance. It was a pretty place, this town of Portland. Hopefully a few murders wouldn't bring it down.

I sat back in the chair and prepared for the night. Drinks, dinner and entertainment. It would be one of our first attempts at a more traditional date. I let my mind turn to visions of possibilities. Lustful yearnings for a perfect ending.

"Hey, I'm ready" she said. I still couldn't get over her look. A quiet little secretary who fetched the coffee. "So, where are we going?" she asked. I told her about Beast. A place that had gotten rave reviews. Our reservation wasn't until seven which gave us time to kill. I suggested we go back to her place. She told me "no" that would just have to wait. We'd go have some drinks for a couple hours, instead.

We went to a place that predated us both. The beer was good but extremely expensive. The crowd was depressing. The men all looked identical, wearing their shades of tan and blue. The women weren't doing that much better. It was a restaurant that had been around since the nineteen fifties. From the look of it, some of the patrons were too.

I watched an exchange with befuddled amusement. A woman in her thirties at the bar. She was coming on strong with a man in his sixties. Laughing at his jokes far too loudly. "Is she a hooker?" I asked. "Kind of." "What does that mean?" "You really don't get out much do you?" "Not really." "She's not a hooker, just looking for a patron to support her art." It took me a minute to figure out what Julie meant. My brain was still feeling a little off. Then it all came together as I kept watching the exchange. A woman past her sell-by date making a desperate bid to meet a man of means.

Julie explained to me that it was a tradition of this place. Somewhere women went to introduce themselves to rich men. It was kind of funny but quite a bit more sad. The woman at the bar seemed to get her man. "It's nothing that hasn't been going on for centuries. Women are attracted to money and power like men are attracted to big tits." I was surprised at Julie's candor which, by now, I shouldn't have been. In addition, what she said made complete sense.

Hours later we were both praising the meal at Beast. The food and wine had both excelled. It's then that she told me a bit of news in her life. Something of real significance. "I think I'm going to move back to the East Coast" she said. "I've had enough of the rain and I miss my family." I didn't know what to say. I certainly wasn't happy about the news. I was enjoying things quite as they were.

"When?" "I don't know. Not right away or anything. Maybe a year from now. Portland has run its course." "What about the derby?" I asked. "I'm getting too old. Seriously. My body just can't take it the way it used to." "When did you decide this?" I asked. "I've been thinking about it for months now. I'm just waiting to finish out the season." She could tell I was upset and seemed to like it. I guess she enjoyed the thought that she would be missed. "Don't worry, you'll get your money's worth before I go. Especially, if you keep taking me to places like this."

She kept her word. At least for the evening. Maybe the discussion had made us both more aware that the arrangement was finite. Soon things would need to come to an end.

CHAPTER SIXTY-FOUR:

It was a note by note refrain of a previous tune. But this time it wasn't about grief. I sat in The Cube feeling sick from the stench. Hersh was hard at work across the aisle. A man walked off the elevator looking determined but confused. He asked for something at the front desk. My phone rang and I watched the desk clerk speak. "There's a man here to see you. He says it's about the NBK case."

I could easily have sent him away. Another curiosity monger or member of the press. There were no new bodies to claim. So, I dismissed that possibility off hand. This man was here for something else.

As I got near him, the possibility grew. It couldn't really be this easy. Although I was reluctant, I shook his hand. Introductions were made as usual.

"I'm Bill Prodsky. Are you one of the detectives on the serial killer case?" "I'm one of them. The rest are actually back up in Seattle. What can I do for you?" "But you're one of them?" "Yes, I'm officially attached to the case. What can I do for you?" "I'm Natalie's boyfriend. I'd like to confess."

My head went dizzy with what he said. I told myself it was just another fool. Another confession about waffles and wheelbarrows or spacemen telling him what to do. There had been dozens on the case because of the notoriety. I usually pawned them off to someone else.

I took him into a room for interrogation. I made sure I also read him his rights. He declined counsel and said he just wanted to start talking. The tale he told was an essay in psychosis.

He had met Natalie ten years ago. From the beginning he knew she was the one. She asked him to prove his love to her by killing. He wasn't inclined to say "no." It had started in the Midwest. They had met in Detroit. Some small bar in a suburb called Royal Oak. She'd lure the men with promises of sex. Bill would kill them once there. Natalie loved to watch the men suffer.

She claimed that it wasn't a sexual thing. It was about revenge and justice. She told Bill that any man sick enough to go for anonymous sex in motels didn't deserve to live. Bill, on the other hand, got off on the thrill. Natalie always fucked him right there by the body. They knew all about DNA and were careful about not leaving evidence.

I asked him about Eric but ended up focused on Ronaldo instead. He knew all the details including the ones not released to the press. His confession was more than credible. He knew far too much about it. He was clearly connected to the crime. When it came to Eric, he knew quite a bit less but I knew better than to keep pressing. I couldn't screw this up with my own obsessions.

As this was going on, decisions were made. The C of Ds declined to notify the task force until after things had begun. He'd later tell them he had assumed the confession was false. Just another whack-job seeking glory. By the time we realized we had the actual killer, the confession had already begun.

I had the case file at hand, including the photos. I ran through them all one by one. I picked out a photo and asked Bill straight out. "Did you and Natalie kill them?"

"Scott Pinket, Detroit 2002? "Yes."

"Doug Timmons, Detroit 2003?" "Yes."

"Mason Whitney, Detroit 2004?" "Yes."

"Charlie Riggs, Chicago 2004?" "Yes."

"Melvin Howard, Orlando 2006?" "Yes."

"Dean Miller, Atlanta 2006?" "Yes."

"Tyrell Watson, Atlanta 2006?" "Yes."

"Craig Whittier, Boston 2009" "Yes."

"Frank Potanalli, Boston 2009? "Yes."

"Mitch Bloom, New Hampshire 2010?" "Yes."

"David Manning, Boston 2010?" "Yes."

"Eric Thurman, Portland 2012?" "Yes."

"Ronaldo Thomas, Seattle 2012?" "Yes."

I closed the folder. "You missed a bunch" he said. I pulled out a notepad and got ready to write. My head was still processing events as he spoke. By the time he had finished, four hours later, my hand had cramped up badly. There were eleven more victims, twenty-four total.

"Bill, I've got to ask you something." "Shoot" he said, as friendly as can be. "Why did you come in today and confess? I don't get the feeling your conscience is bothering you and you needed to unload." "Conscience? That has nothing to do with it." "What is it then?" I asked. "I didn't want Natalie taking all the credit."

CHAPTER SIXTY-FIVE:

When I walked out of the interrogation room, I was met with thunderous applause. A large crowd had watched the proceedings. Among them was the C of Ds who said "Thank God you didn't fuck it up" with a smile. Gillian was also among them. Members of the task force had flown down by helicopter the moment they were told of Bill. A few looked put out that it had ended this way. That they hadn't solved the case with their own brilliant leg work. Most however just seemed relieved. They were pleased that it had all come together.

Gillian walked up to me. He was shaking his head. "You lucky bastard. He really just walked in and started talking?" "Pretty much." "You lucky bastard" he repeated with even more force. It wasn't a kind remark. I made sure to point out that I knew I was just the secretary. A man simply taking notes. It had been their hard work, not mine, that had assembled the file used to guide the confession.

"You should be happy" I told Gillian. "That a mass murderer is off the streets? Sure" he said. "No, that he named Eric Thurman among his victims." It was as close as I would ever come to saying I might have been wrong. "Yeah, I guess." I was losing my sympathy. Gillian was being a prick. Getting a good break always mattered as much as the rest. He was just angry he wasn't the one who caught it.

I made conversation with the others about how it had played out. How this man had just confessed to twenty-four murders. During my tales, Bill was led away by the Feds. Arguments ensued about how the case would be handled from here. I was exhausted and needed a beer. There were many offers to buy.

I wanted to interrogate Bill further. But the task force had it covered. They promised to investigate the details thoroughly. They claimed that they had no more interest than I about Bill and Natalie claiming victims that belonged to others. They were comforting words but I knew it wasn't so. People wanted these cases done and gone. They'd been unsolved and nagging good cops across the country. Victims families had tortured themselves with ugly theories about their loved ones. Imagined slasher film endings for their kids. Thanks to Bill, it could finally be put aside. Ancient history and television fodder. Everyone could move on in peace.

When Natalie was told what Bill had done, she couldn't believe he was that stupid. Bill had ruined it all. She couldn't understand why he would do such a thing. Why he would just walk in and give his confession. Both of them would probably get the needle now. She'd attempted suicide only to be condemned to death. Bill's ego hadn't allowed otherwise.

CHAPTER SIXTY-SIX:

A single photograph destroyed it all. There'd be no more nights of exploring desires that terrified. Deviant needs would remain unsatisfied for all parties concerned. Now, there were only lies.

It started so casually. Most of these things do. I wanted a photograph to leer at. I didn't have such a thing. I had never asked. Maybe because I knew she was a ghost. A mental configuration of want and pleasure. A projection that would fade in the light.

I trolled the company website. Black tuxes and little dresses. It was a formal affair. A holiday bash thrown by the bosses. Every law firm had one. It was there I saw a man that I recognized. Elegant and rich with power. Hersh had posted him on his board. Not a body but a victim of sorts. He was connected to Radovich. This man had been one of his targets. An ear to bend. A policy to pressure. His name was Senator Alvin.

Alvin was the Chairman. Head of the Commission. A state panel he controlled decided the future of the South Waterfront project. Casinos and gambling. Restaurants and hotels. Hundreds of millions had been bet on the outcome.

If the only photo had been taken a few seconds later. Or framed two feet to the left. Then I never would have known. I could have continued to be blind and enjoyed my ignorance. But it was a composition with many layers. Within image lies truth.

It showed Julie in conservative black. She was as tempting as could be. She was standing in the background and looking at the Senator. It wasn't an ordinary glance. I knew the expression well and all that it implied. The Senator belonged to her.

The confrontation took place in her living room. Classic rock played on her radio. John Lennon was on as I walked through the door. It turned out to just be a commercial. Kisses were exchanged. Drinks were offered. I soon got to the point. "How long have you known Senator Alvin?" "Who?" "Don't lie to me. I saw the photograph on your company website." "What were you doing on that?" "Looking for a photo of you." "Why?" "Because I wanted one. Now, answer the question."

Julie took a defensive position and sat in a chair. She was more than a little angry. "Well?" Her expression was one of superiority. Condescension dripped from her words. "You're hilarious. I really don't know who you mean. We had a bunch of guests at the holiday party. That's why they have it.

Believe it or not, they don't go around introducing everyone to the paralegals."

"Don't lie to me!" I yelled. "Are you jealous? Is that why you're acting like such an ass?" "Answer the question." "What if I did know him?" "Are you admitting that you know him?" "No, I'm not. I'm just trying to clarify our relationship. As far as I knew, it wasn't exclusive. Are you saying otherwise?" "That's not why I'm asking." "What about Emily?" "What?" "What about Emily? It's pretty obvious from the way you talk about her that you're in love with her. So, she's the one you love and I'm the one you fuck. Is that the way it works?"

Julie looked like she was enjoying the battle. I told her I was kept informed on the Radovich case. The questions I was asking were about the investigation. It was official police business. Her response was undiluted. Pure in its disdain. "You mean the way your questions about Eric were?" She stood up and walked towards me. "You know, it's not the invasion of privacy that bothers me nearly as much as the hypocrisy. If you want to hear about my personal life, in full, graphic detail, because you get off on it, just come out and say that." "That's not why I'm asking." "Are you sure?" "Yes. Just cut the shit. Alright? So, you did have an affair with him?" "No. I didn't. I don't know the man." She walked to the door and opened it. "Now, get out."

Her words and actions were filled with deceit. She was full of secrets and information that could damage. I knew it right then, at that very moment. The truth appeared before my eyes. Julie could no longer be trusted.

CHAPTER SIXTY-SEVEN:

I sat in the chair drinking chain coffee. We had decided to meet in the Pearl. It was crowded with shoppers and Northwest trophy wives. A spattering of hipsters were added to the mix. I watched her from a distance. Blond hair in the wind. Sweat did nothing to diminish her beauty. She rode her bike through traffic. She waited too long and got stuck behind a streetcar. Normally she'd glide on and go right past. This time, there wasn't enough room to get through.

She arrived with a grin. She seemed glad to be there. Her happiness always surprised me. Somehow, I expected it to be more of a chore. She needed some books on wedding planning. She was taking the task on herself. We went to Powell's, a block of saved words. She was sure to find what she needed.

Her smile was contagious. My eyes wanted to travel. To comb over her entire figure. But I tried to be polite. The good, supportive friend. I focused on my surroundings instead. Lines at the counter. Aisles of books. A mix of the new and used.

"So, are you coming to the wedding?" she said. It caught me off guard. "I didn't know that I was invited." "Of course you are" she said. "But only if you want to be." Her understanding of the situation made me self-conscious. I almost felt embarrassed. "You don't have to tell me now. You can think about it. Billy and I both want you there but I would understand if you don't want to." I wondered how much she really understood. If she could see inside my thoughts. I needed to be careful. To not cross a line. There was a script that needed to be followed.

"No, I'll be there." She was relieved by my answer. She gave me a hug. Her fear of complications had been misguided. "Great. Are you going to bring your rollergirl?" I considered several answers knowing that I would have to explain. I went with the simplest one. "I don't think so. I think we're through." "Really? What happened?" Lies and manipulation. Deceitful practices. How would I describe the situation? I said "things had run their course" and left it at that. She could tell I didn't feel like explaining.

Then Emily said I could always take Angie. Her tattooed co-worker at the bar. Bubbly as she may be, Angie was a heartbreaker. She had just dumped her latest beau. Maybe that's what she should have had inscribed on her body instead of poetic quotations. A warning to potential lovers. "Use at Own Risk" might have worked.

"Does Angie even read poetry?" I asked. "I don't know. Why?" "That one tattoo she has." "Which one. The

Celtic cross?" "No, the quote from T.S. Elliot." "Oh, right. The cross. I'm so stupid. No. I don't know." Emily was more absorbed in the books than in our moment of conversation. An old lady looked at us and gave us a warm smile. I'm sure she assumed that we were a couple.

I excused myself to go up to the third floor. Books on film and music. Emily said that was fine. She wouldn't be long. I searched for a biography on Wire. I failed to find it or anything interesting about the people who created music. I soon moved over to photography. I scanned through a book of decayed buildings by a German Photographer who had gone to Detroit. Portraits of the death of a city.

I put it aside and found a book of nudes. It was more pornography than art and the price was raised accordingly. Enjoyable women in alluring poses on every single page. I got embarrassed when someone saw me looking.

The next book was more tasteful. Black and white nudes made it seem more like art. This wasn't material for short-term thrills. The women in this work were exquisite. Abstract and distant from the living. They no longer felt of flesh and blood.

I saw Emily appear with a stack of books in her hands. "Looking at smut?" she said. It took me a second to recover. My thoughts were not where they should have been. She gestured to the book in my hand. I told her she had it wrong. The smut was on another floor. It was in an aisle marked "True Crime."

CHAPTER SIXTY-EIGHT:

She was lying face down. Her body unclothed as if challenging you not to give into instinct and forget rational thought. Every tattoo seemed precise as if she had been born with each. Derby queen and dominatrix. Lover and liar. Blood poured from the place her face once was. It had been removed by a savage beating.

The usual zoo of chaos and floodlights. Julie's house was ablaze with activity. A man stood in the corner. He was handcuffed and naked. He was also covered in blood. His eyes had that look. A demonic possession. His soul had been taken long ago.

It was Senator Henry Alvin. Honored Chairman of the Commission. Husband and father of two young kids. He was too far gone to even stay covered. An animal after killing its prey. He stood in total silence. Not what I expected. I imagined him howling at the moon.

"What the fuck?" Gillian said. He was amazed by the scene. It was ugly, even for veterans like him. There was blood on the floor. Blood on the walls. Blood all over the heavy Spanish furniture. "Has he said anything?" I asked. "No, he's too far gone to get a word out." I looked at the Senator and remembered him in his tux. So elegant and poised. A man with considerable power. He was crying now. A child's sob. His mind was no longer functioning.

Paramedics injected him with something to keep him calm. Hersh flew across the room. "What the hell are you doing? We need to interrogate that man. Don't drug him up!" The paramedic said the man needed sedation. He was at risk for hurting himself and others. "A little late for that, don't you think?" Hersh replied. He nailed it with perfect timing.

Nothing felt real. It was kept at a distance. I just observed the scene unfold. My interactions were automatic. My mind was set to pause. "You know, after all these years I still don't get it" Gillian said. "What?" "How normal people end up doing sick shit like this. Tina said he even sodomized her after she was dead." I glanced again at her naked corpse. Her body was still perfect. Lovely curves. Smooth skin. A poem to all things erotic. "Did you know her or something?" Gillian asked. "Yeah, I knew her. Her name was Julie Landsdown." "Your Julie?" "Yeah. My Julie."

I told him that I needed a minute. He said he understood. Just another casual falsehood. Alvin was clothed and led away. I saw the crowd gathering outside. Johanson was one of the uniforms on the perimeter. I tried to give him a smile. He either ignored me or didn't see the effort.

For some inexplicable reason I thought of St. Piss and his calling card with pre-paid minutes. Maybe that's when it began. My separation from the living. They all felt different, now. Gillian, Hersh and all the rest. Trapped in another world. A universe parallel to my own existence. They only saw the surface situation. The facts, the evidence, the gathering of material to convict. They were just tourists in a place like this.

CHAPTER SIXTY-NINE:

I was allowed to lead the interrogation. Hersh had no problem being the second. I was more experienced and he understood how much more I knew about the murder than he. However, I had to make sure my history was obscured. My personal relationship with the victim made me a liability in the eyes of some. What I was doing was against policy. It only happened because I had insisted that Gillian be complicit that events unfolded as they did.

ROLL TAPE

"How are you feeling Henry? I'm Detective John Dudek." "Who?" Alvin replied. "Detective John Dudek. I'd like to ask you a few questions. Do you want to tell me what happened?" He just stared at me.

"Henry, why did you kill her?" "She betrayed me." "How?" "She told me it was our secret. BITCH!" He yanked against his restraints. "Calm down, Henry. What did she do? Did she tell someone?" "She gave him photographs." "Who? Who did she give photographs to?" "Radovich. Jackal." "She gave compromising photos of you to Radovich? How do you know?" I asked. "He told me. Then she told me. She admitted it. Guilty." "When?" "Tonight. When..." He stopped himself. Stared at the walls. "When you, what? Henry?" His eyes suddenly met mine. "I killed her" he said. "You killed Julie Landsdown?" "Yes."

I gave him a moment for his mind to calm down. His words were obviously of great importance. "Why did you kill Julie, Henry?" I asked. "She gave them photographs." "She gave photographs to Radovich who tried to blackmail you with them? Did you kill him too?" He seemed to find my question off base. "No. They did." "Who did?" "The Mexicans" he said. I was thoroughly confused. "What Mexicans?" "They own three of the Indian casinos. Small ones." "That doesn't make any sense, Henry. Why would Mexicans own Native American Casinos?" I asked. "To launder money."

I had to take his statement at face value. "Do you have their names for me, Henry?" "Soto." "He killed Radovich?" I asked. "No. He had someone from Mexico brought up to do it." "Someone to kill him?" "Yes." "Did you get the name of that man? The man brought up from Mexico to execute Radovich?" "No."

I weighed the words he was saying against his savage brutality. The animal howling at the moon. There was a truth to them in spite of their source. A logic to every answer. "I'm still a little confused. Why was Radovich blackmailing you?" I

asked. "So South Waterfront would get approved and built."
"Why were the Mexicans so against that project?" "To protect
their own casinos."

I had just calmed him down and risked throwing it all
away. I needed to bring up the cause of his meltdown. "Let's
go back to Julie. How long have you known her?" "A year.
More." "When did you begin having a sexual relationship with
her?" "Eight months ago. I knew the first time I met her at the
law firm what sort of girl she was." "What sort was that?" I
asked. He didn't answer the question. I decided to just let it go.

"When did you find out she was blackmailing you?"
"Two weeks before they killed Radovich and his family. She
killed them." "Who killed them? I asked. "If she hadn't done
what she had done, those kids would still be alive." "Who?
Julie?" "Yes" he said. "Is that why you went to see her
tonight? You wanted to make her pay for getting the Radovich
children killed?" Henry looked confused. "What? No." "What
then? What made you go there tonight to see her?" I asked. "I
was going to warn her." "About what?"
"Soto told me she was becoming a threat. I went to warn her."
"But you hate her. Why would you care?" He looked at me
like I hadn't understood a thing. "I love her" he said.

I tried not to focus on the woman I knew. The one he
had left bleeding on the floor. I had to stay focused. To do my

job well. Hero cop above all else. "So, how did it go from that to the way things ended up, Henry?" He thought about his response before answering. "I remembered the photographs. I mean. I never forgot them but seeing her again. It was just too much. She betrayed me. She needed to pay." "So, you killed her. You killed Julie Landsdown?" He looked ready to leap at me from across the table. "Yes, I already told you that. Yes. Yes. Yes. I killed Julie Landsdown." "Calm down, Henry. You're doing great."

I gave him a moment to try to relax. "Why did Sako...?" He cut me off. "Soto" he corrected. "Right. Why did Soto think Julie was becoming a threat now? Wasn't she a threat already, back when she first gave Radovich the photos?" He looked me in the eye. "You" he said. "What?" His words seemed calm and measured. Designed for maximum effect. "He was afraid that she would tell you everything."

END TAPE

CHAPTER SEVENTY:

County Sheriffs served the warrants. Casinos were raided and searched. Alvin may have been unhinged but his facts proved correct. At least when it came to certain crimes committed.

I was present for one search, twenty miles from the coast. A small casino up in the mountains. The surroundings were white. Snow covered firs. It would have been beautiful except for the scars. A timber company leased much of the land for pennies on the dollar. They cut down huge swathes. Clear cutting. They claimed it was good for the environment.

The books were found and confiscated. They proved to be false. A set used for show, designed for misrepresentation. It took an entire team of computer forensics specialists to eventually track down the real story. It had been just as the senator described. A money laundering service. Mostly for profits made from drug sales in California. The casinos were run by the Mexicans.

Soto was picked up at his home. A modest place in Newport. He was read his rights and said very little. He just instructed someone to call his lawyer.

Like Gillian before him, Hersh was brushed aside the more wide-spread the tentacles spread. After it was established that it was cartel related, the FBI once again stepped in. No expenses were spared and a vast network was uncovered of alliances between Mexicans and others. Some casinos had gone willingly, some were forced, but there was an outcry from every corner. Some citizens used it as an example of how gambling promoted crime. Others claimed the exact opposite. Those people said that this story was evidence of why gambling should be more mainstream. Giant casinos should be run by public corporations. It was the small ones that were always dangerous.

In all of this great discovery, a girl's murder seemed trivial. It was as if she had never died. The Justice Department was more about the deals. Turning criminals into government witnesses. Soto, himself, agreed to such a thing. He said he would turn on his bosses back in Juarez. He even gave up the name of the hit man. But of course, he was never found. He had killed at least a dozen more but he was good at his job and well protected by others.

Senator Alvin had his own struggles. He wasn't qualified to be insane. After a series of interviews with psychologists, he was declared a rational man. His team of lawyers appealed the ruling. They technically lost but swayed public opinion. A plea bargain was agreed. He would serve ten years for second degree murder.

During his allocution he claimed to remember very little. He just remembered needing to see Julie. When he was shown the photos of his victim, bloody and mangled, he couldn't believe that he was the one who had done it.

As for my involvement, I had made a mockery of procedure. The prosecuting attorney told me repeatedly how thankful I should be that Alvin cut a deal. If it had gone to trial, all the details would have come out. Details about my relationship with Julie. As far as the department was concerned, they just wanted the whole thing buried.

Julie was cremated quietly. The roller derby league held an informal memorial service. It was in the basement of a well-known club. Videos were shown of Dom talking about the league. How the community of it had changed her life. A few of the girls cried. Most just got drunk. One briefly mentioned a counseling service if anybody needed it. I was invited but felt too awkward to go. I heard about it after it was over.

Gillian tried to be sympathetic, even supportive. He gave me a growler of his home-brewed IPA. Later, he invited me over and I took him up on his offer. It was good to be surrounded by life. His wife and kids made me feel quite at home.

Gillian grilled in the drizzle. The awning offered little protection. A wicked wind was blowing strong. It didn't matter to him. He was determined. It was grilled salmon all around. He asked how I was doing in that confidential tone. The one cops use to induce trust. I decided it was better not to get into the matter. The things I had been really thinking. Instead we talked about beer and sports. His kids were wound up and running around. His wife apologized as she had once before. I reminded Gillian how lucky he had it. He said that he knew he was blessed. He couldn't picture his life without them. He couldn't imagine going through it all alone.

CHAPTER SEVENTY-ONE:

The rain had come back in a major way. It was more Red Sea than Noah's Ark. But it took more than fierce downpours to keep me away from The Pig. I had important business to tend to.

Angie was still on duty. She was mercifully well-covered. I didn't want to think too much about her gallery of self-expression. She gave me a smile and launched into her story. So much drama about the break-up with her beau. I liked Angie a lot but I wasn't in the mood. I already had a chat show going on inside my head. She was just adding to the noise. When she finished her story, she asked how I was doing. I said I had never been better.

Forty minutes later, Emily arrived. I was already on my second pint. She gave me that look. The one that had hooked me. I still knew what I had to do. She recommended the pork chops and insisted I try them. I acquiesced to her demands. It's then that I told her I'd been thinking of Powell's. Of the conversation we'd had there.

"I've been thinking about it more" I said. "I don't think I'll be able to make it to the wedding." She stared at my beer. You could tell she was hurt. I hated to cause her such pain. She nodded her head, more to herself than me. "I'm really bummed to hear that. But I get it. I really do." The thing is that I believed her. She actually understood. Which made it that much more terrible. I wanted to be strong and be there for her on her big day. Instead I was being weak and melodramatic.

It got worse from there. I had more I needed to say. The words came spattered around the usual interruptions. I had thought about waiting until we could be alone. To have this conversation somewhere more private. My theory had been that this way was better. That the circumstances would mean less had to be explained. Maybe that was true but it was a questionable choice surrounded by requests for more ketchup.

"I think I should also stop coming here so much or spending so much time with you, in general" I said. It was a statement she did not expect. "Why?" "You know why." "But why now? Is it because I'm engaged?" she asked as if that could explain all that had happened. But maybe that was part of it. Maybe this whole time I had been living in a world of fantasy. A place in my imagination where I would lure her away. She would see that her true love had always been right in front of her. But John Hughes was nowhere to be found.

She wouldn't let up. "I think that sucks. We should talk about this more later. Come back after we close." "I'm not going to do that. This is hard enough. I really don't want to drag it out." She started to get angry. She wanted to talk it through. The customers wouldn't leave her alone. Iced-teas needed refilling. Table four needed another round. Everyone wanted her attention.

"You didn't answer my question" she said. "Why now?" I thought about it a second. I wasn't really sure. "I don't know. Maybe it has something to do with Julie. There's lot's going on with me right now." She almost snapped when a man asked her for a lemon to put in his Heff. She said she'd get to it in a minute. "Is that why? Because I've been so caught up in planning for the wedding, I've been a really shitty friend to you?" She had been preoccupied but that had been a blessing. The last thing I wanted was her sympathy.

I watched her walk away, tray in hand. Pork Belly and a pint of Pilsner. It was somebody's night to experience a small moment of bliss. Beer, food and good conversation. Maybe someday I'd be over her and we really could be friends. But right now, that was asking the impossible. She came back to the bar and apologized again. She blamed herself for not being there when I needed her. How could she be? She was still a member of that other world. The one that I was no longer a part of.

I paid my bill in full and said goodbye. I left her with one final suggestion. "You should play Billy Idol at the wedding." "Billy Idol?" "White Wedding. Great song." She laughed, in spite of her mood. "You're sick" she said, as I walked out the door. It was a nice way to say good-bye.

CHAPTER SEVENTY-TWO:

I went looking for Allison at Sacred Heart. I found her quickly enough. She was taking a break with a book in the library. A collection of interviews about the environment.

"Allison. I need you to come with me, please." She seemed a little nervous. "It's not raining right now, let's just step outside. We need to have a talk." I expected her to argue and put up a fuss. She didn't do any such thing in the least. She just smiled a little and grabbed her backpack. It was filled with materials for study.

We walked past a little courtyard with a crucifix made of wood. I kept walking further. I wouldn't say a word. At least not until I got her outside.

We walked out the door. "Where are you taking me?" she asked. "Just somewhere we can talk. I don't think you want anyone to hear this." I could tell from her face that she was both confused and frightened. I told her it was for her own protection.

The clouds had broken. Sunlight slanted through the gaps. It reminded me of a painting by Van Ruisdael. I spotted a bench back by the trees. I told Allison we should go there for our talk. I expected resistance. Once again I was wrong. Maybe she understood that it was her time.

She sat on the bench encircled by hedges. We were in the center of a formal garden. The flowers were ugly. They were still waiting for spring. The Virgin Mary needed a paint job. All the same, I appreciated the privacy. At least here they couldn't see us from the school.

I was surprised Allison was being so docile. She seemed more curious than annoyed. I finally said the difficult words I had come here to express. "Allison, I know what he did to you." "What who did to me?" "Your brother." "I don't know what you're talking about." "I know that he raped you."

Her expression changed to one of calculation and cunning. "That's disgusting. Why would you say something like that?" "Quit lying!" I yelled. She was taken aback. Tears came to her eyes. I was pulled from my anger by her youthful pose. The way she sat reminded me of a child.

"Allison, I'm trying to help you." She looked up at me with tears in her eyes. "I don't know what you're talking about." I put my hand under her chin and made her look into my eyes. "Yes, you do, Allison. He raped you."

A moment passed. It felt like an eternity. Finally, she broke down completely. Tears poured from her eyes. I gave her a few minutes to embrace her sadness. Facing the truth was a difficult business. Especially when it was so ugly.

"How do you know?" she asked. "We found Eric's computer along with everything else. He kept a very complete diary. A lot of it was about you." She shook her head as if that would destroy it. As if that would make reality, itself, alter to her needs. "He talked about the first time when you came home drunk. He bragged about how he had finally gotten you."

She kept shaking her head. It was starting to look mechanical. A bizarre amusement or animated sign. "Even that wasn't enough for him, though. Was it? He gave you ruffies next time. He even took pictures." She finally stopped her gestures of denial. She clamped her eyes closed to try to stop the crying. It was a battle she could never win. "Those were on his computer?" "Yes. He also sent them to Worm and Dave." The terror ran through her. It was hard to tell how much was the things that had been done to her and how much was the shame of others knowing. So much had been killed inside.

"Why didn't you tell your parents?" "They never would have believed me. Would you if your daughter came to you and said something like that?" "Yes. You also had the photos." She shook her head again. "No, I didn't. He showed them to me once, just to taunt me, but I could never find where he kept them." "You could have gone to the police." "Do you have any idea what that would have done to my family?"

I saw a group of girls leaving the grounds. They didn't look like Allison. They barely looked old enough to drive. I wondered what their problems were like. Unhappiness with teachers? Dissatisfaction with their bodies? Parents who pressured them too much?

"He said he was going to do it again. He said he was going to drug me again, tie me up, and wait for me to wake up. He said it would be much more fun if I was awake and knew what he was doing. That's exactly the way he put it. It would be more fun..." "Jesus" I muttered a little too loudly. "I believed him. That he was going to do it. He'd been after me since I was fifteen. It started with him saying he was just fooling around and didn't mean anything. Later though...He could be such a bastard. I hated him."

"Did you tell any of your friends?" She shook her head no. "So, how did it happen?" She told a story so sordid it made me ill. The details disgusted thoroughly. She had pretended to have negotiated a deal of sorts. Something Eric would go for. She had told him she was done fighting. She knew he could take her whenever he wanted. She was done resisting his attempts to have her. Tired of waiting for his next act of abuse. She offered to give in. But she said that it had to be on her terms. She wanted to be the one in control. Allison had learned about all of Eric's experiences and exactly how to appeal to his deviant nature. She had heard the stories and learned the details from Julie. Any discomfort Dom had about disclosing such things vanished in the smell of weed. Just two friends joking around.

Allison told Eric to check into a motel somewhere out in Gresham. He paid in cash and signed in using an assumed name. I questioned why he would do such a thing. Why he would go along with any of Allison's instructions. Eric wasn't stupid. Quite the opposite, in fact. He must have been suspicious that it was a trap. Her answer seemed credible, given the warped nature of the entire situation. "He thought the risk was worth the potential reward. A night with his little sister was something he had wanted for years."

Allison arrived at the motel twenty-minutes later. She had braced herself with drugs and alcohol to carry off the performance of her life. She had learned from Julie and knew what to do. She ordered him to take off his clothes. He had been trained well and was eager to comply. Being tied up was part of the thrill. He didn't even resist when Allison put the plastic bag over his head. She said it was to increase the intensity of his orgasm. Only when the oxygen ran out did he finally put up a struggle. But it was too late by then. Allison had him bound tightly. She refused to loosen her grip around the bag. A pig led to the slaughter. He was dead not thirty seconds later.

"Am I under arrest?" "No, but you will be. Probably before the end of the day. When they do it, don't say a word, OK?" She nods. "It's important you understand that. Don't say a word. Not to them. Not to your parents. Wait until you can talk to a lawyer." "Will I be sent to jail? I don't want to go to jail." "I don't know. You'll have to talk with your lawyer about that but the case is weak." "What do you mean? I did it." "Shut up. Just don't say that or anything else and listen to me, OK?" "Yes." "You have a documented history of abuse by your brother. Some pretty severe mitigating circumstances. You also have something else going for you. Somebody else already confessed to the crime."

I told her again just to maintain respectful silence. The police had people like me who would try to force a confession. The only person that could jam her up was herself. A guilty conscious could get her tried as an adult. Sent away for twenty years or more. If she played it right she could get off entirely. There was a very good chance that she would be acquitted. "And this conversation never, ever, took place. It would screw both of us if anyone ever found out." She nodded again as she ended the last of her tears. Eric had taken so much more than her body. The girl named Allison barely remained.

CHAPTER SEVENTY-THREE:

You sat in the shadows awaiting the debut. The world premier of your greatest masterpiece. Your unfinished symphony of hatred and violence. Something you had worked on for close to two years before your untimely death. Pitch perfect in detail. Masterful planning. You were a prodigy in the art of evil.

Your protégés had arrived. Dave and the Worm. They had prepared just as you had laid out. Diaries and diagrams, they couldn't screw it up. All they had to do was follow your instructions. The Worm helped with the set-up but left before the main act. Dave told him that he was a pussy. It really didn't matter. The real work had been done long ago.

It was a Tuesday afternoon. Partly cloudy and grey. Typical Portland weather. The students gathered in the cafeteria for the first shift of lunch. Today's special was fish tacos. There was also pizza. Mr. Gerber was the monitor. Mr. Just Say No. He was castigating some boys for running. It was dangerous he said. Someone could get hurt. There were at least two hundred kids in the room. Their ages ranged from eighteen to under thirteen. Just another day of bullying and failed math tests. Just another day at school.

Janelle got up from the table to get her usual Diet Pepsi. Her friends were harassing her for being a slut. They had heard about the parties she'd attended at PSU. All the things she'd done with Denis. She tried to play it off like it was all meaningless fun. She wasn't even sure why she'd done it.

The clock struck eleven forty-five. The timers were about to detonate. Placed in gym bags and knapsacks. Dave had put them against the column, just as Eric had drawn. A blueprint had been sketched. Placement determined. Maximum impact was required of each device. There were three bombs total. All built over months. You had learned your trade well, you hateful bastard. Bomb making skills had been passed down from the internet. Al-Qaida just one of many mentors. They were simple devices made of common ingredients. They proved to be highly effective.

The first blast occurred. Then the second and the third. Nails flew through the room at high speed. They were the ones Dave had bought at Home Depot. They weren't the right size. They were a little too large. But they still made effective shrapnel. Janelle had five rip through her body. Three in her lungs. One in her kidney. Another piercing her thigh. Pretty in Pink turned crimson. She didn't die right away. That would come eleven minutes later.

There were forty-one killed by the initial blasts. Those chosen few didn't even know what hit them. Suddenly, it had all just come to an end. There were others hit by the explosion. Limbs removed. Skin burned. Eyeballs blinded. The screams came from everywhere as the room filled with smoke. Nobody knew what was happening. Mr. Gerber stood brave trying to say no to his own death. A chunk of metal had punctured his liver. He tried to tell everyone to just stay calm. He told everyone it would be alright.

Students tried to exit through the emergency doors. The ones that lead right outside. Dave had sealed them shut with chain locks, five minutes earlier. He was disappointed he couldn't stay to watch. He wanted to see the panic inside. Like pilgrims in Mecca or those shoppers at Walmart, many would suffocate standing. They were packed so tightly they weren't able to breathe. The door handles bent from the force of pressure but the locks just wouldn't give way.

I can see your vampire smile as others flee into the halls. Anything to get themselves away from the carnage. You had made the calculations and determined the delay. The exact moment for your next little trick. The hallway they would exit through was already prepared. They fled the burning cafeteria down a single corridor. Hundreds jammed into the narrow path, hoping for escape. Your timing was off but only by seconds. Your goals were still achieved. Two more blasts from bombs in a locker. The one belonging to Denis, the Worm. The door of it ripped one of the jocks in half. So much for his plans to play football. More nails and shrapnel. A confined place called hell. Screams, confusion and mayhem. Many died right there. At least another twenty. Your goal of a hundred was already in sight.

Those that survived the bombs in the hallway emerged from the smoke. More than a few looked like zombies. Flesh had been seared. Limbs mangled beyond recognition. A few survivors would spend their lives as cripples.

Dave took a position at the end of the hallway just as your plan said. His body was pumped full of adrenaline. He had thought of this day for over a year but he had no idea how much he would enjoy it. You were both having a really good time.

That bitch Ashley emerged from the smoke and the fire. The cunt who rejected Dave at the Green Dragon. She was screaming so loud you could hear it over the chaos. Dave waited until she got a little closer. Then he pulled the trigger. A modified rifle. It was easy to make automatic. Dave sprayed Ashley with the bullets as if each were a kiss. He peppered her entire body. Pretty legs and lovely breasts. None of which she shared with him.

After she fell to the tiles, he moved the gun in a more precise and methodical way. Horizontal movements back and forth. A slight change in elevation each time. He sent a swarm of bullets, insects of death, down the hallway to attack. Their stings proved lethal. His technique quite effective. They ran right into the gunfire as if they wanted to hug it.

You couldn't believe their stupidity. You were finally proving your point. You were so much smarter than them. You loved how they kept coming. How they fell so easily into your trap. They figured it out but it took them so long. Morons one and all. They finally realized what they were doing. How they were running into a kill zone. They turned around and ran the other way.

Dave reloaded. There were plenty of clips left. Part of the mother lode you hit in the Dalles. He inspected the damage. Just for good measure, he shot Ashley again a few more times. She probably didn't even remember how badly she had treated him. All he had wanted was a little conversation. What he got was attitude instead. She thought she was so much better than him. He wasn't even worth the time to ignore.

The memory enraged him as he walked through the piles of the dead and wounded. He shot a few more in the head. A girl he didn't know was lying on the floor. She was twitching really strangely. It reminded him of the deer he had once hit by accident. That road by the cabin. He wondered if she appreciated how merciful he was being as he shot her again.

He heard a voice. It was loud and deep. A figure emerged from the smoke. It was the principal, Mr. Williams. Hands held high in the air. He begged Dave to stop what he was doing. He gave him words of reassurance that it would all be Ok. All he had to do was put down the gun. Dave answered with a bullet. Williams' offer of help was far too late to make a difference.

Dave strolled through the halls looking for stragglers. He disappeared around the corner. I imagined the bodies stacked one atop the other. A few squirming with their last bits of life. The alarm was shrill. The strobe lights flashing. I saw your skeletal figure silhouetted in the haze. I saw your face. Your look of satisfaction. You took pride in your student's fine work.

Miss Kamden with a K was hiding under a desk just waiting for it all to pass. She heard Dave walk in and held her breath. He saw her. There she was pleading. He admired her lips. Imagined the feel of them. He put the thought out of his mind and pulled the trigger. He had to stick to the plan.

Then Dave heard the sirens. It had all gone so quickly. The fun times always do. But you had provided one last flourish. A bit of flair and grandeur to end the final movement. Dave took a position on the second floor. A perch with quite a view. He watched them arrive, one after the other. Fire trucks, ambulances and police. There were no timers involved. This had to be done manually. It was a perfectly executed play. Dave waited until they gathered and built in numbers. He showed remarkable discipline. Then with a command from his cell phone he set off the remaining devices. The ones targeted at the first responders. The explosions were disappointing. He expected the cars to lift off the ground. Instead, it was more of a general blast. Not pretty but effective. Twenty-six more dead. You had exceeded expectations. Your total was now over a hundred and twenty.

Dave knew what was left. He wasn't scared in the least. He was happy to be part of it all. It had gone as you had always promised. Maximum fatalities. Everything about it proved how clever you were. The way the bombs had been built and so carefully placed. The way the predictions had been made of their movements. Every calculation had been accurate and precise. The body count could not be argued. Fuck Columbine and Virginia Tech. That was little league shit. You had shown them how it was done.

Dave took that last five minutes to climb up to the roof. He noticed that a large section of the school was on fire. He saw the crowd in the distance. The parents and survivors. The news crews broadcasting live. I saw you there with him, arm around his shoulder. You both had reason to be proud. He put the rifle aside and pulled out a pistol. He put it into his mouth. You stood there smiling. So impressed with yourself. You laughed when he pulled the trigger.

Nirvana played. The cheerleaders danced. I sat back in my chair and raised my glass. "Here's to you, you evil fuck." Your diaries sickened. Your plans disgusted. But Dave had let you down. Without you, he didn't have a chance.

CHAPTER SEVENTY-FOUR:

It was narrowly avoided. Columbine Redux. The Worm had broken first. Dave, eventually followed. The interrogation was videotaped and later shown at trial. The image of the kid who wanted to be mass murderer.

ROLL TAPE

"Where are the guns, Dave?" I asked. "What guns?" "Your pal, Worm, told us about your trip to the gun show. What did you do with the guns?" "I don't know what you're talking about." "Where are the goddamn guns?! I yelled." His calm was making me angry. "There aren't any."

I decided to take a more low-key approach. My voice barely above a whisper. "Where are they, Dave?" He answered with confident assurance. "I really don't know what you're talking about. What guns? I don't have any guns." "So, the Worm lied? We're going to find them anyway. At this very second, there's police at your house with a warrant to search it. So, why don't you just tell me?" He seemed more annoyed than shaken. "You can't do that." "Yes, we can. We are." "Whatever. You're not going to find anything." "Yeah? You sure about that? You better be."

Right on cue Gillian walked in. He handed me a slip of paper and left. I read the address out loud. "415 Salmon River Road. That address mean anything to you, Dave?" Panic flashed in his eyes. "That's your family's cabin up in Mt. Hood. Your mom says you've been up there a lot, lately. What are we going to find up there?" Dave tried to remain defiant. "You can't go up there. It's not your jurisdiction." "Yes, we can, Dave. The search warrant has already been issued. So, you want to tell me now what we're going to find? Or should I just have you taken back to your cell now so you can start getting used to it?"

I let the moment sink in. The battle was over. His resolve began to crumble. "Dave, talk to me. It's over. You're just making it harder on yourself by not cooperating." I could see the struggle going on in his mind. I waited as he reached a painful conclusion. "They're not in the cabin. They're in the tool shed. So, are the rest of the supplies."

"What supplies? What else is there?" I asked. I swear he almost smiled. "What else is in the shed?" I asked again. "Bombs. Enough to blow the whole school into a pile of rubble." "Sounds impressive. It must have taken you a lot of time to build them all." Dave seemed very proud of himself. "We've been working on this for over a year."

"Did you and Eric and Worm all think of it together?" Dave shook his head. "No. It was all Eric's idea. He just asked us if we wanted to be part of it." "And you said yes?" I asked. "Yeah. Why not?"

"Why did you want to be a part of Eric's plan to blow up Adams?" "Because they're stupid and deserve it" he said. "I don't believe you. That's why Eric wanted all those people dead, not you. Why did you want to be part of it?" He looked down at the table. Thought carefully about the question. I prodded him once again. "Dave. Help me understand your side of all this. Why did you want to be part of Eric's plan?" His answer came out in a mumble. I could barely understand him. "I just got tired of being invisible."

END TAPE

CHAPTER SEVENTY-FIVE:

After those days, my nightmares continued. But they, eventually, became less frequent. Time doesn't heal but it numbs. I still drank too much and listened to the same old music. I tried to discover new bands to add to my collection. A few were Ok but none really did it. Most of them just felt like echoes.

I was to be tried for heresy. The date had been set for the twenty-ninth of April. I had sinned against the department. Word had gotten out about my conversation with Allison. How I had coached her. She claimed all she told them was that I offered to go with her. That I was trying to convince her to turn herself in. She promised she never gave them any details of the exact exchange. But there had been eyes upon us as we talked.

It wouldn't have been difficult for someone at the school to have seen me arrive. I had practically dragged Allison across the grounds. An inference could be drawn about what had taken place. Especially since I had difficulty explaining why I had gone there alone. There was also that previous complaint by her mother. Something regarding my inappropriate behavior. It all raised more questions than answers.

In addition, there was that earlier failure to follow procedure. The one involving Senator Alvin. I shouldn't have been the one to take his statement. Stories were even leaked, not one of them true, about my strange fascination with the occult.

During this time I had been suspended with full pay. In all honesty, I appreciated the break. I spent my days in bars, none as good as The Pig. But the beer was cold and cheap. My evenings were usually spent watching movies. Early Scorsese, Jean-Pierre Melville and the occasional comedy or two. I went to a few concerts but quickly lost interest. Standing alone wasn't all that much fun.

The South Waterfront project moved toward completion. Architectural models were shown. It was to be a showcase project. Big and glitzy for Portland. A place that once prided itself on modesty and good sense. The Native American casinos, the ones that were legit, were going to have a tough time surviving. They would, of course, but on a smaller scale. There was always someone desperate enough to bet their last dime.

It was all gaining momentum as my hearing drew near. I had been a good detective but none of it mattered. Where there's smoke there's fire. I told myself I no longer cared.

It all went away with a call from the mayor. He didn't appreciate my persecution. The chief concurred as did the Public Relations Department. All internal investigations were dropped. When I asked what had precipitated this sudden turn of events, I was given a very brief answer. The public needed its heroes. It wasn't true. It had more to do with politics. It still worked to my favor. I went from villain to hero. I was soon the poster boy for all that was good.

I was paraded out before the press. The Detective That Had Stopped a Tragedy. The questions asked were about how I had broken the case. No one talked about Julie or Allison. It was an issue of morals and taste. My exploits had been local but my fame grew large. The New York Times ran a profile. I even got an interview on Sixty-Minutes. I made sure to give credit where credit was due when I was asked about Natasha and Bill. I had even tried to get Gillian on the interview with me. The producers of the show declined. They said that the story wasn't about a particular case. It was the story of a lone detective.

I ran into Angie, once. She was with her latest guy. She always seemed to have one. He seemed a nice enough kid but he had those stupid ear things. The big plugs that deformed earlobes. I wrote off my hatred for such adornments to just being cranky. What did I care what the kid wanted to do with his ears? As for Angie herself, she was looking seriously pretty. A death trap waiting to be sprung on young love.

Eventually, Allison was set for trial. Many thought she would be found guilty of first degree murder. Others, however, knew better. They predicted the reaction to her brother's horror. His reputation had grown exponentially since his diaries had been leaked. The more they read, the more they thought they understood. I hoped, for their sake, they never would.

CHAPTER SEVENTY-SIX:

I sat alone in my chair engaged in my usual routine. Stone Roses wanna be adored. I was contemplating my future and dwelling on the past. My habitual process of self-mutilation. I had downed two bottles of Pale Ale and was contemplating a third when I heard a knock. I hadn't been expecting anyone. I never did. I opened the door to find a face both familiar and new. An angel appeared to me weeping.

I let her inside. She didn't say a word. I put aside my own temptation to speak. This wasn't the time. It was, what it was. She leaned close and gently kissed me. There was no bitter aftertaste. No greasy interference. It was sweet and perfect. Warm and giving. She took me by the hand and led me to the bed. She gently took off my clothes.

She was the one hurting. Or, should I say, she was hurting too. She revealed herself to me. Naked and open. Long-limbed body, a study in grace. Silence remained unbroken as more kisses were exchanged. Words would come later when explanations were offered. Right then all that mattered was being with each other. Pleasures of the flesh and of the soul.

Over three hours passed of blissful indulgence. The long wait had only increased our hunger. There were more skilled or experienced. More expert in technique. But nothing about it disappointed. It was the stuff of great love songs with a soundtrack of silence and rain. Portland weather continued to be ever changing.

Only later did she explain the events which had brought her to my home. Part of me didn't care to hear. But she insisted on telling me. Of offering a reason. She had found out Billy had been cheating on her for quite some time. A single incident had sparked his confession. She had seen him with someone else. It was far worse than she predicted. The scale of his deceit had been enormous. He had been with many other women. It had been going on for years. He claimed that he loved her but that he had a problem. He didn't even understand why he did it. She listened to all of it. Contemplated every word of his guilty admission. Then she told him the two of them were through.

She said to me she had always loved me. For years she had just put it aside. She thought of herself as Billy's girl. Now that he was gone, she could finally say it. She wanted me in every way. So much more than just a friend.

As much as I wanted to believe in the Hollywood ending, this was as yet to be determined. I figured I was a reststop. A break from the pain. Given time, she would return to Billy. She assured me otherwise. She was sure what she was doing. She said she would never treat me that way. I told her to use me all she wanted.

I told her I was planning a long trip away. Maybe a few weeks. Maybe, forever. The gloom of Portland had taken its toll. I was going to drive down the coast all the way to LA. I asked her to join me. To come along for the ride. She said "yes" which filled me with excitement and promise. She loved the ocean and wanted to lie on the beach. She wanted to wear a bikini in the sun. I made a crack about Aphrodite rising from the sea. Then the words came to an end as I pulled her against me. For an old man, I was doing just fine.

She fell asleep atop the sheets. I was thankful for the view. Her body was unmarked. No scars or ink, except for the one from her youth. She had a tiny line on her shoulder from a bicycle accident. A sudden meeting with the sidewalk as she fell. She was perfect in her imperfection. Physically and in every way.

I covered her with a blanket and turned off the light. I sat there in the darkness. I made plans for our trip. The Oregon coast down to Northern California. Maybe a few days in Monterey. Then down to LA. for a week in Santa Monica or Venice. After that we could decide the rest.

The sun burst through the window. Its rays woke me from my happy dreams. I touched her face softly to make sure that it was real. I listened for the whispers. The rumors and accusations. I listened for the dogs in the distance. All I heard was the sound of her breathing.

DOGS IN THE DISTANCE

SUGGESTED PLAYLIST:

Stone Roses: I Wanna Be Adored

Psychedelic Furs: Pretty in Pink

Nirvana: Smells Like Teen Spirit

Sister Mercy: This Corrosion

Soundgarden: Fell on Black Days

Sex Pistols: Submission

Nine Inch Nails: Closer

Billy Idol: White Wedding

The Stooges: Gimme Danger

Joy Division: She's Lost Control

Thom York: Black Swan

Wire: Lowdown

DOGS IN THE DISTANCE

Kevin Leicinger is the author of several novels including FERAL BEASTS, KAIJU and BRIGHT SHADOWS. He currently lives in Los Angeles.